MAKING THE CUT

MAKING THE CUT

SOPHIE WIGGINS

The
Book
Guild

First published in Great Britain in 2025 by
The Book Guild Ltd
Unit E2 Airfield Business Park,
Harrison Road, Market Harborough,
Leicestershire. LE16 7UL
Tel: 0116 2792299
www.bookguild.co.uk
Email: info@bookguild.co.uk

The manufacturer's authorised representative in the EU
for product safety is Authorised Rep Compliance Ltd,
71 Lower Baggot Street, Dublin D02 P593 Ireland (www.arccompliance.com)

This work is entirely fictitious and bears no resemblance to any persons living or dead.

Typeset in 11pt Minion Pro

Printed and bound in Great Britain by CMP UK

ISBN 978 1835742 426

British Library Cataloguing in Publication Data.
A catalogue record for this book is available from the British Library.

For 'dance mums' everywhere

Prologue

"WHAT DO YOU THINK, Lydia? Is it as bad as it looks? Or is it all put on for the cameras?"

I'd been listening to a few of the women from work discussing a reality TV show. I didn't really want to join in. I was more interested in eavesdropping and hearing what people thought about it from an outsider's perspective.

"It's tame," I replied, sipping my coffee. "The reality is way worse."

But the reality would never be believed.

Backstage had started in the US a few years earlier, and naturally been picked up by TV bosses in the UK, who thought we would lap it up. And we did. Granted it may have been a niche audience, but dance kids and dance mums alike were hooked. We were amazed at the skill and talent of the kids, but more than that we were entertained by the level of competition and bitchiness between the mums. It was addictive. The teacher, Miss Jenny, was a vile piece of shit, who abused those kids emotionally, all in the name of entertainment. But the girls' parents – well, the mums anyway – watched on from the viewing galleries, condoning the insults and gruelling routines

Miss Jenny doled out every episode, so it was easy for us to justify tuning in to watch the exploitation of kids. We told ourselves that if their own mothers could stomach it, so could we.

We watched on as the elite team of pre-pubescent girls had their self-confidence eroded as quickly as their friendships. It was in our living rooms four or five nights a week and gradually we became desensitised to the cruel comparisons and barbed comments from Miss Jenny. She was becoming a caricature of a dance teacher, no doubt encouraged by the production team to come up with ever more shocking ways of pitching the kids against each other, making unreasonable demands of the ever-obedient mothers, and win, win, win at all costs. The ratings demanded it.

And we watched on, knowing that dance teachers everywhere would also be watching, comparing, and expectations from now on would be so much higher. We were aware that our kids weren't at the same standard as the kids on that show. And we were also aware that the teaching staff at Victoria Coppella Studio would be inspired to reach that standard. They were ambitious and wanted to be the best. We knew that our lives as we knew them would need to be given over to the dance school if our little angels were to succeed. No longer would we be able to make our own plans for the weekend. No longer would our salaries be our own. No longer could our spouses and any other children we may have be taken into consideration. The dance classes, which started as a Saturday morning hobby for my toddler, were now my life. I couldn't get out of it if I wanted to. The demands increased – slowly at first, building momentum until my life felt as though it was no longer my own. We would all go on to spend years sacrificing our time, money, and sanity in the hopes of what? I never even knew what drove my behaviour, what made me so willing to do the things I did.

I often wonder how different our lives would have been if we'd never gotten into all this. I would have been at home more. My money would be my own – there might even be some money in my account now, rather than living almost to the limit of my overdraft every damn month.

And Annie – what would she be like if we'd never come this far? I had naively expected her to become more confident as she grew up, scared of nothing as she became used to getting up on stage in front of hundreds of people and performing. It never occurred to me that being confident on stage might be very different to being confident within herself. And I would never have believed it if someone had suggested it might actually destroy her confidence. How could it? How could a child get up and perform in front of an audience, often solo, and then be overwhelmed by self-doubt, self-criticism – even self-destruction? I genuinely believed that all my efforts were about giving Annie the opportunity to do something that would not only keep her busy but would benefit her in other aspects of her life. As Annie has grown, these delusions have revealed themselves to be exactly that, and more and more I begin to regret not posting that damn letter twelve years ago.

1

Missed Opportunities

"I'M TAKING ELLA TO ballet at the weekend. You should bring Annie," my friend Helen suggested.

"Ah yeah, that sounds good, how cute!"

Visions of little tots in pretty tutus were going through my mind. I'd had a go at ballet as a child but hated it, and thankfully my mum realised I was not a natural, so she put up no argument when I didn't want to go.

Annie and Ella were born just days apart and loved spending time together. Helen told me she had been in touch with the VCS studio, and they were happy for us to just turn up. No leotard or ballet shoes required. "Don't spend your money on that stuff until you know she likes it," Helen had been told.

That's good, I thought. *At least they're not roping us into anything that'll cost a fortune.*

We arrived at the studio the following Saturday morning – Helen, me, and two excited little girls with matching Angelina Ballerina backpacks containing their water bottles and, for Annie, nappies and wipes. At almost three, she still wasn't potty trained, but Miss Heather – the 'baby ballet' teacher – assured me this wasn't a problem. "We don't have parents in the room, but you're welcome to stay and sit in reception or go and get a brew in the café," she said. "Don't worry, if there's any problem we can come and find you, but I promise they'll be fine."

And they were.

As Miss Heather took their chubby hands and led them to the circle of baby ballerinas, Annie looked back over her shoulder; her eyes sparkled with excitement, as she bounced across the studio floor.

An hour later, they came out of the studio holding Miss Heather's hands. "They were brilliant!" she told us.

"Did you like it?" I asked Annie, not really needing an answer. Her chubby, rosy little face beamed, her eyes wide as she bounced from one foot to the other, telling me all about it.

"We did sitting in the circle with all the other girls, and I sat next to Ella, and I did sit next to Miss Emma as well, and we did 'naughty toes and nice toes' and then we did skipping round and pointing our toes, and galloping like a unicorn, and then we did twirling round in a circle with our arms in the air…" She spoke at a hundred miles an hour, her giddiness making my head spin.

In all honesty, I didn't really care about what they had been doing – Annie was happy, so I was happy.

Annie was hooked. All week she would tell me and Rob and her grandparents and the nursery staff, and anyone else who would listen, about everything she had done at ballet class and how excited she was for next Saturday.

After a few weeks, I took her to buy her first leotard – sky blue and with a matching skirt: a kind of a voile fabric with pale blue dots on. I bought the regulation pink ballet socks, and the icing on the cake – the first pair of ballet shoes. Tiny pink satin shoes, which were so small they looked more like they belonged on a keychain than on a little human's feet. Annie took them out of the box as soon as we got home. "Just trying them on to show Daddy," she said.

"That's fine," I said, "but make sure they go back in the box afterwards so they're still nice on Saturday." Back in the box they went, until half an hour later, when Grandma came round, and Annie was 'just trying them on again to show Grandma'.

Saturday morning lie-ins became a thing of the past. Baby ballet was the earliest class, at 9am. We'd meet Helen and Ella in the car park, and then brave the chaos of the reception area together.

The noise was almost unbearable. Kids shouting, crying, even just talking but at excessive volumes it seemed. Mothers (and occasionally fathers) stood around trying their best to gossip while also trying to keep their little poppet still as they attempted to scrape baby hair into something resembling a bun. Teachers would come into reception from their various studios shouting instructions for parents and children alike, adding to the volume. The windows would be steamed up from the sweat of kids running round, parents running round after them, and the whole area always smelled of what I think was probably a mixture of sweat, the expensive perfumes of the dance mums who rocked up at 9am looking like they'd spent four hours in hair and make-up, and the polish used to maintain the appearance of the beautiful wooden sprung floors.

Parents would scramble to the reception desk with their various enquiries – the curved desk offering no suggestion of where a queue might be formed, so the two ladies behind it were like bar staff on a busy Saturday night, having no clue who to serve next amid the din and line of people waving their money around. There was a locked box to drop envelopes of cash in, but you had to drop in the correct amount (you would never get any change), and you wouldn't get a receipt either, so naturally not everyone was happy doing this.

My almost lucky escape came one Saturday, not long before Annie would turn three years old. Annie and Ella came out of their class into the sweaty reception area. There was no space to get them changed, and I couldn't face the fight to get to an equally crowded changing room. Sod it, we were only going around thirty metres to get to Helen's car, and the weather was warm and sunny. The girls were flushed and sweaty from their exertions, so we quickly replaced ballet shoes for trainers and made a run for it across the car park.

"Er... excuse me, ladies!" came the shrill voice from behind us, the tone like a headmistress who has caught her charges smoking in the toilets during lesson time. It was one of the two reception ladies – I later learned her name was Gladys. *It must be something serious to drag her away from the carnage inside the reception.*

"Those girls should *not* be leaving the studio like that!"

Helen and I looked at each other, questioning the statement silently. "I'm sorry...?" Helen replied, holding her hand over her eyes to shield from the sun.

"You need to get them changed into proper clothing. They'll catch pneumonia going outside without proper clothes on! And have you even considered who might be walking around here looking at little girls in the wrong way?"

"Oh, okay, well, we're nearly at the car now, so..." Helen replied. I said nothing. I'm quite good at come backs when I'm prepared for a situation. Caught off guard, I'm pathetic. The imaginary arguments I would have alone in the shower or in the car were epic; I was well-rehearsed, witty and cutting in my responses. But situations like this... like I said... pathetic.

Gladys interrupted Helen, with that same air of authority. "For future reference, the girls should be getting changed at the studio. They should not be coming and going in their ballet uniform. Do *not* let Miss Victoria see those girls leaving dressed like that!"

Again, Helen and I looked at each other, flabbergasted. What the actual fuck was that about? Gladys turned on her heel and the conversation was over. She could only have been more dramatic if she had a cape to whip around and a hat with a feather in it. We watched, wide-eyed and jaws almost hitting the ground, at her attempts to flounce. I looked at Helen, then Annie. I tried to suppress a giggle but failed. Annie started too. Then Helen and Ella. The four of us stood on the car park watching the stroppy bitch throw the studio door open. She wore heels clearly too high to be able to balance well given her short, dumpy stature. Despite my laughter, I hated her. I hated her condescending tone. I hated the wrinkles in her chin, which were packed with caked-on powder and framed with whiskers of varying lengths. I hated that she came out of the building wrapping her cashmere cardigan tight around her, as if the fat around her middle was not enough to keep her warm. I hated that she felt she had the fucking right to speak to us like that in front of our children. And I really fucking hated myself for standing there and taking her shit.

Helen is usually better at handling sticky situations than me, but even she was speechless as we got into the car. "I'm fuming," she said, through a forced grin, hoping the tone would be picked up by the girls, rather than the words. "Me too," I responded, pulling down the sun visor to check Annie in the mirror.

Annie was incredibly sensitive to tense situations – more so than most kids her age. She had that sixth sense for picking up on vibes and atmospheres, an ability to read the room that would usually only be learned over time, by observing behaviours and body language. She was looking out of the window, the little crease that I called her 'worry dimple' clearly visible, as she pondered the telling-off we'd all received. She was not old enough to put into words how she felt, but that didn't stop the feelings being there, even if she didn't know what they were. Annie lived in a dream world of tutus, princesses and unicorns, where all almost-three-year-olds should live. Any shift in atmosphere was picked up quickly. It worried me. More than anything in the world, I wanted to shield her from the adult crap she would learn about way too soon, wrap her up in soft fleecy Disney pyjamas and warm blanket fresh out of the dryer and hold her safe in my arms. Rob would say I 'wrapped her in cotton wool'. I absolutely would have done if this could be seen as a reasonable thing to do and not something that would scar her for life and likely have me sectioned.

Helen and I were on the same page as far as discussing the situation – we didn't talk about it in front of the girls. We didn't want them to hear us swearing, and we certainly didn't want the conversation to be repeated by either of them within the studio setting.

Not that that was an issue for me. Annie wouldn't be going back. I got home, put *Dora the Explorer* on, and started ranting to Rob. He made coffee, not even really listening to me. He clearly didn't think it was that big a deal, and as usual he thought I was being oversensitive and overreacting. "Maybe she was just looking out for them?"

Rob always played devil's advocate. I think that's how he saw himself. The way I saw it, he never had my back. Sometimes it might have been necessary to look at a situation in a calm, objective manner, but other times – like now   I needed him on my side, and it infuriated me that he would respond this way. If he'd been there and heard how that woman spoke to us, maybe he would have felt differently. Actually, he probably wouldn't. He would have apologised profusely and considered his hands slapped. He would have made sure Annie was always dressed correctly and would make a point of kissing ass to make up for this, the most serious of crime ever to be committed. Rob always took the path of least resistance; anything for a quiet life. More than anything, Rob needed to be liked. "No way," I said, hands on hips as I glared at him. "You weren't there. She was on some kind of power trip. It was like she was having a bad day and just really wanted to have a pop at someone, and we were in the firing line. Well, I'm not putting up with that. I'm not paying good money to that place to be spoken to like that, by some demented bitch receptionist!"

I wrote our notice letter.

Dear Miss Victoria

Please accept this letter as notice that Annie will not be coming back to dancing.

I would strongly recommend that you speak to your reception staff about the importance of valuing their customers, and about appropriate communication.

My friend and I were followed by the older receptionist onto the car park, and shouted at by this woman. This was in front of other parents in the car park, but also in front of our own children. This is not acceptable.

The parents of the children in your school are your bread and butter. Without them, you would have no dance school.

I will not be spoken to like that by someone whose wages I'm paying, and I would suggest you consider whether this person is someone you are happy to have as the face of VCS.

Yours sincerely
Lydia Moffatt

As I read the letter to my disinterested husband, I was conscious that I was raising my voice, when I noticed Annie stood behind the door which was slightly ajar. I pushed it open, and she looked up at me with big tears balanced on her lower lashes, her elf-like chin trembling.

I couldn't do it.

Some might say I was too soft – either with Annie, or with the dance school, or both. And for my sins, yes, I probably was.

I justified my inaction at the time by telling myself that Annie shouldn't suffer because I was angry at some silly old bitch with ideas above her station. And that's probably true.

Ella never went back after that. But Annie insisted she still wanted to go, even if Ella didn't. I was surprised by that. Annie liked to have Ella by her side, like a comfort blanket. In my mind, I reconciled this as being the sign that I was doing the right thing. She must be really dedicated, even at her young age, if she was going to go it alone. I couldn't deprive her of the opportunity.

But my regret, years later, is that the letter was the real 'sliding doors' moment – an opportunity to have changed the course of our lives, and I never even realised that until it was too late. If only I had posted that letter.

Gladys had not only spoken down to me in front of my daughter, but she was also going to get away with it. I was silenced. Gagged. That was the first time I had to suppress my anger and resist the urge to fight back at VCS. Over the following years, I would get used to it. But suppression does not dissipate. Like red hot embers in the gut, smouldering, building, suppression is the heat that builds quietly, just waiting for the moment it can burst into flames.

2

Chickenpox

"OH FUCK, WHAT'S THIS?" I muttered under my breath. I was having a cup of tea with my sister when my phone rang, showing the number I recognised to be Manor Park Primary School. It was 1pm, so I knew it was likely to be illness or injury.

"Hello?"

"Hello, is this Annie's mummy?" came the sweet high-pitched voice of Mrs Aspen, the school office administrator.

"Yes, it is."

"Oh good. I thought we should let you know… Annie may be coming home with chickenpox." She sounded reluctant to say the words, maybe expecting a tirade of abuse from a parent who was going to struggle to take time off work. "Unfortunately, a few of the children in Annie's class are off with it at the moment, and Annie looks like she might have one or two spots coming up." I could imagine her holding the phone from her ear as she waited for my response.

"Oh no, how's she doing?" I asked. I knew chickenpox was doing the rounds and remembered having it as a child and feeling rough.

"She's looking a little washed out, to be honest. Are you able to pick her up at all?" she asked nervously.

"Yes of course, I'll be there in five minutes." I was already slipping my trainers on, while putting my coat on and cradling the phone between my jaw and my shoulder.

My mind raced as I drove to Manor Park to pick Annie up. *Do I need to take her to the doctors? Is there anything they would be able to give her? Do we have calamine lotion at home? (No, of course not – why would we?) Will I need two weeks off work to look after her? Do we have Calpol at home? Do I need to change the bedding every day? (Of course not, it's chickenpox, not nits, you fucking idiot.) I must let Erin's mum know she won't be able to go to her birthday party tomorrow. I must let dancing know...*

Fuck.

Dancing. It was Annie's pre-primary ballet exam on Tuesday.

There had been three extra lessons a week since sodding Christmas for ballet alone to prepare for this exam. Pre-primary ballet, for fuck's sake. Like it even mattered. It had cost a small fortune in those lessons, not to mention the new ballet shoes Miss Heather insisted on. Never mind, couldn't be helped. Nobody's going to want their child picking up the pox, so I thought I should let them know.

Annie looked poorly. Her little face was ghostly white, apart from the two giveaway spots on her right cheek, and another one which looked to be making an appearance on her forehead. Her eyes were heavy, and she looked generally sorry for herself. She was quiet in the car, a sure sign she was not feeling good. After a quick detour to the chemist to stock up on calamine lotion, we walked through the door, and Annie went straight to the sofa, dragging the blanket down from the back of it, and curled into a tiny ball.

"Here you go, sweet," I said, offering a teaspoon of Calpol to try to keep her temperature down. "How do you feel?"

"I'm itchy and scratchy."

I moved her hand away from the spot on her leg that she was about to go for. "You mustn't scratch, or it will leave a horrible mark on your skin. I'll get you something to put on it."

"Ewww…" she said, scrunching at the smell of the calamine lotion I dabbed gently onto her spots. Thankfully there weren't many of them.

"I know it's gross," I said, "but it will help it to stop itching so much. You must let it dry without touching, okay?" She nodded. "Why don't you try and have a little sleep?" I suggested. No encouragement needed. Her eyes closed, and she seemed to be dozing when she suddenly sat bolt upright.

"Mummy! My ballet exam is in a few days! Will the spots be gone tomorrow?"

"Sorry, sweetheart, they usually take at least a week or two to go. The good news is you will be able to stay off school next week, and I'll take some time off work to look after you. But I'm sorry… it does mean no ballet exam, and no lessons for at least a week either."

"But, Mummy…" Tears had already started filling her big brown eyes. "Miss Victoria said it's very important that we have to do the exam, and we can't be ballerinas and wear tutus in the shows if we don't do it."

"Don't worry, I'll speak to Miss Victoria. I'll see if we can just do it on a different day when you're feeling better." She seemed to be pacified and dozed back off into a deep sleep.

Miss Victoria answered the phone straight away, taking me by surprise. I think I was expecting her not to be able to hear the phone amid all the din at the studio, but then I remembered it was still in school time, and it was Friday afternoon, not Saturday morning.

"Oh, hello, Miss Victoria. This is Annie Moffatt's mummy. Annie's in Miss Heather's baby ballet class?" I knew she wouldn't know (nor would I have expected her to know) the name of every kid at the dance school; there seemed to be about a million kids, after all.

So, I was surprised when she said, "Ooh Miss Heather's been telling me all about Annie. We were saying what a travesty it would have been if she'd left when her little pal left. She's a real natural, you know. Beautiful little dancer."

"Ah thank you, I'll let her know you said that. Anyway, I just wanted to let you know I've had to pick her up from school this afternoon. She's got the chickenpox, so she won't be able to come to ballet tomorrow morning, and I'm afraid she won't be able to do the exam on Tuesday either."

"That's such a shame," Miss Victoria said. "She would have done so well in the exam." She sounded genuinely disappointed. I was honestly surprised she cared. After all, what difference did it make to her? We'd paid for everything up front so there was no impact on her financially. And there were hundreds of kids doing these exams – why did she care? Anyway, it was unavoidable. It wouldn't be fair to anyone to let her go while she was still infectious. Miss Victoria assured me there would be more exams in a few months' time, so Annie could move classes and pick up with them. I wasn't sure how Annie would feel about that, but I'd cross that bridge when I came to it.

The weekend was rough for Annie. The spots seemed to multiply under our very eyes and were clearly driving her up the wall. She was feverish, and restless. As always, Rob worked all weekend, so it was down to me to nurse Annie – not that I minded. I enjoyed the cuddles and having her sleep snuggled up to me. I'd missed that since she stopped having her afternoon naps. Even though I hated seeing her feeling poorly, I also relished being needed for comfort.

Monday rolled around slowly after a full weekend of barely moving from the sofa. Annie was ready to go back to school. Well, not really, but she knew she would have to go to school if she wanted to go to dancing.

"Mummy, I'm fine, see," she said, her pale face forcing an unconvincing smile as she twirled round in the hallway.

"Sorry, kiddo, you can still pass the chickenpox to other people, so you have to stay off school for a few days." Her head lowered. She knew the response she would get, and she knew she wasn't well enough. I noticed she hadn't mentioned the ballet exam, and I wasn't going to bring it up either, though I suspect it weighed heavily on her little mind.

After a quiet morning of colouring in and doing jigsaws, we'd just sat down together on the floor to have a teddy bears' picnic lunch on the carpet, when my phone rang. "Hi, Lydia, it's Miss Victoria from dancing."

"Oh, hi, Miss Victoria," I said standing up and trying to disguise the fact that I had a mouthful of peanut butter sandwich and teddy bear crisps. Annie's ears pricked up, but I left the room. I had no idea what the call was going to be about, so thought it best that she didn't hear any of it.

"I've got some good news," Miss Victoria said, sounding excited. "I've phoned around all the parents of the little girls on Annie's exam line, plus the ones who are due to do their exams before and after Annie. They've all had the chickenpox, parents and children, so if she's feeling up to it, I'm happy for her to still come in." *Wow*, I thought. That was really going above and beyond what I would have expected. She must have made about fifteen phone calls to parents, maybe more. I was so taken aback I didn't know what to say.

"Oh... oh wow... that is so nice of you." I swallowed the last of my sandwich. "But what about everyone else? The teachers and reception staff?"

"I've spoken to all of them – even spoke to the examiner and Fiona, the music girl, and they've both had it too, so there's no reason for her to miss it if she feels well enough."

This woman must be a saint. I knew she had a full day that Monday of back-to-back exams, so for her to go to all the trouble of making these calls almost brought a tear to my eye. "Depending on how she feels," she continued, "she could come in a little earlier and have a quick run-though with Miss Heather, seeing as she missed Saturday's lesson, but there's no pressure. She doesn't really need it, and it might be too much if she's not one hundred percent."

"Okay, well I'm sure she will be excited to do it, and we'll see how she is tomorrow before we decide whether to come early or not."

"Not a problem, whatever Annie decides is fine with us."

After we ended the call, I stared at the phone, not quite believing that she had done that for Annie. It might not seem like much, but the point was that she didn't have to. I hadn't asked her to, she hadn't offered – presumably as she wouldn't want to get Annie's hopes up in case one of the girls might have been vulnerable – and I would never have expected it. A warmth washed over me, and I smiled. Miss Victoria really did care for these girls and wanted the best for them. She didn't want them to miss any opportunity that came their way and didn't want Annie to have to move to a different class to be able to take the exam next time around.

Annie was over the moon, as expected. She wasn't even worried about going to the studio covered in calamine lotion.

I waited nervously in the smaller studio as the girls were taken through, hair scraped into neat buns and caked in hairspray with an unnecessary amount of hair grips to hold it together. Annie had looked close to tears as Miss Victoria roughly dragged a brush through her hair, scraping some of the spots on her scalp and pulling so tight it gave her a surprised, face-lifted expression, more suited to that of a Hollywood wife than a five-year-old. Her surprised expression was mirrored by my own when Miss Victoria told me to just put my five pounds in the tin for the hair, but I would need to give the pianist money to reception. *Five pounds?* I wondered. *For what?* Turned out it was for the privilege of having hair styled by Miss Victoria and seven hair grips. *I'm in the wrong job*, I thought.

Still irritated by that, I asked one of the mums who the pianist was. She laughed at me. "Oh no, there isn't an actual pianist. They use a CD now."

"So why do we pay £4.50 for the pianist?"

"I'm not actually sure, to be honest. We've always paid for a pianist for exams since my eldest daughter was here and she's fifteen now. Although now I think about it, they did used to have a lady come in and play piano for exams, so she would have needed paying, I suppose."

"It's just something you have to do," chipped in another mum without looking up from her phone. I'd seen her around the studio many times. She seemed to have an air of authority, as though she owned the place. I didn't question it further. I would eventually come to find out this mother – Belinda – had had her own aspirations of becoming a dancer. Her dreams had been crushed when she had a serious neck and back injury, slipping on stage and tumbling awkwardly into the band pit below. Watching her later, I could tell from the way she swaggered around that she had never quite accepted that the dance world wasn't meant for her. And so, she lived her dreams and ambitions through her daughter, Libby, her five-year-old 'mini-me', who seemed to be horribly competitive for her tender years.

The other mum sipped her coffee, blank expression on her face. It either hadn't registered with her, or she didn't care, that she was paying for something that didn't exist.

17

I looked on the exam notice board. Eight exams today, each with six students on a line. Same every day this week and for two days next week. I quickly did the maths. Forty-eight students paying £4.50 each; £216 per day; £1512 taken by the dance school in just over a week for doing nothing other than a token amount paid to an ex-student to pause and start the CD as needed. She wouldn't be receiving £1512. Seemed like a complete scam. The numbers for hair slightly higher – same number of students, five pounds each, would mean £1680. The profit margins on those hair grips were astounding. *I'm definitely in the wrong job*, I thought. And there I was at reception handing over a five-pound note, which gave me no change, to pay for the imaginary pianist.

My irritation was set aside, but not forgotten, by the time the results came in a month later. Annie received a distinction in the exam, with a score of 98% – the highest pre-primary ballet result in that year group. I was so proud, and so were Miss Heather and Miss Victoria. I think that was the point that they started taking more notice of her.

3

Attention

IN THE WEEKS AND months that followed that first exam, I found myself caught up in the attention Annie was receiving, and all the opportunities that were presenting themselves, now that Annie had, it seemed, been noticed as a promising dancer of the future.

Most of the girls Annie's age were doing tap and modern classes now, as well as ballet. Miss Heather started doing acro classes too. "Mummy, please can I do acro?" Annie asked me one Saturday. "The bigger girls who do acro did a show for us and it looked so good, and Miss Heather said she thought I would be good at it, so can I do it?"

I cringed. The cost had tripled already with the tap and modern classes. Rob would have a fit if I agreed to another one. Then again... I didn't smoke, didn't drink, didn't have any expensive hobbies of my own, and I worked full-time in a shitty office job I hated, so why could I not do what I wanted with my money?

Fuck it.

"Let me have a chat with Miss Heather first," I said.

"She's in the studio now, Mummy. Go and talk to her now before the next class." She grabbed my hand, pulling me to the small sweaty studio used by the junior classes.

Miss Heather sat in the corner with one of the 'bigger girls', who was stood back to the wall, feet in first position while she chugged from a bottle of water and chatted with Miss Heather. Bigger seems a ridiculous word to use to describe the girl. Although she looked about fifteen, she was tiny. *I bet she hates it when the teachers call the older classes the 'bigger girls'*, I thought. She wore an aubergine-coloured leotard, and pink footless tights. She was so thin. Her little arms and legs looked so fragile, and I noticed she had a pair of pointe shoes next to her. *Must be stronger than she looks, though.* She bent down to put her pointe shoes on, bending entirely from the waist. The movement revealed her spine, vertebrae so sharp they looked like they could rip through her pale skin. Her back had fine, dark, downy hair on it. I suspected she was anorexic.

A childhood friend of mine had developed anorexia as a teenager, so I was familiar with the symptoms. I knew – and understood why – it was not unusual for young dancers to suffer from eating disorders. Dance clothes left nothing to the imagination. Every lump and bump there on show for all to see. I remembered my own early teenage years, studying myself in a full-length mirror, squeezing enormous handfuls of imaginary fat between my thumbs and fingers, feeling disgusted with myself, but being grateful that I wasn't on the gymnastic squad or swimming team at school. Nobody ever had to see my body. I'd envied the girls on the gymnastics squad – defined muscles and smooth, sleek silhouettes in their jewel-toned leotards and catsuits. I think even if I had looked like them, I would never have had the confidence they had. I could have had the perfect body and would still have stood hunched over waiting for my turn – doing my best to round my shoulders in a way that would minimise my newly developing breasts, and legs crossed as if bursting for the loo, but really as a way of reducing the amount of cellulite-covered flesh on show. It was ridiculous. I'd never been big, and I'd never had an abundance of dimples on my thighs. Maybe everyone felt the same, but they certainly didn't show it. I shuddered at the thought that this was something that might affect Annie. I pushed the thought away as I approached Miss Heather.

She smiled brightly. "Hiya, Lydia," she said as if we were old friends. I found Miss Heather to be warm and friendly on the occasions I had spoken to her, and she was obviously good with the little ones. She had a kind of ethereal softness about her that made her seem 'safe', and the girls all adored her.

"Hi, Miss Heather, Annie wants to join your acro class. Would that be okay?" I asked her.

"Yes of course! I'm starting a new class for the six- and seven-year-olds in a couple of weeks, so it would be lovely to have her." Miss Heather's big blue eyes lit up and she beamed at Annie.

"Oh, well she's not six for a while yet," I said, sensing Annie's disappointment through her hand, which loosened its grip. "Is that a problem?"

Miss Heather grimaced. "Miss Victoria wanted them to be six really. Aww but little Annie..." She looked down sadly and saw Annie, who was now looking at the floor, not wanting Miss Heather to see the tears that would no doubt be welling up. "She's my favourite," she whispered to me.

"It's okay, not to worry," I said. I looked down at Annie. "It's only seven months until you're six, darling. It's not that long. It'll soon pass." She looked up at me, tears balancing on the rims of her eyes. She nodded and tried to smile, but I could see her bottom lip quivering, and she tried to pull me away from Miss Heather.

I told Miss Heather to put her name down to start in April, thanked her, and we started to walk out of the studio. We were almost back at the car when I heard Miss Heather calling me. We stopped and turned to see her heading to us, the wind blowing her blonde hair all over her face. "Next Saturday. One o'clock class. Keep it to yourself," she said quietly, giving Annie a cheeky smile, drawing her into a secret to be kept between the three of us. I didn't need to look at Annie to see the excitement on her little face.

When I told Rob, he was his usual quiet self. "How much is this one going to cost?" he asked. I gave him the details. "But she can wear whatever she likes, no uniform for this one, just the class fees," I justified. "And Miss Heather said they shouldn't really start until they're six, so she's making an exception for Annie because she's so good."

"She said I'm her favourite," Annie chipped in, not looking up from the Fisher-Price figures she was lining up in front of the fireplace in height order, each exactly two centimetres apart.

"I'll bet," Rob said, cynically. I hated him when he was like this. If Annie had been a boy, no expense would be spared on opportunities to nurture a world-class footballer. It would have been an investment in his future.

But dancing was different. He thought it was a waste of money. My money, but a waste, nonetheless. Rob never gave me a penny towards the costs, and I never asked him, partly because I didn't want to cause an argument, but mainly because I didn't want him to know how much it was costing. Rob thought I was an idiot for paying for dancing. Ballet was okay, he said, but the dance school were just reeling me in, and he often asked where it would end.

It didn't matter what he said. I would do what I wanted, and what I thought was best for Annie. *Some people spend more money on wine than I do on Annie's classes.* So, fuck Rob.

If I had any worries like Rob's, they were eased by the praise Annie received. I could justify the money if she enjoyed it, and she was good at it.

Miss Heather came out of the class the following Saturday with Annie. "Oh my goodness," she said dramatically. "Wow. Just wow!" Annie giggled.

"What did you do?" I asked Annie.

"Let me show you," Miss Heather said, getting her phone out, and flipping it to show a landscape video. I watched, as my little girl, who still did 'naughty toes and nice toes' in ballet class, did forward rolls, teddy bear rolls, handstands, and cartwheels. I had no idea she could do any of these things. And she could do them well, as far as my untrained, and slightly biased, eyes could see. She looked flexible, springy, and light on her feet, as if she'd been doing these classes for months. She was in her element, and I could hear Miss Heather and Miss Emma shouting "Well done, Annie!" The class were cheering her on as she did three cartwheels in a row, followed by a forward roll, from which she stood up, without so much as a wobble, arms outstretched like a gymnast. I looked at Miss Heather.

"She's really good," she said, seriously. "Really good."

Annie was hopping foot to foot. "Do you need the loo?" I asked her. She nodded and then ran off to the toilet.

"Honestly, Lydia, she was sooo good," Miss Heather said again, gently touching my arm. "She's a natural, honestly. She'll be an amazing dancer and she's so flexible."

I hadn't noticed Miss Victoria creep up behind us. "Look at this," Miss Heather said.

Miss Victoria watched the video. "Wow, she's amazing!" she said. As she walked off, she looked over her shoulder. "One to watch there, Miss Heather."

I was so proud. What mother wouldn't be?

4

And the Money Kept Rolling In...

"PLEASE COULD YOU FILL the car up with petrol?" I asked Rob one Sunday evening, as I ironed Annie's school shirts.

"It was only filled on Monday... why does it need filling already?" I knew this was not a conversation that would end well.

"Because we've been at the studio every night last week, and then a trip to Sheffield this weekend, so it's almost on red. I'll give you the money."

"It's not about the money for petrol, Lydia. Well, not really... It's about the amount of money that gets spent on dancing overall." I knew it. I rolled my eyes, though it was hard to argue when I knew he was right. Dancing was costing a small fortune every month now.

Miss Victoria had kindly organised a coach trip to a huge dance convention. I didn't really want to go on the coach as I knew the other mums would be on the gin or wine as soon as it set off. Plus, Annie got travel sick, so we decided to drive instead.

"How much has this weekend cost?" Rob asked me, accusingly.

"I have no idea, Rob. I wasn't keeping tally. Not much, though…"

The weekend had cost more than a family holiday abroad for a week – aside from the petrol cost, there was an entry fee, both for the kids and for the mums. The food at the convention was extortionate school cafeteria shite – stale sandwiches curling up at the edges, and limp salad that had certainly seen fresher days. There were bacon and sausage rolls available, but Belinda bought one and the bread disintegrated when she picked it up. No thank you. We all bought lunch, and then decided – on realising the sandwiches were inedible – to go to the pub next door to the convention centre for a proper lunch, again with wine. The girls had all chosen workshops and classes they wanted to take part in. All at a significant additional cost, and the teachers of these sessions (practically celebrities as far as the girls were concerned) were all selling their own merch, so of course the pressure was on, because… you know… 'for the memories'.

There seemed to be an infinite number of pop-up stalls selling dancewear in every style, shape, fabric you could think of. Everything from tiny baby tutus to commercial dance outfits – some funky, some definitely slutty, I thought. Most of Annie's group had decided they wanted to buy the 'iconic' Lola Lovell crop top and shorts sets, all identical in style – lace over Lycra with a high halter neck – but in (as we were told by the rather intimidating old boot running the stall) forty-six different colours. Wonderful, the mothers all chirped, the girls could have matching outfits in their own colour choice. *Yes, wonderful,* I thought. *For fuck's sake.* I really hoped my overdraft limit would hold out until Monday and not financially embarrass me in front of this coven. Annie chose a pale silvery-blue, and in truth I did love it. It emphasised her pale skin but in a flattering way, and would make her stand out from the crowd, while still being part of it. And she was so pleased to have something the other girls had, so she could feel like part of the gang. Libby had raspberry pink, Jemima went with a peacock blue-green, Holly chose a deep 'Cadburys purple', and Phoebe settled on a rusty orange colour, though I could see she really wanted the raspberry pink. It wouldn't have mattered which one Libby had – Phoebe would always want that one. Forty-six colour choices, and Phoebe wanted that one. Seriously, there was no difference visible to the naked eye, between the raspberry pink and the fuchsia, but it was obviously a massive difference to Phoebe. After much debate, Becky made the decision for her. As I'd gotten to know the mums over the last couple of years, I knew there was a huge rivalry between the mums, which clearly rubbed off on their daughters.

As the afternoon classes were getting ready to start, we had gathered in one of the open areas big enough to accommodate all thirty-two kids and their mothers/grandmothers.

"Can I have your attention?" Miss Victoria shouted over the din. She batted one of her own grandchildren away, telling her to go and sit down with the other girls. "Girls, mums, grandmas! I know the girls have their next class in twenty minutes, so I wanted to do this now… come on, girls, *shush* please. This is very important."

We looked at each other. Do what now?

"Miss Stacy, Miss Jessica, Miss Heather, and I have been super busy for the last few weeks, putting together a surprise for you all." The girls glanced at their friends excitedly, eyes wide open. What could it be?

"Miss Stacy, please could you come up to show the girls."

Miss Stacy was Miss Victoria's daughter. They shared numerous mannerisms, as well as their hoarse, scratchy voices and their unwavering commitment to all things dance. Miss Stacy tiptoed in between all the girls sat on the floor, carrying a costume bag.

"Now, we know you've all been watching *Backstage* on the telly, and loving how professional and smart all the girls look, so we wanted to do something for you." With that, she dramatically unzipped the Barbie-pink cover to reveal – not a costume, but a uniform. Miss Jessica stepped forwards to help her get the various bits out of the cover, and Miss Heather also took her place in the line to transform into a clotheshorse. Between them, they held up a leotard, a crop top, a pair of shorts, a pair of leggings, a t-shirt, a tracksuit, a onesie, a pair of sliders and a beanie hat – all bearing the VCS logo in black stitching against a marbled turquoise background.

Gladys, the old bat from reception, who I now knew was Miss Victoria's mother, shouted, "Victoria, do you want these as well?"

"Oh yes, I forgot about them." Miss Victoria cackled. Gladys stepped carefully round the crowd – her fat, swollen ankles visible under her voluminous pleated skirt – foretelling the physique Miss Victoria and Miss Stacy were heading for as they got older, though in truth both of them already had pretty unsightly 'cankles'. This had always surprised me, given their chosen career paths.

Gladys wheeled round a small cabin-sized four-wheel suitcase with a holdall sat comfortably on top. Again, these were mostly marbled turquoise with black edging and were adorned with the VCS logo. She took her place at the front of the crowd next to Miss Heather and did what I suppose she thought was a funny gesture, twisting her hands towards the bags, as though modelling them for a shopping channel.

I didn't think it was funny. I thought it was fucking ridiculous. Their generous surprise was going to cost all of us a fucking fortune. Nausea hit me and my bowels turned to ice. I could feel the colour draining from my face, blood being replaced by a sickening numbness, making it hard for me to speak.

"Fuck," said Sheryl, the mum next to me, under her breath. I looked at the other mums, who seemed impressed at the design skills, and delighted at the thoughtfulness of the teachers. I couldn't speak. I could only look at Sheryl, widen my eyes and take in a sharp breath, which I hoped conveyed something like 'yeah, fuck'.

I spotted Annie looking amazed at these beautiful garments. "Just like on *Backstage*," she mouthed to me.

Why had they done this? Why did they bring these beautiful, expensive, fucking insane uniforms all the way to Sheffield? Why could they not have shown the mums back at the studio? Preferably when the kids were not around. This was a deliberate move, I thought. It was going to be impossible to get out of buying these now, even though I couldn't afford it. We didn't know the cost yet, but I knew it would cost more than my wedding dress had. For fuck's sake, they were children and would outgrow them in less than a year.

"Now," Miss Victoria continued. "There's no obligation to buy any of these. You can buy as many or as few bits as you want. They weren't cheap, but we want to present ourselves as best we can, don't we, girls?" The girls all nodded enthusiastically, mesmerised by the uniforms. "And the teaching staff have spent an awful lot of time in designing them, and getting samples so we could make sure we get the best quality. So they make us look like a really professional team, just like the girls on *Backstage*. So... if we do decide to start a competition team..." This was left hanging.

The girls could read between the lines, their eyes widening with excitement. I could read between the lines too, but felt much less optimistic...

The noise levels picked up again as the girls twittered excitedly about which bit they 'just *had* to have'.

"Like I said, there's no obligation to buy any of them, but... when we got the sample made, we were so excited we took the liberty of ordering them for everyone who was coming this weekend, so speak to your mummies. I have some price lists which I'll give to your mummies. Then," looking at us, "if you want to buy today, they're in the van and you can have them ready to wear tomorrow." She smiled, so proud of herself and all she and her team had achieved in designing an unnecessary, no doubt unaffordable set of clothes to be worn a handful of times. There were no words to describe the hatred I felt towards that woman in that moment.

I looked at the price list and my head began to spin. I could hear the girls, their voices getting louder as their excitement built. I felt dizzy and had to lean against the pillar at the side of me to stop myself from falling as I began to feel unbalanced. It had become unbearably hot all of a sudden.

I could hear snippets of conversations between various mums and kids. I tried to listen out for anyone who might be voicing the panicked thoughts going round my brain. But there were none.

"OMG, I want all of it!" one said.

Leotard £85.00

"Me too, they're so *Backstage!*"

Crop top £65.00

"Mummy, can I have them all?"

Shorts £40.00

"Yes, you can, but it's part of your birthday present."

Leggings £55.00

"Miss Victoria, please can I get Ava's now?"

T-shirt £45.00

"Miss Victoria, please could I have Tilly's as well?"

Tracksuit £135.00 up to age 12, then increasing to £145.00

"Better not tell my husband about this," said another.

Onesie £85.00

"Ah…what they don't know can't hurt them, right?" laughed her friend.

Sliders £35.00

Miss Victoria was coming round with the machine for card payments and a notebook.

"Only if you promise to be a good girl for the rest of the weekend."

Beanie hat £40.00

The words started to blur on the page.

Suitcase £155.00

"Are you okay?"

Duffel bag £75.00.

Sheryl was speaking to me. "Lydia, are you okay? You look a bit pale." *Get yourself together*, I thought, *and do it quickly.*

"Haha, no I think I'm having a heart attack, looking at this list," I tried to joke, but knew it wasn't landing.

"Yeah, me too," Sheryl said, looking at the piece of paper that had now ruined the whole weekend. "There's no way I can afford this. Wish we'd known about this in advance."

I couldn't take my eyes off the paper, scanning the numbers and quickly trying to add it up. Over eight hundred pounds. Dropped into conversation so casually. Sickening me to my stomach. Spoiling the whole convention experience.

Then I remembered I had pawned some jewellery last week (in anticipation of this weekend costing a bit more than I expected, and definitely a lot more than I wanted Rob to see on our bank statements). The cash was hidden at the back of my phone case. Just over five hundred. I could worry about how I would explain my missing wedding and engagement rings if and when Rob ever even noticed. The nausea started to wear off. Immediate crisis averted. I could get part of the kit, if not all of it. The rest would have to be for Christmas. Annie was fine with that. I think she really wanted to wear the Lola Lovell outfit anyway but didn't want to be the odd one out: We settled on the leotard, tracksuit, sliders and beanie hat, so there would be a little cash left over, for any other nasty surprises that might crop up.

I looked at Sheryl, could see her bottom lip trembling, and she was starting to flush from her neck upwards. I could see she was desperately trying to hold back the tears, not let anyone, but especially her daughter Rosie, see her like this.

"Can I lend you the money?" I whispered. "Just maybe get the tracksuit and beanie for now and pay me back when you can."

"No, absolutely not!" Sheryl took a step back. "I couldn't let you do that. But thank you so much for the offer. It's so sweet of you but I couldn't."

I felt bad then. Rosie seemed a nice enough kid, always polite, and Annie seemed to like her. I knew Sheryl was a single mum of three kids. Rosie was her youngest and was the only one still at home. I didn't know her that well, but we got along okay, and I knew she had more than one job to support her kids – the elder two being at university – but I wasn't even sure what her jobs were. All I knew for sure was that she stood out amongst the dance mums. She didn't have highlights in her mousy hair. She had no acrylic on her nails, though she had clearly painted them herself for that weekend, the slightly chipped edges giving it away. Her clothes weren't even noticeable, let alone designer, like everyone else's seemed to be. Well, apart from mine, of course. Sheryl was doing the best she could for her kids, but it wasn't enough. Not for the dance world.

"Honestly, it's fine," I said. "Please let me do this for Rosie. It's an absolutely shit thing they've done, springing this on us like this, putting us in this position. It's just fucking thoughtless, and cruel. Please, Sheryl, I want to help. I can't let Rosie feel left out. Please let me." I wasn't waiting for an answer. I was getting the cash out of my phone case. *I can fake not being hungry at dinner time*, I thought.

Rosie was coming over. "Sheryl, please take it," I pleaded, offering the notes as discreetly as I could. It would be embarrassing enough to have to borrow money from another mum, without any of the other mums – or even worse, the kids – knowing about it.

Sheryl regained her composure, not wanting Rosie to see her deflated. She took a deep breath, I assumed to gather the stoicism to keep it together. "No." She put her hand out to affirm she would not be budging on this. "I'm completely out of my depth here. There's no way I can keep up financially with all this. I wanted Rosie to have the same opportunities that her sisters had, but things are different now, and I just can't afford it."

"But please, I can…"

She took hold of both of my hands and looked me square in the eyes. "Thank you so much, I appreciate the offer, and the kindness behind the offer, but I can't. It's a uniform this month. Next week it will be something else. I'm spending more than half of my wages on this now, and I just can't keep doing it. I feel like I'm drowning."

As Annie came over, bouncing around, babbling about being on a team, and looking like they are on *Backstage*, I watched Sheryl and Rosie leave, Sheryl's arm around Rosie's hunched shoulders. I saw the tell-tale jerking that told me Rosie was sobbing hard. I knew it would be breaking Sheryl's heart right now, but she was right. Even if she had accepted my offer that day, the financial pressure was relentless. To accept my offer would have only been delaying their inevitable departure from VCS – I could only have offered a very expensive sticking plaster.

At dinner that evening, I ordered a kids' meal for Annie, and a pizza for myself – the cheapest item on the menu. We had taken over a whole area of the Italian restaurant, leaving only a couple of tables for 'walk-ins'. The noise was immense. It was setting my nerves on edge, and I wanted to scream. I couldn't stop thinking about Sheryl walking away like that, and knowing she was right to do it, however hard it had been. The vision of poor Rosie, her dreams unaffordable, sickened me to my stomach, and I left most of the pizza.

I joined in the conversations about classes and leotards and teachers and all the rest of the shite the mums were talking about, but the dirty trick Miss Victoria and the teachers had pulled played heavily on my mind. It was thoughtless, cruel, and I hated her for it.

Back at the hotel, Annie was too hyped for bed. She wanted to play with her friends. We could hear the shouting and laughter in the Premier Inn corridors and opened the door. Other mums were stood in their doorways. Most had opted to share rooms despite the animosity I knew was simmering below the surface between so many of these women. Two-faced bitches. The kids were taking turns doing tumbles down the corridor, then they started mickey-taking some of the acts they'd seen during the day. Little bitches. I noticed Annie about to join in and I shot her a look – don't you

35

dare. She understood the message and cartwheeled away from the conversation.

Not a single person had even noticed, let alone cared, that Sheryl and Rosie weren't there.

Standing in the doorway to that hotel room, I felt I had betrayed Sheryl, a woman I barely knew, by staying and not standing up to Miss Victoria. Not asking where all this would end. I realised my position in this pack of dogs. At that point I was only half in. I was attending classes and events as required, but not really committing to – or wanting to commit to – the culture of the school. I was there for Annie, to support her and be there with her for the things she loved. But I knew there was going to come a point soon where I would have to get on board and join in with the bullshit sycophancy, unquestioningly handing over every penny I had, and essentially becoming another one of Miss Victoria's cash cows. Commit or get out. I knew the sensible choice would be to get out now, before I went bankrupt and risked my marriage for this. But I knew my choice had already been made. I wanted Annie to be happy. At all costs.

The rest of the convention passed slowly for me, but all too quickly for the girls. Apart from a flat tyre for Miss Victoria's bastard uniform van in the afternoon, which I found secretly hilarious, the Sunday was relatively uneventful and forgettable. I just wanted to get home and get in my own bed. I'd had a knot in my stomach that I couldn't shift since the incident with the uniforms and Sheryl leaving. I was stepping into the lion's den, with my eyes wide open. Nobody was forcing me. I was doing it voluntarily. I hated myself for being an absolute pussy and not taking a stand like Sheryl had, but I would hate myself more if I deprived Annie of the opportunities that could be missed if we left.

I never saw Sheryl or Rosie again at the studio. A mutual friend told me months later that they were doing okay, and having made the decision to leave, Sheryl had gotten over the guilt and forgiven herself, while I felt I had sold my soul to the devil herself.

Primary School 1994

"AND THE WINNER OF the James Halford Award this year is... Lydia Hartley!"

Oh no, *I thought, feeling like the embarrassment was going to literally kill me; the heat from blushing spreading throughout my body and threatening to boil me alive from the inside out.*

I wanted to do well in my tests, but I absolutely did not want to win another stupid award. Why did they do this to us? I won it last year and thought I was going to die on awards day. It was meant to be a good thing – a reward for hard work and doing well throughout the year. Not for me, though. For me, this was more like a punishment, a humiliation I thought might actually be the end of me.

On a hot, humid day in June the previous year, the hall of Manor Park Primary School had filled with the whole student population, and their parents, as well as all the teaching staff on one of the hottest days of the year. I had felt hot, sick, and my heart was beating so hard I thought it was going to come up into my throat and choke me to death. I had stomach ache, and despite trying to distract myself and calm myself down by looking for my mum in the sea of faces, the griping wouldn't go away. I was terrified that I would need the toilet and wouldn't be able to hold it in. I tried counting the holes in my new, shiny black patent slip-on shoes that my mother had bought me. I would not have normally been allowed slip-on shoes, but I recognised this as being my mother's way of trying to get me excited about the day – to get me to look forward to it so I could wear my new shoes. I'd have happily worn my battered old Clarks sandals for the rest of my life to avoid this.

As I was in Junior 3, I had to sit through all the other younger class awards first. I looked down the line of cross-legged kids. Most of my class had zoned out by the time we got to Infant 3 anyway, so that helped. I could see Stephen Whittaker examining the revolting contents of his nose that he had just pulled out. Adam Clarke was gazing, open-mouthed, at the artwork on the walls as if he hadn't seen it every day for the last three months. Sarah Wilkie was repeatedly rolling her knee-socks down as far as they'd go on her ankles, and back up again. Christopher Barratt had pulled the laces out of his shoes and was now struggling to get them back where they should be. And Jody Thomas was picking a scab on her knee. This was all good. Maybe they wouldn't even notice my name being called out. It calmed me a little. All I wanted in the world was to be ignored. For the rest of my class to carry on about their business and not even register that I was living my worst nightmare. Nothing to see here.

"And now on to Junior 3, the winner of the James Halford Award for the second year running... Lydia Hartley."

My own name sounded hateful. How had I never noticed how horrible it was? Why did my parents call me something *so ugly and weird? They must have known it would draw attention to me, the absolute last thing in the world I ever wanted.*

I stumbled slightly as I stood up, partly because I was shaking so badly, and partly because my legs and feet had gone numb from sitting cross-legged and tense for almost two hours. I walked up to the stage, feeling every set of eyes in the hall, and every set of eyes my imagination had also invited, to look at me, to watch me make a fool of myself. I was terrified. Would I trip up? Would I poo myself? Would I actually vomit as I felt I might?

As it turned out, I did none of those things. I went a horrible shade of beetroot, and sweated profusely, but I managed to get to the stage without dying, shake Mr Allan's hand and receive my certificate and trophy. I even managed the return journey back to my place on the floor without incident.

But here we were again. I had deliberately answered a couple of questions wrong on each of the tests. I remembered last year Mrs Murray had said there were only a few marks between me and Dawn Emery and only a single point between Dawn and Trevor Bailey, so I thought I could probably sway it so I still did well, but not well enough to actually win anything. I hadn't banked on Trevor's nanna dying having such an effect on his grades. Amanda Jones' parents had been paying a tutor, and she was always telling me how she was going to beat me this year. Fine, I thought, you'll get no competition from me. *But the tutor hadn't been enough.*

When Mrs Taylor had called my name out, I wanted the earth to open up and swallow me. I was instantly reminded of how much I hated hearing my name being called out. I'd had my fingers crossed for Dawn, Amanda, and Trevor scooping the trophies, but to no avail.

But worse than that, despite the heat radiating across my face, I could feel something worse – the bitterness of my so-called friends. Carly and Tina sat behind me, whispering just loud enough for me to hear, but not Mrs Taylor.

"It's all right. My sister said when people get trophies, they get their heads kicked in at high school," Tina said.

Carly giggled. "Yeah, I heard that as well. And I heard if you're a swot, you actually get your head flushed down the toilet to flush your brains away."

"Ewww, that's so gross! But it might teach her a lesson and make her stop thinking she's better than everyone else."

I didn't think I was better than anyone else. I didn't even think I was as good as anyone else. I was good at maths and English, and maybe science. But I was rubbish at sports, and I was rubbish at music and I was rubbish at art. And I was rubbish at making friends. And I looked weird. And I blushed whenever anyone paid me any attention I didn't like. I spent playtimes with the other girls, but never really felt like they liked me very much. I thought they only let me play to make the numbers up and so there would be someone to be last to be picked for team games. And now two of my so-called friends hated me. And high school would soon be here.

Better stock up on shampoo.

5

Making Friends

THE MONTHS THAT FOLLOWED the convention in Sheffield were a blur of non-stop activity at VCS. The teaching staff and Miss Victoria had been inspired by everything they had seen in Sheffield and were buzzing with ideas. To anyone outside the school, and even to me now with hindsight, they took a very 'scattergun' approach – if it's something we can do, we should. Regardless of whether the kids wanted to, regardless of whether the parents wanted to (or could afford to), not a thought that the kids might have homework, or need to get to bed at a reasonable time. The logistics of having so many plates to spin was never a consideration, and often teachers would get tired and stressed and start shouting more at the girls, just because they themselves had overlapped rehearsals.

The teachers wanted to compete. They felt they had a strong enough school to hold their own in a competitive environment and they wanted to show the world. They hurriedly drafted a contract for parents of the 'chosen ones' who had expressed an interest in joining the competition squad. At that time, they were only interested in putting their best dancers out in each of the age categories, and Annie was so excited to be picked for her age group, along with her friend Holly.

As well as competitions, there were auditions for various summer school places, ballet school places for the older girls, a couple of TV shows that were going to be piloted, musicals (often to include acting and singing – neither of which the school offered classes in at that time, though naturally the opportunity was there and they would come to jump on it), modelling opportunities, masterclasses, panto audition… it never ended.

But most pressing was Starstruck – VCS's dance extravaganza. Done only every two years, thank fuck, the effort that went into a show (which really would only be watched by friends and family of the students) was actually quite admirable. Rehearsals started in September, though teachers had been having creative meetings and parent meetings long before, increasing gradually from extra half hours here and there, to long, full days at weekends.

The three weekends before the show's run started were spent at the Adelphi theatre – a beautiful old Victorian building in the centre of town. Somewhat dilapidated in parts, it still had many of its original features and had an old-world charm that attracted visitors from around the country. It was relatively large for a theatre of its age, and every year hosted ballet companies from Russia, West End musical companies, stand-up comedians, semi-professional drama companies doing boring plays about detectives and murder – blah, blah, blah – very Agatha

Christie and clichéd, I thought. Not my cup of tea. It was also the venue for the Christmas pantomime – which this year would be *Cinderella*. Panto auditions were also on my radar, but I wanted to get Starstruck out of the way before I worried about the next thing.

We were allowed to watch the Starstruck dress rehearsals, which I thought kind of ruined the surprise, but I suppose Miss Victoria wanted to dangle a bit of a carrot for the mums who had given up their Easter weekend, and Mother's Day, for this.

As Annie was still only seven, she and her contemporaries were still not old enough to have real dressing rooms – instead they all (I think somewhere between 180 and 200 juniors) flooded a large area at the back of the Adelphi.

Miss Victoria had arranged with the theatre that we could leave costumes and shoes there after the final (yes final – there were three) dress rehearsal, so nothing would be forgotten on opening night. All had to be hung up on rails that bordered the circumference of the atrium, which would be our home the following week. They had to be on labelled coat hangers, with clear plastic bags attached to each one containing the shoes for that costume, and any tights, hair accessories or props. Easy. I was grateful we wouldn't have to keep lugging seven costumes backwards and forwards for the week.

This was Annie's third Starstruck. Her first one had been when she was only really a toddler. The girls formed a long line across the stage and performed 'Tulips from Amsterdam' – hair wired into upturned braids, poking out under white Volendam hats. Great for those who had long, thick hair, less so for the rest of the tots, like Annie, who had shoulder-length wisps of baby hair. They wore costumes that I assumed to be like the Dutch national costume but combined with a cutesy baby tutu. Despite the insane cost of it, I loved it. I thought Annie was adorable, even though her braids weren't thick enough to hold the wire.

By her second Starstruck, Annie was doing more classes, so there were inevitably more rehearsals, more costumes, and more accessories. Could it really have only been two years ago that she did 'English Country Garden' (ballet), 'My Boy Lollipop' (tap – gave me the ick; I hated that one. Way too sugary for me and I imagined the audience to be full of dirty old men getting off on watching these little tots licking fake lollipops), and 'Happy Working Song' (modern – from the Disney film *Enchanted*, which was Annie's favourite at the time)?

I think that the third Starstruck was probably the point I started to feel like a 'dance mum', and not an outsider. Sarah (Holly's mother) and I had gravitated to each other as our kids would soon be competing together. It was in my mind constantly that this 'friendship' we had drifted into would soon be tested as the girls would inevitably be competing *against* each other, but I would deal with that as it happened. I mean… we were all grown-ups… We became friendly with a few other mums, though I wasn't sure I would ever call them 'friends'.

All girls were now – as was a requirement to be part of the competition squad – doing ballet, tap, modern, acro, contemporary, and hip-hop as a minimum. For extra brownie points, Annie, Phoebe, Libby, Jemima and Holly also did an additional ballet class, and a commercial class, as well as drama, which had been added only recently to the school's curriculum. In truth, Annie didn't like the drama class, probably because there were boys in it, and boys were still disgusting to her. But she didn't want to not do it. Fear Of Missing Out...

Sarah and I had buddied up and often took turns to drive the four of us for rehearsals. Annie got on well with Holly, who was also quite an introverted child.

Phoebe and Libby were 'frenemies', as were their mothers, and Sarah and I both found their antics hilarious. A while ago, Phoebe's mother, Jo, whispered to us about how Phoebe had been 'scouted' for something or other after last year's school nativity. Wow, we would say, that's amazing. I've no idea how Jo didn't see through my fake enthusiasm (I have been told more than once that my facial expressions give away what I'm really thinking). Later Belinda would tell us, in the same conspiratorial whisper, that Jo was wildly exaggerating, and that Phoebe had happened to be on the front row of 'Away in a Manger' when a parent, who happened to work for the local paper, took an admittedly cute shot of her, singing as though her life depended on it. The picture was a quarter of a page, and Jo was understandably proud, but her tales of Phoebe being scouted were somewhat embellished. Belinda's version of events was that as the parents were all stood with Jo and Belinda cooing over the pictures in the paper (six pictures in all, but Phoebe's was the biggest apparently) in the playground, another mum, whose brother worked in Paris as a children's fashion designer, made a comment to the effect of "Aww she's so cute. She should be doing some modelling…" That was it. There was no follow-up. No modelling contract had been forthcoming. No lucrative deals with BabyGap, JoJo Maman Bébé, or anyone else. Nothing. But Jo had dined out on this for several weeks now, and Sarah and I (and Belinda of course) loved to hear the story being retold, as the embellishments got more outlandish each time. But as much as we saw the situation for what it was, Belinda was really pissed off about it. It took me a while to figure out exactly why, but eventually I realised it was as simple as Phoebe getting a bigger picture in the paper than Libby.

Lesley and Jemima were still a bit of an enigma. I got the impression both mother and daughter felt they were far superior to everyone else, even though ninety-nine per cent of students and parents also had a similar air about them. Lesley was horse-like, but well groomed. Her long, thick hair was immaculately styled into bouncy curls, with honey blonde and ash brown highlights, and I never saw her with dark roots. Her face was fully made up at all times. Contouring, which must have taken hours, looked like it was slimming her already long face down, but I couldn't criticise. She always looked like she'd stepped out of *Vogue*. Immaculate clothing, very expensive looking, but no obvious designer branding anywhere. Her handbags were made by Coach or Hobbs, and always understated and classy. Her sunglasses, always perched on her head regardless of the weather, were Stella McCartney, Tom Ford, or Givenchy, depending on her mood, but again always understated. She would waltz into the studio, bag casually draped over the crook of her arm, in heels I couldn't even imagine wearing, yet she glided across the potholed, gravel car park without incident.

Jemima was a brat. I couldn't stand her, and though I would never have spoken of her badly in front of anyone other than Sarah, I knew most of the girls and mums found her annoying. She had a frizz of uncontrollable red hair, and had a bitchy resting face, despite being only seven years old. Her pale green eyes always seemed to be judging. Jemima was also an only child – I suspected possibly an accident – and it seemed unlikely she would ever have any brothers or sisters, as Lesley and her husband Dominic were both career-minded. They enjoyed exotic holidays several times a year, leaving Jemima at home with Lesley's mum, Nancy. Both of Jemima's parents worked away regularly, often hosting 'scheduling meetings' with both of their own mums to coordinate their diaries. Work schedules were the highest priority. After that came golf for Dom, and hair/beauty appointments for Lesley. They would also block out time for socialising because it was important to them... for their wellbeing. After that, they would look at whether either of them were available for any of Jemima's activities, and give consideration, before committing, to whether they might be too tired, so would need grandparents to step in. So, I understood why maybe Jemima acted out a little bit, but it didn't stop me from disliking her.

We saw more of Lesley's mum, Nancy, than we did of Lesley. Nancy was lovely – one of the kindest people I've ever met. She would do anything for anyone, and she did pretty much everything for Lesley and Jemima. It pissed me off that sometimes I would see Nancy looking tired, and she would tell me about how busy Lesley had been – going to Dubai last week for a work thing, and then a hen party in Croatia at the weekend, and she's had to have a day off today to have a rest and get some much-timed 'downtime' before a full day of beauty appointments tomorrow. *Yeah*, I thought, *it must be truly exhausting for her. Poor Lesley. All pampered and beautiful, no doubt, while her own mum wears herself out running round for Jemima.*

So, on the night of the final dress rehearsal as the girls changed into PJs and onesies (it was 11pm on a school night), we hung up costumes on pre-labelled hangers as instructed, ready for the opening night. Accessories were in clear plastic bags, with names written on in black permanent marker. The rails around the atrium looked surprisingly well-organised given the number of costumes they held. We had pulled two tables together for our little group, and had all claimed our own places at them. We had set up mirrors, make-up, wipes, hairbrushes and a billion hairpins at each station. The show was on Wednesday, Thursday, Friday and Saturday nights, with a matinee performance on Saturday.

As we all started to leave the building, I stopped. "Oh, shit," I said, rummaging in my bag. "I think I've left my car keys on the table."

I saw an eyeroll from Jemima. She had been whining for twenty minutes about needing to get home to bed. Like she was the only one. I ignored her and looked at Sarah. "Could you take Annie, and I'll run back for them?"

"Yes, no probs. We'll walk slowly so you can catch us up."

"Shall I come with you, Mummy?" Annie asked.

"No, it's fine," I said. "You go with Holly and Sarah, and I'll catch you up in two minutes."

Sarah and I had planned this in advance. I went back to our table in the atrium, which was now eerily quiet. Not a soul around. You could almost sense the presence of ghosts. I had stashed gifts in my handbag and one of Annie's costume bags. The mums had all clubbed together so the girls could have the same. I set up each make-up station with a 'good luck' card, a teddy bear with bow matching the colour of each child's tap outfit, as they were all different, and a silver necklace with a ballet shoe pendant, beautifully gift-wrapped by the jewellery shop. We figured if Miss Victoria was confident nobody would steal hundreds of thousands of pounds' worth of costumes, a few presents for seven-year-old girls were unlikely to attract attention from any would-be thieves.

Belinda was going to come straight from work the next night, so would be there earlier, and would bring helium balloons to attach to the girls' chairs. Jo would bring Libby. Sarah was picking Annie and me up a bit early so we could get something to eat before getting ready. We had no idea what Jemima's plans would be. No doubt Nancy would be bringing her, and her mother would watch from the front row of the stalls, assuming she wasn't too tired.

My Friend

BACK WHEN I WAS *around nine or ten years old, a family moved in a few doors away from us. Mum, dad, a son who was about sixteen, so practically an adult as far as I was concerned, and a daughter who was my age.*

I was skipping on the drive one day when Kelly walked past with her mum and their dog, a ratty little terrier.

"Hello," the mum said. "We heard there were some girls on the street around Kelly's age. Are you Lydia or Joanne?"

"Lydia. Joanne lives over there." I pointed at the big house over the road.

"Well, hi, Lydia. This is Kelly. Say hello, Kelly." Kelly was clearly mortified to have her mother be so bolshy and practically force people to make friends with her. It didn't bother me. Joanne was a bit odd and never played outside of her house, so I didn't have much to do with her. I was desperate to have someone I could play with, so I was grateful for Kelly's mum's interference.

"Wanna play?" I assume that's how we became friends. I think I must have instigated our friendship, as Kelly was even more introverted than I was. Kelly went to the local school, having moved only a couple of miles from the next

village, while I went to another school, which was closer to the house we lived in when I was four.

I struggle to remember now what friendships were built on at that young age, but we were like sisters, always at each other's houses.

I remember when we were a bit older, Kelly used to get the Jackie magazine every week, and we would pore through it, devouring anything and everything we could that taught us the things we didn't want to ask our parents about. Thursday night was 'Jackie night' and I would run up the road to Kelly's straight after tea and we'd read the problem page first. Boyfriends, periods, bras, bullying, early sexual experiences... I guess these are the things we talked and bonded over, all seeming a million miles into our futures. We were just on that cusp of childhood and adolescence.

Kelly's mum once bought her a box of tampons, so she could have a look and get used to the idea before she actually started her periods. It seemed bizarre to me as periods were still such an alien concept that I didn't really believe there was any truth in it – I thought it was probably some kind of urban legend.

Kelly and I were, I suppose, very similar in our personalities, and our levels of maturity. We were happy in our own company, and neither of us were really interested in spending time with other friends from school, so we became very close.

The only evenings we didn't see each other were Mondays and Wednesdays. On a Monday, I had swimming lessons, and on Mondays and Wednesdays, Kelly went to ballet class. She never really spoke much about the classes one way or another. I assumed she must have quite enjoyed them, or she would have told me, but equally I never really got the impression she was passionate about it. It was just something she did. Same for me with swimming.

I remember once going round to Kelly's house when she was practising for a ballet exam. Her mum had cleared the dining room of all furniture to give her the space she needed. Her mum sat on a chair in the corner and pressed 'stop' and 'play' on the cassette player periodically. I watched for a while as Kelly would lift one foot daintily and bring it into the inside of the opposite knee, then slowly the grounded foot would raise onto tiptoes. Although the movement itself didn't look particularly difficult to me, there was a grace about the way she did it that I knew would be incredibly difficult.

Kelly was wearing shorts and t-shirt, and a pair of pink satin ballet shoes with ribbons tied around her bare ankles. Her tanned legs were slim, but the muscles when she stood up on her toes defined themselves, to show to the world how much effort went into this simple move.

The raised leg was slowly stretched out to the back, and I saw her hip bone move to allow that back leg to turn out and face the wall instead of the floor. I'd always thought ballet looked quite easy, but then having watched the strength Kelly had in her muscles, I knew differently. While anyone could stand on their tiptoes, or stretch a leg out, to do it gracefully, and without shaking or wobbling, took real control and that was definitely not easy.

I watched quietly, and when the tape finished, Christine told Kelly she had done okay but should practise a lot more before the exam.

"I was talking to your friends' mums at dancing and they're all practising for at least an hour and a half every single night," she told her.

I was shocked – not at the amount of practice needed, but at the idea that Kelly had friends that I didn't know about. Not school friends, but dance friends. They were also the same age as us, these girls I had never even known existed, and they would also have those toned leg muscles that I knew I would never have. My best friend was part of something I would never be a part of, even though she never saw them outside of classes or even mentioned them in passing.

As we went to different primary schools, we followed the natural path into their respective associated high schools and so were still separated during the day.

Kelly found the transition from primary to high school much easier than I did. We both had that 'nerd vibe' which dictated who our school friendship groups would eventually be. But whereas I very much blended into the background of high school (at least in the first couple of years), Kelly seemed to have the best of two very different worlds. She stayed out of trouble and did well with her schoolwork as she was, essentially, one of the brainy and studious kids, while also being considered by her peers to be one of the cool kids based purely on her loose association with some other more popular girls who she knew from her dance classes. She never cared about popularity, though. Popular meant attention, and despite the confidence she had when she danced, Kelly actively avoided any kind of attention. She was shy around boys, and hated anything that would make her stand out. Kelly was just cool enough that she was never expected to join the more rebellious faction of the school year group, but she was protected from bullying because of who she danced with.

I wasn't so lucky.

6

Showtime!

WHEN THE FOUR OF us arrived at the Adelphi the following afternoon, it was still fairly early. The show would start at 7pm and Miss Victoria wanted everyone there for 5pm. We arrived around half an hour early, but the place was already buzzing with excitement. There were kids and parents all over the place. Some of the little ones were already in full costume and make-up, ready to go on stage in three hours.

The concourse around the atrium was packed with the youngest dancers and their mothers – tiny little things in tiny little tutus, hair curled into ringlets, one or two still sucking dummies. I wondered how many of those pretty pastel tutus would make it to the stage covered in blackcurrant juice, the mothers incurring the wrath of Miss Victoria, who had specifically warned people at the dress rehearsal "No eating or drinking in costumes, unless it's water!" Some mothers must have had death wishes.

We made our way through clogging clouds of hairspray and glitter to our table in the atrium. Belinda was there already, and the pink star-shaped helium balloons were tied to each improvised vanity station. She was standing, hairpins in mouth, spraying and scraping Libby's hair into the sleekest of buns, as Libby sat playing a game on her mum's phone. Jo and Phoebe had arrived but gone off somewhere to find something to eat.

We had brought a picnic tea – sandwiches, mini sausages, crisps and chocolate brownies – so Annie and Holly demolished it quickly so they could put on their costumes. On the way in, Miss Victoria had been at the door handing out instruction sheets, so as we tucked into our sandwiches, we read through.

JUNIORS

Ballet – Cinderella

Pink dress, white tights, white ballet shoes, tiara.
Hair to be in a tight bun at the crown – not right on top,
not a low bun – AT THE CROWN! If anyone doesn't know
where the crown is, please ask someone who does know!
Children will not be allowed on stage if they have dirty
tights or scuff marks on their ballet shoes, so please be
careful!

Fuck me, I thought, *she's upped her game since the last show – not allowed on stage! Imagine, after paying all that money and spending months doing extra lessons, being told they can't go on because there's a speck of dirt on their tights. I mean, there's having high standards, and then there's being obsessive and bloody unrealistic.*

Tap – Rat Pack Tribute

Striped costume, tan tights, black tap shoes, pillbox hat,
gloves
Hair to be in low bun, with NO WISPY BITS! Children will
be inspected at the side of the stage. We've done three
dress rehearsals, so we know everyone has the gloves and
hat. Any child who does not have all accessories will not
be allowed on the stage.

Again, what the actual fuck?

Modern – Disney

Glitter dress, tan tights, tan shoes
Hair in high bun with curly hairpiece and headband
Curls should be immaculate. Do whatever it takes to
remove any frizz. Any messy hairpieces, or missing
headbands, and your child will not be allowed on stage.

Commercial – Girl Pop

Black pants, vest top, hoodie, headscarf, white pumps
Hair in high bun with curly hair piece. Headscarf must be
secured with hair grips and tied in a tight knot.

*What, no threat? And finally, after hair up, hair down, hair
up, no hair change!*

Contemporary – Ghost

Pale blue dress, blue shorts, bare feet, blue hair ribbon
Hair to be half up half down with blue ribbon in a bow.
Hair should be curled into loose ringlets if possible.

Again, no threat, although I think there will likely be about six and a half minutes to get changed into the contemporary dress and ringlet the hair. How on earth…?

Acro – The Eve of the War

Catsuit, sequinned hair accessory to be worn on the left above the ear.
Hair in low bun, but any wispy bits must be smoothed down or… you guessed it… your child will not be allowed on the stage!

Ah, there it is. Yet another hair change, and the obligatory threat.

I considered myself to be pretty organised, but this instruction was scaring me. I would never have sent Annie to the stage with bits of costume missing, but now I was tense and felt anxious. I kept checking the bags attached to the hangers to make sure everything was there. I was glad the girls were all in all of these dances together, the pressure shared between us. But I wished we had an extra set of hands for the ringlets. I'd brought the chopstick curler, which was on the shopping list we were given a few weeks earlier, but I hadn't even tested it to make sure it worked. Some dance mum I was…

The back page of the instruction advised 'all parents and children in the auditorium at 6pm sharp' – 6pm *sharp*? I didn't remember the last show being quite this bossy. I looked at Sarah, who was reading through her copy, eyebrows raised. "Hmm, interesting," she said, folding the papers carefully and placing them gently on the table. "Not sure it needs to be in that tone."

Belinda chipped in through the side of her mouth, which was full of hair pins. "It's only so the girls all look professional on stage, so they all look the same. Otherwise, it looks a bit of a mess." *Oh fuck off, Belinda.*

"Yeah," I said. "I agree with all that, but they're not professional dancers. They're little girls. They're seven years old, for fuck's sake." The girls were too busy looking at the game Libby was playing to take any notice of my language.

"I know," Belinda said, applying about half a can of spray to Libby's head while the girls stood there breathing it in. "But it's always been like this. It's why VCS has the reputation for being the best around, because of the high standards."

Does it?

I had never researched any other studios, so wouldn't have known that. But Belinda was a bit obsessed. Libby had to be the best dancer at the best dance school. Otherwise, there was, or might be, someone better than her, and that was not an option for Belinda, who had lived this herself in her younger years, so she understood it way better than I did. To me, expecting the same standards of young children as you might expect from senior dancers seemed a bit much. I hadn't brought Annie here for that. I brought her so she could do something she enjoyed and spend time with kids outside of her school group. The thought that the costume police could fail her at 'inspection' and stop her going on stage absolutely horrified me. How cruel would that be? Was it an idle threat or would she actually carry it out?

Nancy came in the atrium with Jemima. "Ah, could Lesley not make it tonight?" I asked her.

"No," she replied, trying to find a space on the table for all of Jemima's stuff (everything was left here overnight – what the hell had she brought with her?). "She was tired after a busy weekend and having such a late night last night with the dress rehearsal." Sarah and I glanced at each other, and I saw Belinda's eyes roll. Did she mean the same dress rehearsal we were all at last night? Okay then...

Jo and Phoebe came back in with copies of the show programme for us all as a keepsake. I had refused to buy one – £7 for a list of names, some nauseating messages and a load of adverts.

'To our bright shining star. Break a leg!'
'Shine like the star you are'
'Mummy and Daddy are so proud of you, our little star'
'We love you to the moon and stars'

All made me feel nauseous. Almost all of the messages had the word star in them. And I reckoned ninety-nine per cent also had the word 'amazing'. Amazing, amazing, amazing. Vomit.

'You'll be amazing'
'You are amazing'
'Our amazing ballerina'
'Shine like the amazing star you are'
Revolting.

Mine stood out in its bluntness – '*Good luck Annie, love from Mummy and Daddy xx*'.

The girls had hair done and make-up on as per instructions given in class – 'so you can see it from the back of the auditorium, but not too much'. Very helpful. The girls had their ballet costumes on under their onesies, as we all trundled down to the auditorium.

I loved the smell of the theatre – it reminded me of old books – kind of aged and musty, but likely to contain something exciting and magical…

Miss Victoria had to ask three times for everyone to be quiet. Annie was sitting on my knee with her finger on her lips, mimicking Miss Victoria, who was on stage waiting for silence. She'd had her hair done especially for tonight – no doubt the *Gazette* would be in attendance, so one must always be photo-ready. The noise died down enough for her to be heard. Anyone else would have needed a megaphone, but Miss Victoria was plenty loud enough.

"Thank you, everyone, for coming here a bit earlier tonight so we could do this. It's the law that we run through all the housekeeping arrangements with you…" I'd heard all this before, so zoned out… fire exits, no photos, don't leave your kids overnight or something to that effect… I was mentally going through the bags again, worrying that a glove had gone AWOL, or some kind of dirt fairy had waved her wand over the white tights. Half an hour the lecture lasted. The kids were getting antsy. They wanted to be back in the atrium with their friends, doing gymnastics on the concourse (if they could find a space).

"And finally, before you go…" I zoned back in. "Can I just say a massive, massive thank you to all of our amazing teachers, amazing children, and the really amazing dads who no doubt pay for all this!" The crowd laughed at her joke, a crowd that included only three or four dads as far as I could see.

Er... and the mums?... No?... Nothing?... No, nothing. I bet at least half of the dads of these kids had no idea how much was being paid for all this.

Back in the atrium, the girls were practising their ballet, Jemima taking on the role of Miss Heather. Another girl from their class, a skinny little elf-like creature – I think she was called Kelsey – came to join them.

"No, you can't join in," Miss Jemima said to her, pale, freckly arms stretched as though to physically block her. "This rehearsal is only for the kids on the front row."

"Oh, Jemima," Nancy said softly. "Are you sure she couldn't join it? It would be very kind of you to let her join in and rehearse with you."

"No, Grandma. She's not on the front row, so she can't do this bit." She turned her back on Nancy and faced the line of four girls. Kelsey didn't seem particularly bothered and skipped off to another group of kids who were happy to play, but I was furious. Not just with Jemima, but with Nancy, for letting Jemima speak to another child like that. Was that it? 'Oh, Jemima'? No wonder she was such a horrible child – nobody ever told her off. Little bitch.

Soon enough, one of the chaperones came through to the atrium, and blew a whistle, which stopped everyone in their tracks. "It's showtime!" she shouted. The kids screamed and mums cheered. The atmosphere was electric, and it was hard not to get caught up in the buzz of it all. Annie was full of energy and couldn't wait to get on stage. As they were gathered up by the chaperones, she held Holly's hand tightly, both of them jumping up and down with excitement. We stood at the sides and watched as they lined up neatly to be taken through the stage door. Annie waved at me, and I waved back, giving her a thumbs up. I had tears in my eyes, and so did Sarah.

But no time for getting emotional. They were back after a few minutes, and we began the first of the hair and costume changes. This one wasn't too bad as there was twenty minutes before the next number. Didn't stop the nerves, though, on that opening night. I was all fingers and thumbs doing Annie's hair. But I knew by Saturday, I would be calmer.

After the first change, we became more confident in our hairdressing skills – even the bastard ringlets weren't too bad, though admittedly this was probably because Annie's hair was still quite thin and wispy. Sarah had more trouble with Holly's as her hair was very long and very thick, so I helped her out once Annie was done.

The evening flew by, as there was so much going on, with little time even for coffee in between the costume and hair changes.

As the girls went to the stage for their contemporary number, we started to unpack their costumes ready for their final change, when Nancy screamed. "No, no, no, nooooo!"

Everyone in the room looked over, panicked.

"What is it?" Belinda asked, going over to the rail where Nancy stood, face ashen, hand to her mouth in horror.

"Oh fuck," Belinda said calmly, pulling the hanger off the rail. Jemima's ivory-coloured catsuit had been hung with the legs doubled back over the hanger so it didn't trail on the floor. The bag containing the hair accessory – named in marker pen as instructed – was hung around the hook, but the labelled side was turned inwards and had smeared permanent marker all over the costume. The ink on the bag must have been wet when it was hung up.

"Okay, think," Belinda said, more to herself than anyone else, as we looked on in horror, not knowing what to say to Nancy. There was no way Miss Victoria, or whoever was guarding the stage from scruffy dancers, would let Jemima on stage looking like she'd been climbing the chimney. But how could we get the marks off? And in about ten minutes. There was no way.

Nancy crumbled into a wailing heap on the floor. Belinda ran off to find a teacher to see if there were any emergency costumes, while the rest of us went round the room seeing if anyone had any similar costumes that might pass the stage-side inspection. Nope. Nothing even remotely similar.

And then the girls came back through. Jemima saw her grandma on the floor in tears, and then saw the costume. "What did you do?" she shouted accusingly to her grandmother.

"She didn't do anything, Jemima," I said.

"So, what happened to my costume?" she demanded, hands on hips. "What am I going to do now?" Her eyes filled with tears, and I felt a little bit sorry for her, but was also seriously irked at how she spoke to me. Petulant little madam.

"Belinda's gone to see if…"

Belinda came back in the atrium with Miss Heather. They were shaking their heads. Miss Heather looked close to tears.

Jemima became hysterical.

"Miss Victoria said no costume, no dance, and she's not happy for her to go on in a dirty costume. I'm so sorry, Jemima."

"But it's not dirty, it's pen that's smudged," Jemima choked through her tears.

"I know, sweetheart, but Miss Victoria said no. She said, to the audience, it would look like it's just dirty, so she said no." She crouched down and held Jemima's hands as her howling increased. "Now, I know it's upsetting for you right now, but we will have a look in the studio tomorrow and see if we can find an old costume that might work that Miss Victoria will allow, so even though you can't go on stage tonight for this dance, hopefully you'll be okay for tomorrow. How does that sound?"

Annie and the other girls had started getting changed and having their final buns sleeked and sprayed into place. Jemima sat sobbing and refused to speak to her grandmother, who she felt had clearly been responsible for this catastrophic event, turning her back on her dramatically as Nancy attempted to apologise for something she hadn't even done, at least knowingly. It was a shame Lesley hadn't been there to deal with this.

As the chaperones led the girls to the stage for their acro number, Sarah and I went to find coffee. There was really nothing we could say to ease the situation and the tension between Jemima and Nancy, and there was no need for us to endure it too, so we made ourselves scarce.

As we walked past the stage door towards the bar area, we heard the voice of Richard Burton's 'No one would have believed' speech, introducing the story of *War of the Worlds.* I loved *War of the Worlds* and couldn't wait to watch this performance to 'The Eve of the War' on Saturday evening. The music was so dramatic and invigorating…

We got our coffees and walked back slowly, not wanting to get back to the atrium before the girls. At least then we could focus on our own kids, and not the unfolding drama. I wasn't into all that. Some people thrived on it. Jo and Belinda had stayed with Nancy and Jemima, absorbing every detail of the conflict between grandmother and granddaughter as if it were a soap opera. Later they would re-tell the story countless times, embellished by Jo no doubt, and Belinda would transform into the hero of the story as she was the one to go and fetch Miss Heather. This was a totally irrelevant detail, but it meant Belinda's name would feature in the story – any opportunity to be involved, as though the mere fetching of a teacher would ensure she went down in dance mum lore.

I hoped the incident with Jemima's costume hadn't distracted Annie or any of the others, but they came back buzzing with adrenaline.

I took all of Annie's costumes home that night, and Sarah did the same. Just in case.

7

Saturday – Last Shows

SATURDAY CAME AROUND SO quickly. After months spent rehearsing for what seemed like hours and hours every day, it was almost over. All that time and in the blink of an eye it was done.

Following the drama of Wednesday night, the Thursday and Friday shows had gone fairly smoothly. Phoebe lost a hair accessory, and Libby's ballet elastic pinged off during the number, but other than that it was uneventful.

The four of us – Annie and myself, Sarah and Holly – arrived in town just after lunchtime. It was a beautiful spring afternoon – the first day we'd had that was warm enough to not really need a jacket. We'd brought the usual bags of goodies and a picnic lunch but decided to eat on a bench outside the theatre, just to soak up some rays before going inside the theatre.

"Oh my God, I'm so excited," Sarah said, squeezing Holly so hard she nearly dropped her sandwich, "but are you sure you're okay with the hair?" We'd agreed that

Sarah would watch the matinee performance, and I would help Holly with costume and hair changes, and then I would watch the evening performance, and she would help Annie.

"Of course! It will be fine. To be honest, now we've got the hang of the ringlets and the timings, I think it'll be fine. If need be, the girls can help too. Just make sure you leave me your curler."

"Will do." Sarah was bouncing her knees, like an overexcited child.

As we went into the foyer, a crowd was gathered at the far end, just in front of the atrium. "What's going on there?" I asked, unable to see anything other than people.

"Ooh, must be the photos!" Sarah said. I peered through the crowd as best I could for someone of five feet, two inches. Several long tables had been lined up, and they were covered with individual photos of the kids. Underneath each one were several others, showing the same kid in all their other costumes. Naturally the table was becoming untidy as mothers, fathers, grandparents and God knows who else scrambled for the pictures of their little darlings.

"How much are they?" I asked a young, slightly punky-looking girl with bright pink hair and giant holes in both earlobes.

"Fifteen for one, forty for three, seventy for six," she said, I assumed for the billionth time that day, if her bored tone was anything to go by. Shitting hell. Seventy quid, just like that. Nearly a full day of torture at work to earn that and spent in a nanosecond.

Just bite the bullet, you'll regret it if you don't, I told myself.

"Okay, can I order one of each of these?" I asked, having located Annie's bundle.

"Nah, you don't order them. You can just take them today," said Punky Brewster.

"Ooh that's good," a random mother cooed behind me.

"Hang on a sec," I said. "Is there only one copy of each of these, then?"

"Yeah," Punky Brewster said, loudly smacking her chewing gum. Gross. "But you can take them to this shop in town and they'll copy them for you if you want any more."

"Hmm, not really the point I was trying to make. What if someone else had bought the pictures of my daughter?"

"Well, they wouldn't, would they? You're obviously her mum, so why would anyone else buy them?"

Oh God. I mean, she was probably only in her teens or early twenties but still…

"Oh right, yes, I think you're probably right," I retorted, unable to control the bitchy sarcasm spewing from my mouth, though it was clearly lost on her. "Although, what if I wasn't? Hmmm? What if I was some random paedo looking for pictures of little girls?"

I gritted my teeth as I tried to keep a lid on it. For a brief moment, a delicious fantasy flashed through my mind – grabbing this young idiot by the ridiculous holes in her ears and smashing her face into the table, sending photos flying all over the place…

Her supervisor/mum/colleague, or whatever she was, came over, bringing me back to reality. "What's the matter?" she asked, more to Punky than to me.

"This lady wants…"

I interrupted. "Hi, nice to meet you." Trying and failing to wind myself back in. "I'm the mum of one of the kids on display here and wondered if you had thought about the implications of what might happen here?"

"What do you mean?" she asked vacantly. Fucking hell. Another one. Definitely the girl's mother.

"You're selling pictures of little girls and teenagers in a public space, to anyone who will hand over the cash. Do you not see a problem with that?" My head cocked to the side. Despite how irritated I was, I did enjoy watching her confusion.

The other mums had quietened to listen, and I heard a couple of comments – 'yeah, she's right actually', 'ooh good point', 'shit, never thought of that', which only added to my fury. How had these fucking imbeciles never thought to even question this?

"Well… no… I mean we're only selling them to the parents, aren't we?" For the love of all things holy… She seemed uncomfortable, but only because people were now starting to watch, not because I was practically accusing her of selling child pornography to paedophiles.

I smiled as best I could with anger threatening to bubble over at this woman's stupidity.

"And how do you know who the parents of each child are?" I asked her, reducing my volume carefully, to try to avoid attracting any more attention as I could see Annie pulling away from the crowd.

"Well… we don't, but we…"

"Okay, that's enough. If you aren't understanding why this might be an issue, then you really have a problem, especially working for a company that takes pictures of children." I rolled my eyes. "Now, I'm going to buy the pictures of my daughter, because I want them and because only by me buying them myself can I rest assured that they are not being sold to a paedophile who has walked in here, into a public space, where anyone can buy these photos. I will, however, be reporting this whole thing as a potential safeguarding concern."

I paid for Annie's pictures, turned on my heel, and walked back to where Annie, Sarah and Holly had distanced themselves. Sarah had bought Holly's pictures from another teenager manning the stand.

"I'm so sorry about that," I said. "I just can't believe they are being allowed to do that. We used to have to order the pictures and then they would come back with the kids from the studio in a couple of weeks. That was fine, no issue with that. But this... this is insane!"

"You're right," Sarah said, dipping into a big bag of Smarties and then offering them to me and the girls. "I'd never even given it a thought. Anyway, we've got our pics now so no perverts can get them! Last day of Starstruck for another two years. Let's just enjoy it!"

Already my spirits were dampened by the photo debacle, but we walked into the atrium and my heart sank further. All around were bouquets of beautiful flowers in a variety of sizes and colours; there were more balloons and wrapping paper everywhere.

"Oh fuck, I forgot about all that," I said to Sarah under my breath.

"Me too, but never mind. The girls don't care about sodding flowers anyway – they're children for fuck's sake. Just another way to 'one-up' other mums if you ask me."

She was right. I knew she was right. Local florists would have made a fortune that day on all this lot. And the kids couldn't have cared less.

Sensible me had justified it to myself. The show had cost a small fortune in extra lessons, costumes, good luck gifts, eating out, photos and other incidental things we don't even think of – even the car park was going to cost £20 for today. Annie had enjoyed every second of the week, so it was all worth it, but she did not need or care about flowers.

But another part of me started feeling guilty. Even though Annie didn't care about flowers, and neither it would seem did Holly, were they the only ones here who did not have them? It certainly looked that way. Jo, Belinda and Nancy had all brought flowers for their girls. I even questioned why they would get flowers delivered to their homes (and these were definitely not supermarket flowers) and bring them here to the theatre – why not just leave them at home? I knew the answer, of course. If nobody sees what you're doing, sees what you're buying, sees how extravagant you are, sees how 'amazing' your child is, what's the point? I could pretty much guarantee that if flowers had been banned from the theatre, those kids would not have had flowers at home. There's no point wasting money on something that isn't screaming 'indulgence', is there? I knew all that, but I still felt bad. I knew from past shows that it was tradition to get flowers for the final performance, so I did know about it. I suppose I had just forgotten.

I needed to put all this negativity to one side and focus on what needed doing. Hair and make-up first. The girls had been watching some of the older girls doing their own, so wanted to have a go, which was fine by me – I could always tidy it up with a couple of baby wipes if they made a mess of it, but we kept the colours fairly neutral so there was not much scope for make-up catastrophes. Lipstick would only go on just before being called to line up, so no worries there.

I felt calm, calmer than I thought I would, looking after the two girls – double the hair changes, double the costume changes. We had used the last three nights to think about ways we could do it quicker, and had got it down to a fine art.

Belinda was watching the show that night too, so was looking after Phoebe for Jo in the afternoon. Nancy was going to watch the final performance too, assuming Lesley was up to being a backstage mum, of course.

Between the three of us, we were pretty confident we could do this.

All five girls were ready and raring to go over half an hour before the matinee started. Naturally the mums were mostly on their phones, looking at social media. I logged on to Facebook. I hadn't been on it all week as there just hadn't been the time. There were 827 messages on the VCS page just since Wednesday. Most of them had been 'good luck' messages, but the last 300 or so were from those who had seen the show. Once again, the sycophancy nauseated me.

'Oh my God – best Starstruck ever'

'Amazing, amazing, amazing – best teachers in the world'

'Thank you so much to the VCS staff for all their hard work in putting together this world-class extravaganza!'

'Teachers and kids alike – just amazing'

'I have no words – just incredible what VCS have put together'

'Every show gets better and better – amazing!'

'Truly amazing!'

We got it. It was amazing. I mean, I was sure it would be. Nobody could argue an incredible amount of work hadn't gone into it, but I still couldn't help rolling my eyes. I could see around the room the countless mothers scrolling what I imagined would be the same page I was looking at.

The afternoon flew by in a non-stop whirlwind of activity, hairspray, glitter and noise. Sarah and Jo were buzzing with excitement and pride when they came back through – hugging all the girls, not just their own.

"I'm so proud of them all," Sarah said. "Honestly, just wait until you see it. It was incredible!"

"Phoebe, what happened to your aerial?" Jo asked her daughter. She appeared calm, but knowing Jo, no doubt she would have been pissed that Phoebe literally missed a trick.

"I was scared to do it."

"Well, you better make sure you do it tonight when Nanna's watching."

Fucking hell, Jo, give the kid a break, I thought. *Let her just enjoy the experience with her pals.*

We had a booking at an Italian restaurant for the ten of us for dinner between the matinee and the evening performance. Finally, I could sit back, relax, and watch the performance that had cost six months of my life and about a billion pounds. I was nervous about not being backstage with Annie, but I knew she would be fine under Sarah's supervision. She was a sensible kid and was as self-sufficient as an eight-year-old could be.

The restaurant was packed with dance kids in onesies and glitter in their hair, and their mums, occasionally dads as well who had rocked up to watch the final show. Rob had watched on the Thursday evening and had no interest in watching again. He hated it all. Said he didn't understand it. He said he enjoyed watching Annie but found every other number to be nothing but long-winded torture.

As I sat there watching Annie with the other girls, I felt kind of sad that the week was coming to an end. She'd had a fantastic week. There had been no tears – from Annie, at least. No doubt there would be later when the last of the costumes were packed away. The studio would be closed for two weeks after the last show, so the teachers could have some much-needed R&R. I recalled the feeling after the last show two years ago – going from non-stop lessons and rehearsals to two weeks of nothing had felt like brakes being slammed on, causing emotional whiplash. As much as I moaned about it all – and I knew I did – nothing made me happier than seeing Annie happy like this. She'd been having a couple of minor fallouts at school in recent months, so I knew dancing gave her a distraction from that as much as anything. Annie dwelled on things a lot, so distraction was key.

My heart swelled with pride that evening watching her on stage. Mums would always be biased and think their kid was the best, so it would have been pointless to say it out loud, but I really thought she was. And she was in the centre of the stage, front row, for every number, so clearly the teachers thought she was good too.

My eyes misted up as I watched the ballet, and it was only as they stood in finishing positions that I noticed

Jemima was missing. I didn't give it too much thought, though; my attention was on Annie. I didn't know either of the ladies I was sitting between, but I was so proud I couldn't resist pointing Annie out to both of them. Like they cared.

When they tapped on to stage for the second number, I noticed Jemima had appeared, but again didn't pay much attention to her.

To their credit, the teachers – and their borderline neurotic obsession with getting everything perfect – had pulled off an incredible show. The babies were adorable, the seniors looked (to my untrained eye) to be world-class, and every group in between tracked the journey they would follow, the improvements and developments in the techniques they would learn as they got older. Annie's journey was still in its relatively early stages, but watching the older kids gave a real insight into what might lie ahead for her.

As expected, the finale – *War of the Worlds* – did not disappoint. Richard Burton's opening speech gave way to the dramatic orchestral intro, which set my heart pounding and turned up the atmosphere in the theatre ten-fold. The girls pulled off their tricks with immaculate precision. Annie and Holly delivered perfectly mirrored aerials, landed without even a hint of a stumble, and I couldn't help cheering.

Naturally, Miss Victoria did her end-of-show speech, with the obligatory flowers for teachers, and for herself. Every time I saw this, I noticed how robotic the presentation of flowers was. I wondered who paid for them. I mean… one way or another, it would be us – the parents – who paid for them, but which of the staff went to the florists to order flowers and then received them on stage as though they were a gift? There was never any sign of emotion or surprise, not even a comment about how beautiful the flowers were. They never said thank you to anyone other than the kid who had the honour of presenting them. The flowers were just part of the routine, a tradition, an expected part of a process. So, what was the point?

There were some almost-tears, which some of the audience seemed to believe, as Miss Victoria spoke about hard work, dedication, the high standards the school held to, and the commitment of all the children to uphold them. She told us how proud she was of each and every one of the children. She listed the recent achievements of past students – a couple were in West End musicals, three working on cruise ships, one had been on a TV talent show, and one was almost through to the final round (how do you even get 'almost through'?) of auditions for a long-running kids' TV programme.

As I finally went back through to the atrium, I was met by Sarah handing me a can of wine from M&S in celebration. She'd arranged for her husband to take us all home, so she'd already started on the wine as soon as the girls were taken for the finale.

We sat, exhausted, and clinked our cans. "To dance mums," she toasted.

"To dance mums."

8

Panto Audition

THE BRIEF REPRIEVE OF the two-week break was over all too quickly for me, but not quickly enough for Annie. I had welcomed some time off from being at the studio almost every night, not to mention the respite for my bank account.

As we walked across the car park that Monday evening, we bumped into Sarah, who had just dropped Holly off. "I'm just popping to the shop for some onions," she said, "but I'll be back soon if you're hanging around."

"Yeah, I'll be here. Takes me twenty minutes to get home, so I'd only be setting straight off again to come back."

Sarah looked at Annie. "Ooh, Annie, there's a poster up in reception about panto auditions! Exciting stuff eh!" Annie's eyes widened in excitement. I had taken her to the annual pantomime at the Adelphi since she was a tot of less than two years old. In truth, I had been going every year since I was a child myself, aside from the teenage years when it would, of course, have been unbearably embarrassing if someone from school had seen me there. It was the highlight of the Christmas season for me, and Annie and I looked forward to it every year – naturally Rob was never interested; he thought it was only for kids. Rob would sometimes accompany us if he had nothing else going on, but quite often he would be at football or a work night out or some such other bullshit excuse. So, it became our little tradition – just me and Annie.

Even as a very young child, Annie had been mesmerised by it – the music, the costumes, the beautiful princess, the evil baddie, but most of all she loved the goofy sidekick: Buttons in *Cinderella*, Wishy Washy in *Aladdin*, or Smee in *Peter Pan*. He was usually played by someone known to the audience, as being a children's TV presenter or something similar. Annie loved the shouting and cheering, and especially the booing. She was usually so quiet, so her loud participation was evidence of how invested she became.

Now she had just turned eight, she was old enough to audition for this year's pantomime – *Cinderella*.

We stepped into reception, which was noisier than usual. Mothers and children alike had two weeks of catching up to do.

"I hope she's going to audition this year," Miss Victoria said, with a wink, as I queued to pay Annie's fees.

"I hadn't really thought about it, to be honest," I lied, "but yes, I'm sure she'd love to."

Annie was bouncing up and down next to me, hands clasped together as though in prayer, and looking at me as though requesting permission. "Yes, I think she'd love to." I giggled.

"She'd be great," Miss Victoria said. "And I know she's the same height as Phoebe, so they could be opposites." I had no idea what that meant, and shrugged – my ignorance apparent as Miss Victoria went on…

"We have to have two teams of girls, so they don't have to be in every show. It's too much for the little ones. So, they have an opposite, who does exactly the same as they do, and shares costumes, dressing room space, props… all that stuff. I know she'd want to be on the same team as Holly, so no good putting them as opposites."

"Oh… well…" I could sense other mums looking over, and I knew what they were thinking. I was thinking the exact same thing. If Miss Victoria had already figured all this out, was it a given that Annie would get a part? If so, what was the point in auditioning?

"Don't worry, we have a meeting before rehearsals start which explains everything you need to know," she continued.

I felt uneasy and could feel myself flushing, and I was sure I heard a mum saying "see, there's no point auditioning if they already know who's going to be in it". I could have been wrong, but it seemed likely that people would feel that way. I know I would have felt the same way if I was listening to this conversation.

I felt excited at the opportunity Annie looked likely to have already got in the bag, nervous about Annie doing an audition, and embarrassed that Miss Victoria was saying all of this in front of other mums and children. Did she say the same things to other kids? Did the kids who did panto always know before auditions that they were pretty much guaranteed a part?

I pretended to brush it off, and played it down to Annie, hoping other mums would buy into the humility I was trying to portray. "Well, we'll come for the audition and see what happens then, but you need to remember there will be more girls at the audition than there are parts." I desperately wanted to manage Annie's expectations, just in case, but also wanted to finish this conversation. The air suddenly felt thick with animosity, directed at me as much as Miss Victoria, even though I didn't think I'd done anything to warrant it.

*

Three weeks later, we crammed into the studio on a sunny Saturday afternoon. Annie had been there since early morning for lessons, so she was looking a little bedraggled. The reception area, smaller studios and all changing rooms were packed. The noise levels were unbearable for me, and I wanted to scream. My stomach was churning, and I felt nauseous, despite having eaten nothing all day. Annie seemed to be taking it all in her stride – I think I was feeling the nerves on her behalf.

I took Annie outside of the studio, and Sarah and Holly followed. The teachers must have anticipated high numbers would attend, so there were a few plastic chairs outside. We sat the girls down and started doing their hair. Over the last few months, I felt I had become something of an expert in this area. I had spent hours watching videos online with Annie, and she was my reluctant 'Girl's World' as I practised the techniques I was learning.

The instruction was 'black leotards and immaculate hair – no jewellery'.

"I'm not keen on the ambiguity," I said to Sarah. "I think I preferred the detailed instructions we got for Starstruck."

"Yeah, I know what you mean. I'm scared in case the hair is the thing that lets them down."

"Mum, will you just stop," Holly said, without looking up from the chin-to-chest position Sarah had pushed her head into. "I'm sure they won't even care what our hair looks like."

"Course they will. You have to look immaculate." She turned to me. "And also 'cute'. Miss Victoria said they like the little ones to look cute."

"Cute?" I questioned. "How do you make hair look 'cute' but also immaculate?"

"No idea." Sarah spoke through the side of her mouth as her teeth held half a dozen hair grips. "We're going with space buns and ribbons."

Annie had already decided she wanted something similar, but we agreed to use 'bun donuts' to give some structure to them, and also make sure they were both the same size. Annie had so much hair by then that we had to use the extra-large donuts, which then made her look like she was wearing Minnie Mouse ears, especially once the little black bows had been added. It was definitely immaculate, probably cute, and Annie was happy with it, although I was sure I heard a couple of sniggers as we walked back through the reception area to line up. I hoped Annie hadn't heard them.

"Who is judging?" I whispered to Sarah.

"I think it's Miss Stacy, Miss Victoria and someone else – I think from the theatre or something."

"It's Jo, from Panto Productions," Belinda chirped. I hadn't seen her arrive, though I knew she would be there. Libby was no doubt top of the list for guaranteed parts.

Belinda had created the most perfect ballet bun I had ever seen on the crown of Libby's head. Not only in the perfect position, but also the diameter and thickness were enviable. Even the shape was a perfect circle. A blonde hairnet captured any wispy bits, and a black bow sat at the base. She was only eight years old but looked like a professional ballerina. I looked at Annie's childish Minnie Mouse ears and felt a panic rising up in me. Was there time to re-do her hair into something classier and more low-key? The judges would all be looking at this beautiful ballerina in the making, with her perfect bun, which seemed to draw up her spine and elongate her neck. How could someone so young have that posture? I guessed it was because her mother continually corrected her.

The panic inside me continued to rise. I was sweating. I could have tried to re-do Annie's hair, but what if they were called in when it wasn't finished? She wouldn't get the part, and it would all be my fault. She would blame me for being the only one of her friends not to be in panto.

Libby touched Annie's Minnie Mouse ears. "Aww they're so cute. I wish my mum would do something more exciting than a boring old bun."

I should have been calmed by this, but I wasn't. I was sweating and could feel my heart thumping against my ribs. The noise of the studio – previously loud – seemed to quieten down and become more like a sound I might have once heard when swimming underwater. My palms were wet, and my throat was dry. My face had gone completely numb, so I had no idea if I was flushed, or ghostly white.

"Are you okay?" Sarah asked me.

"Yeah fine, I think I just need some air."

I'd had panic attacks in the past; thankfully not many, but enough to be able to recognise it for what it was. I took my water bottle out of my bag and a pack of extra strong mints. Someone once told me that whatever coping methods we use to deal with panic attacks, it's probably all 'mind over matter' and more about distracting yourself just long enough for the physical symptoms to pass by. I sucked on a mint, and in my mind, I tried to describe the taste, as if to an alien or someone born without tastebuds. This usually worked, and thankfully the palpitations and sweating started to subside after a couple of minutes.

I felt ridiculous. Annie, Holly, Libby, and now Phoebe too, were leaning on the wall so casually, as if waiting for a bus. Phoebe was excited and a bit hyper, which seemed to rub off on the other girls, and they started being silly. "This is what I'm going to walk in like…" Libby giggled, and started doing what Annie would call a 'sassy walk'. The girls all shrieked with laughter.

They were fine. Annie was fine. And there I was, having a full-on panic attack because Libby's hair looked better than Annie's. I was probably feeling nervous as well, but I knew it was the hair that prompted the palpitations and sweats. *Get a fucking grip*, I told myself.

Jemima rolled up at the last minute, with Lesley in tow for a change. Both mother and daughter appeared to be calm and unfazed, though it was the first audition for all of these girls who had only just become old enough to apply.

Lesley air-kissed her daughter and said, "I'll be in the café having a coffee, so just come through when you're done." No nerves, no words of encouragement, nothing.

Miss Victoria opened the door to the largest studio, and the noise went from a hundred to zero.

She smiled at the students, who were now eager to get in there and do their thing. "Okay, girls," she shouted, though there was really no need to. "Now, you know when you come through, where you need to stand in your lines. So come in quietly, dance your hearts out, and don't forget to smile!"

"Good luck, Annie! Good luck, girls!" I said, almost relieved that they had gone in and now it was quiet.

We sat on the chairs outside in the glorious sunshine, faces turned upwards in hope of getting a tan.

After about half an hour, we went back inside. Without the children making a racket, reception was as quiet as a library. The parents who had decided to linger around whispered to each other rather than talking at a natural volume. I could see foot tapping – not in time with any obvious rhythm – from a few nervous parents. One mum was nibbling the skin around her fingernails, a habit I'd also developed recently. Today my fingers looked as though the skin had been peeled down like macabre fingerless gloves. The pain when I did Annie's hair and caught the raw flesh with a hairbrush, or even worse some hairspray, brought tears to my eyes. Blood, sweat and tears made a dancer, Miss Victoria would say. She never mentioned that this would be the parents as well as the dancers.

We could hear the music, although I didn't recognise it. Something upbeat. Very panto.

Belinda and Jo came back in. They had been for coffees. Belinda was cool as a cucumber. She must have known Libby had a guaranteed place. Jo, by contrast, was having a complete meltdown, which was not helping.

"Oh my God, I'm so nervous," she said, wringing her hands together tightly and then wrapping them across her stomach. "I just feel sick. I've not been able to eat anything for about three days. Not slept a wink either." Belinda was rolling her eyes. If Jo had had the same conversation I had with Miss Victoria (which I suspected Belinda had also had), it had done nothing to alleviate her nerves. Jo survived on coffee and her nerves. She always felt sick about something. There was always something Jo was nervous about, which made her feel sick. That said, it was usually something she had pushed one of her kids to do (which she knew they would likely have no problem doing), and frankly I was surprised she hadn't found a way to take things in her stride a little more by now.

"They'll be fine," Belinda replied, looking bored.

"But how do you know that? How can you be so sure?" Jo pestered.

"Because it just will. If it's meant to be, it will be." Belinda either had a reason to feel relaxed and confident, or she was the most serene, pragmatic person I had ever known. Or perhaps she hid her nerves well. Or maybe she didn't give a shit. Nah, we all knew that was not the case. If Libby didn't get a part, Belinda would go batshit crazy. It was unthinkable.

Jo started biting her nails. "I don't know how Phoebe will cope if she doesn't get in."

"The same as any of them will if they don't get in." Belinda bit back. I was slightly taken aback.

Sarah stepped in before things got tetchy. "Well, I just hope they all get in," she said. "It would be worse if only one of them got a part, or even worse if only one of them didn't get in."

I nodded in agreement. "Yeah, fingers crossed for all of them."

It was a whole week before the results were out.

Annie was ready to go uncharacteristically quickly that day. "Come oooon…" she wailed, dragging me out of the house. "We need to get there quickly."

"The results will be the same," I told her. "Whether you're the first to find out or the last."

"I know, but I just want to know…" Her big eyes pleaded with me to just get her there as quickly as was humanly possible. While all I wanted to do was avoid it. I was nauseous. Excited that she may get in, but terrified that she wouldn't. My palms were sweating, and I could feel the adrenaline pulsing through my body. Fight or flight? *I'll take the flight every damn time*, I thought. I'd even taken some of Rob's propranolol to help with the palpitations I thought were going to cause me a cardiac event any time now.

As I drove to the studio, I started to feel the familiar warning stage of a panic attack. *Not now*, I pleaded with my body. *Please not now.* Annie was nervous too. I could see it on her face – her little worry dimple still there – even though she told me she was excited, and she gazed out of the car window. She had gone quiet, and I needed noise to distract me. I wound down the window as we drove past the road that led to the local recycling plant. If noise could be a distraction, so could smell, and by God, the stench was rancid today.

"Phoooeeeyyy, Annie, is that you?" I asked her and gave her a gentle nudge. "Did you drop your shopping?"

Annie turned round and giggled. "Errr... nooo... that's so gross!"

"I think it might be the smell of stinky cheese. Could it be your feet, Anniebobs?"

"Noooo! I think it's your feet, Mummybobs!"

We turned in to the car park. I could see Belinda just going through the studio door. She lived further away than we did, so I knew she must have driven at breakneck speed to get there so quickly. Like it mattered. But it did. It mattered so much to Annie, so it mattered to me.

As soon as she got out of the car, she darted across to reception, not bothering to wait for me, and barely checking it was safe from other cars on the car park.

I entered the reception to see a huge crowd of girls gathered around the notice board. I didn't have my glasses, so wouldn't be able to see until the crowd dissipated anyway. Annie had wiggled through to the front, so I lost sight of her for a second. I moved to the reception desk – whatever else was going on, fees had to be paid.

Miss Victoria was behind the desk with Miss Stacy. I couldn't look at them. Whatever the outcome, I wanted to hear it from Annie, not those two.

I saw her crouching down to wiggle back out of the crowd – she was beaming, her face blotchy and her eyes full of happy tears. "I got in panto!" she squealed.

I don't think I've ever been as happy or proud in my life

88

as I was in that moment. I hugged Annie tight, and only then managed to make eye contact with Miss Victoria, who gave me a knowing wink.

I scanned the crowd, who were barely moving. It was mostly kids, but there were a few mums in there as well. Of course.

I could tell from Belinda's somewhat smug expression that Libby was in. It looked like Phoebe was too, though I could only see Phoebe, not Jo. She was probably hyperventilating somewhere.

"Holly got in too," Annie told me, just as Holly and Sarah came through the door.

"What about Jemima?" I asked her.

Annie shook her head. "Reserve list."

Ouch. This was not going to go down well with Jemima, Nancy or Lesley. Didn't seem to bother Annie too much, though. She was happy she got in, and even happier that Holly was going to be on the same team as her.

The crowd slowly thinned as the girls all went to their studios, leaving some space for the mums to analyse the teams.

Team A

Felicity Acaster
Beatrice Christie
Camilla Norton
Iris Walker
Holly Richmond
Annie Moffatt

Team B

Charlotte Rushforth
Pippa Rushforth
Verity Clifford
Catherine Rushforth
Libby Bickerstaffe
Phoebe Bates

Reserves

Jemima Roylance
Amy Peters

There was an additional note underneath advising parents of the first meeting for both teams. Reserves not needed.

The teachers had all gone into their classes, and Miss Victoria was speaking to Felicity Acaster's mum, Diane, so Sarah and I paid our fees and walked out of the studio. As we walked out, we were almost mowed down by Jemima, who looked manic in her desperation to see the results. Her grandma trailed behind, carrying Jemima's bag as always. We had just reached the car park when we heard the blood-curdling scream, knowing it came from one very disappointed reserve.

High School

THE FIRST FEW WEEKS *of high school were terrifying. So many bigger kids. So many classrooms. So much space to get lost. Although I was in a form group with a couple of friends from primary school, the only kids I knew in my lessons were Trevor Bailey and Dawn Emery and I wasn't particularly friendly with either of them.*

My quiet nature meant I gravitated towards the 'nerdy' kids – the ones whose homework was always in on time and always correct. I made new friends – Sally, Angela and Amanda – and I was comfortable with them, which for me was quite an achievement. We would go to each other's houses after school to do homework and go into town or to the cinema on the weekends. They were good friends: steady, dependable – and dull as dishwater.

At break times, we would sit on the benches in the courtyard and talk about homework or band practice or some sports competition one of them was doing. And all the time I would be watching another group of kids. The cool kids.

What makes them so cool? *I wondered.* How does one become one of them? Are they beautiful people? *Some of the girls were pretty, but not all of them. Some wore way more make-up and perfume than was acceptable at school, faces caked with foundation so thick it would need to be scraped away to reveal the actual skin tone. Their hair was fashionably styled and coloured, but nothing outstanding. The boys were good-looking or athletic – never both. Were they particularly smart? Or funny? They were all in the higher (but not highest) sets for their lessons, so intelligence – or lack of – didn't set them apart in any way. They certainly seemed funny to each other, though they favoured 'in jokes', so how could an outsider judge?*

Years later, I would come to realise that it was only their level of confidence that set them apart from the rest of the year group. They believed they were beautiful, and clever, and funny, and cool. And their self-belief flooded out to the wider school population, brainwashing others into believing it too.

It wasn't until the third year of high school that I started to pay attention to boys. One in particular – Dylan Woods. He was one of the cool kids, in fact probably the alpha male of the cool kids if there was such a thing at the tender age of fourteen. He was bright and had been moved up into the top set for English, maths and science, and he sat next to me in maths. I looked forward to maths lessons and would make a special effort on Tuesdays and Thursdays to do my hair nicely and make sure I sprayed some Impulse before school.

Dylan had the most beautiful eyes I'd ever seen on anyone, especially a boy. Blue as a Maldives ocean, and thick black lashes that the girls were no doubt envious of, if their caked mascara was anything to go by. But it was the way his eyes creased when he smiled, and he smiled a lot. Sometimes he would smile at me, and I'd have to look away, sensing a flirtation between us, but not wanting to blush, or fall of my chair or embarrass myself in some other stupid way. I couldn't allow myself to believe for a second that Dylan Woods would be interested in boring old me. Anyone on the receiving end of that smile would see the same thing I saw, and he couldn't be flirting with everyone. Or maybe he was. Maybe he didn't even realise he was doing it. I was reading too much into it.

Sometimes Dylan would ask what answer I had written to a particular equation and would move closer to me to see what I'd written. I didn't stop him. I knew he didn't need any help from me. He just wanted his arm to come into contact with mine and see how I reacted. I would pretend I hadn't noticed, because I didn't want to make a complete idiot of myself. I knew he probably did this with girls he sat next to in other classes. And I guessed they probably did what I did. Absolutely nothing. I wouldn't acknowledge the touch, but I wouldn't move away either.

Halfway through that third year, Dylan's friend James got moved up into my English class. As we queued up outside the classroom one day, James was behind me.

"Ah so you're the Lydia that Dylan mentioned," he whispered from behind.

"What?" I was shocked, surprised, and highly delighted that Dylan had noticed me enough to mention me to his friend. A slightly light-headed feeling – nervousness maybe – washed over me. "What did he say?"

James shrugged. "Not much. He just said you were quite cool, and it would be good to have you at the party next Friday. But I said you probably wouldn't want to come 'cos you don't really know anyone."

"Err... well, no... I don't..."

"Although aren't you friends with that Sally girl with the long dark hair? She's usually in this class, isn't she?" His cheeky expression told me he already knew the answer to this.

"Yes, but she's at the dentist this afternoon. But yes, she is my friend."

"Right," James went on, raising his eyebrows as if in question.

"You like Sally? You do know she has a boyfriend?" I asked him. Mr Charles had opened the classroom door, and we filtered in.

"Well, I wouldn't say no." He grinned, and took his place at the back of the classroom.

I couldn't concentrate for that whole lesson. I had butterflies in my tummy and couldn't wait to call Sally later. Her boyfriend Paul was bland, and I found him difficult to be around. He was an awkward conversationalist. I always had the impression Paul had either read books on or been coached in the art of conversation. He would interject some current news story into a discussion about something unrelated, as if he'd been preparing for this for a while and had finally found a pause in the conversation in which to contribute.

Surely Sally would at least want to think about going to the party, although I never got the impression she was impressed with the cool kids, not like me. I was intimidated by them, but also desperate to understand what it would be like to be part of their world. Could that air of 'coolness' rub off on me? Or would it miss the mark completely? Could I morph into something better than I was? Or would I fall flat on my face and become the laughing stock of the school?

I couldn't wait to speak to Sally when I met her later at the library, but she wasn't keen. "We don't really know them," she worried. "Why would they want us there?"

"Because James likes you?"

"You mean because Dylan likes you?"

"Well maybe that too." I chewed the skin around my nail beds. "Forget it, it doesn't matter. I told James you wouldn't want to go because you've got a boyfriend, so we won't go." I flicked through a well-used copy of Pride and Prejudice, *which had been left on the table. I didn't really have any interest in it; I was fidgeting while I pondered whether to push it or let it go.*

"I mean… were we all invited? Did he mean Ange and Amanda as well? Or just us?"

"Just us, I think," I replied nonchalantly, still thumbing through the book. "I didn't ask. Don't really know any more than that. No big deal. Just thought I'd mention it to you. But we'll do something else. Maybe bowling? Or I think that Hugh Grant film is out this week?"

"Hmmm." She was thinking about it.

"Or have you got plans with Paul?"

Sally rolled her eyes and shook her head. "I'm thinking of calling it off."

I looked up, wide-eyed and open-mouthed. "What? But you've been together for like…"

"Seven months. Yep. We're getting on okay, but I'm a bit bored, to be honest. And I don't like the way he kisses." She giggled.

"Ewwww that's so gross! What does he kiss like?"

"Don't laugh and promise you won't tell anyone 'cos I feel really bad telling you, but it's like this…" She sucked

her cheeks in to create a goldfish-like pout, and then somehow made it pulsate. We burst into laughter and were immediately shushed by the librarian.

"Yeah, I think it might be time to get rid. You shouldn't have to endure that. Nobody should be enduring kisses like that!"

"I'll come to the party, but only for like an hour or so. I'm only coming because I know you want to, but I don't want to stay for long. Okay?"

"You're the best." I hugged her and kissed the top of her head.

"Lesbian."

We didn't tell the others about the party. They wouldn't want to go, we assumed, and would probably try to talk us out of going.

The following Friday I was sitting on Sally's bedroom floor. Her usually tidy room had become chaotic, and I sat watching her pull various bits out of her wardrobe and then throw them on the floor dismissively. Sally's room had never looked like a teenager's room; I doubted it ever looked like a child's bedroom either. Tastefully decorated in soft blues and creams, with surfaces adorned with grown-up stuff like lamps, plants and items chosen by Sally's mother to achieve a desired aesthetic, rather than the standard teen décor of posters, books, make-up and magazines strewn around the place. Sally's room was usually calm and restful. Not anymore.

"Why did I agree to this again? I have nothing to wear. I don't want to go!" she wailed.

"Because James wants you to go, and maybe we should think about widening our circle a bit, show everyone that there's more to us than nerds who spend all our time reading textbooks and going to Guide camp?"

Sally sighed. "Yeah, but I don't think I have anything 'cool' enough for a party with the cool kids."

I stood up, holding a blue dress against myself and looking into the mirror. Pretty dress. I guessed Sally's mum had bought it for maybe a family dinner out somewhere, or church, or maybe even just to hang on the back of the bedroom door as it blended so well with the colour scheme.

"How about this? It's really cute, but maybe if we pair it with your Docs, it could look a bit more edgy?"

"Edgy? Me, edgy?" Sally considered the idea for a moment. "That's actually not bad. Maybe if I put on that jacket I got for Christmas as well..." She pulled out a black leather jacket.

"Perfect! And it definitely gives you an edgy look. Right, find something for me!"

We settled on something similar for me, but in pastel pink, and with a denim jacket and Dr Martens of course; at least that way if our chosen look wasn't as cool as we thought it was, at least we would both feel equally uncomfortable.

"Ow, not so harsh!" Sally moaned as I attempted to scrape her wild curls into some kind of style.

"Sorry! I'm just trying to make it look less... you know, like you've been up all night revising."

"But I was up all of last night revising..."

"I know, I know." I smiled at my friend. "But tonight, we're trying to be different. Blend in a bit."

I stepped back, admiring my handiwork. Sally's hair was now in a relaxed braid, with the straggly bits by the sides, that I'd seen the cool girls wear. I handed her a pair of hoop earrings.

Sally applied a touch of lip balm while I changed into the dress.

"You look great, Sally. Seriously, we're going to be fine," I said, noticing her looking apprehensive.

"I hope you're right. What if they laugh at us?"

"Then we'll laugh along. We're going to have fun, remember? And we've been invited, so we must be doing something right."

Sally smiled. "You're right. Let's do this."

9

And So It Begins...

THE THREE MONTHS BETWEEN the audition and the start of panto rehearsals flew by for the mums, although for the girls it seemed to be an eternity.

"How many mooooooore sleeps?" Annie would ask on an almost daily basis.

"One less than the last time you asked."

The meeting had been held a couple of weeks after the lists were posted on the board, so for the 'newbies' it was a good opportunity to meet the other kids and mums who were pretty much going to be our family throughout December.

They seemed okay. Mostly. Felicity's mum, Diane, was a panto veteran. This was her fourth panto season, so she was cool and calm. I did wonder why she wasn't as excited about it as we were, but then neither was Felicity. Sarah and I would ponder later about who wanted this more – Felicity or Diane – as neither really seemed that bothered.

Gabby Christie – mother of Beatrice – was going to be hard work. She liked to talk a lot about herself, and none of it was very interesting, though she did have a very high opinion of herself, which Sarah and I found very amusing. Gabby could have been a dancer herself based on her petite frame, though we would come to find out later that this had always been a dream but never a reality for her. Gabby was tiny, and had cheekbones so sharp you could cut a diamond with them. She smoked heavily, ate rarely, and congratulated herself often. She was harmless enough, but by God did she go on… Beatrice had a peanut allergy, and during coffee after the meeting, Gabby told our team all about the ordeal of going grocery shopping and the difference between 'contains nuts', 'contains nut traces', 'may contain nut traces', and 'produced in a factory which…' I don't know… shelled peanuts or grew peanuts or something. I'd lost interest by then. I got it. Don't eat peanuts around Beatrice.

Liz and Emma seemed okay, though they had an aura of 'we've done this before, so watch and learn'. Their daughters, Camilla and Iris, were in the year above Annie and Holly, so this was only their second panto, but both had sisters a few years older, so Liz and Emma had done this for at least three years with their older kids.

I wasn't sure why, but I found Liz Norton to be incredibly intimidating. She was friendly enough, but seemed to have that way about her that just makes you feel 'less than'. Her blonde hair was in a fairly standard bob – nothing spectacular – and she was pretty but not stunning. Plenty of people were much prettier, and I never felt intimidated by them, so it wasn't that. I never caught her doing it – to me or to anyone else – but from that first meeting I felt as though she had looked me up and down and decided I was not good enough.

Emma was much easier to chat to. She knew Rob from school, and they were friends on Facebook, so we had at least some common ground there. I liked Emma a lot, but definitely more so when she was not around Liz.

Team B was much smaller. Jane Rushford's three daughters – Charlotte, Pippa and Catherine (I guessed she was something of a royalist) – were all on Team B. This, of course, made things much easier for Jane as she would not have to take her turns chaperoning both teams. However, it also meant only four mums available to share the responsibility. I had already heard that Jane's husband was the panto director, hence it was a given that all three girls would be in it – who would argue against it? Miss Victoria? Unlikely, as she would agree to anything that brought money and visibility to herself or the dance school.

Verity's mum, Janine, seemed lovely, but I sensed she was a real people-pleaser and probably a bit of a suck-up. She came across as friendly and warm. Quite motherly, I suppose, which was not a vibe I picked up from most of the others.

Annie was quiet when we came home from the meeting. "Everything okay?" I asked, as she played with some of the chips we picked up from McDonald's on the way home.

"Yep."

"Are you sure? I thought you would be full of beans after getting together with your panto team."

"Yes, I'm okay. I promise."

"Okay then… if you're sure." She didn't look up at me

and sat twirling a chip in a tub of ketchup. "Are you not hungry either?"

"No not really. I think I'm just tired. Is it okay if I just go to bed?"

"Yes of course." I watched my baby girl put her food back in the bag without even looking up. Something was not right. She came round and hugged me and said 'goodnight', but that was it. Something was going on with her.

I rang Sarah to see if she had any clue. "I don't, sorry, but hang on and let me ask Holly…"

I could hear the muffled conversation, but not the words. I could feel the anxiety growing like a balloon in my stomach.

She came back to the phone. "Are you still there?"

"Yes, yes I'm here."

"Holly said she thought Felicity might have said something to Annie that had bothered her."

"Like what?" I asked, nausea washing over me.

"Holly wasn't sure of the details because she missed the first part of it, but something about Felicity telling Annie that clever girls aren't really any good at dancing. Apparently, Annie and Holly were talking about a maths test they'd done, and Felicity said there was nothing cool about being a smart-arse."

"Right…" I felt the hairs on my arms stand up.

"Hang on, there's more. I'm fucking fuming, Lydia. That little cow said to Annie that because she's so clever, she must be really bad at dancing, and she wouldn't be surprised if Annie fell over on stage or got everything wrong."

"No wonder she's in a bloody state!" I closed my eyes and pinched the bridge of my nose.

"What are you going to do?"

"No idea at this point. I'll speak to Annie and see what she says."

As I ended the call, I looked at my hands. Three of my fingers were bleeding and I hadn't felt the pain I'd caused through my anger. I had to take a few deep breaths before I went upstairs as I really had no idea what to do in this situation.

I knocked gently on Annie's door. When there was no answer, I opened it slightly. "Annie, are you awake?" There was no response, but I hesitated, knowing it was unlikely she could have fallen asleep so quickly. I saw her little shoulders heave from the weight of the sob she was so desperately trying to hide from me.

I walked round the bed and saw her pillow was soaked with tears; brown wisps of hair were stuck to her face.

I hugged her tightly to me. "It's okay, Annie, it's okay." I rocked her until the sobbing subsided.

"I know about Felicity and what she said to you." I stroked her hair back out of her face. "Do you know why she was mean to you?"

"No, I never even said anything to her ever before tonight," Annie sobbed.

"Well, sometimes, when girls, especially girls like Felicity who are a bit older, see younger kids who have something they don't, they can get jealous. And when girls are jealous, they can get nasty, like Felicity did tonight. Do you understand that?"

"But I don't have anything she hasn't got..." Her tiny fists rubbed the tears from her eyes.

I stroked her hair away from her face. "It's not always

something you can see, and she might not even be aware of it herself, but I think when she heard how clever you are and she knows how good you are at dancing, maybe she thought that if she's not as clever as you, that's it's not fair you have both things, so instead of doing the smart thing and trying to be more clever, she tries to take something away from you. Does that make sense?"

"Kind of, but she said that I can't be a good dancer, and everyone knows it."

"Okay, so look at it this way. Firstly, she's the only person who has said that, and I think we know that's down to jealousy. Secondly, do you really think Miss Victoria would put anyone on stage, representing VCS, if they weren't going to make her look good? She only puts the best dancers into panto, because the newspapers come and see it, and lots of people come and watch every year and it costs a lot of money, so it has to be good, right? So let me ask you this… do you think Daisy Holmes and Mila Hewitt are bad dancers or good dancers?"

"Oh, they are so good, Mummy. They can do loads of tricks and get distinctions in… like… everything."

"Right. And they didn't get into panto. And you did."

Annie nodded, thinking it through. Then the tears came back, flooding through her lower lashes, each one breaking my heart a little more.

"What is it? What did she say that hurt you so much?"

Annie hesitated, as though saying the words out loud would give some kind of legitimacy to that kid's hateful comments.

"She said that I was bound to fall over on the stage, and that when I did, the music would stop and it would be silent in the audience, and then a spotlight would come onto me, and then the audience would start laughing at me."

I felt sick to my stomach. What the fuck was wrong with that kid? Did she really feel so threatened by a younger child that she was prepared to sink this low?

Anger grew in my belly but was overshadowed by something way more powerful – a mother's instinct to protect her baby. But how? How do you deal with a child like that?

"Annie, I promise you this…you will not fall on stage. And if you do – which you won't – I will be there to catch you, and before the spotlight can even find you, I'll have scooped you off stage and I'll go back and do a little performance of my own so people won't even remember you fell."

She giggled. "Oh God, Mummy, please no! What would you do?"

"Hmm… I'm not sure yet. Of course, we've got enough time that I can think of something, but for now you can choose. Should I do a song or a dance?"

"Neither!" she squealed.

"That settles it – it shall be a dance. I'll show you what I'm thinking…" I clambered off the pink duvet and stood up straight with my arms and feet in first position.

I tried to think of some ballet-type song I could sing along, but my mind was blank. So 'Pass out' by Tinie Tempah had to do. I gave my best street dance performance, complete with lyrics that I didn't even know, so basically made up. It was dreadful and after thirty seconds I collapsed down on the bed. I would not be winning any prizes any time soon, but it didn't matter. Annie was laughing.

I settled her back down and tucked her teddy in with her.

"Do you feel a bit better now?" I asked.

"Yes, I think so."

"Okay, so I want you to get a good night's sleep because you'll be having a lot of late nights soon. And now you've shared your problem with me, half of it is mine, so I hope your worry seems lighter now?" She nodded. "Of course," I went on… "I heard that it's possible to take a full problem away just by the power of raspberries!" I blew a long, loud raspberry on her tummy and she howled with laughter, wiggling round the bed. "Again, again!" she shouted when I broke free.

"No, that's enough for tonight," I said tucking her in. "The problem is all mine now, so I don't want you to worry about it at all now. You leave it with Mummy, and I'll sort it."

"What will you do, Mummy?"

"I'm not sure yet," I replied. "But she won't bother you again."

I wasn't sure how to handle the situation. I hadn't come up against bullying before – at least, not Annie being bullied. Not like this. And I had promised I would sort it, so come hell or high water, I would sort it. I could talk to Miss Victoria. Or I could talk to Diane. Or maybe even have a little chat with Felicity herself. I would need to think this one through, but no way would that be continuing through panto season. No way.

10

Gifts

WE TURNED UP TO the Adelphi early on a Friday afternoon in early December. Opening night with a dress rehearsal in the afternoon. We had more bags than we would have taken for a week abroad, but hoped we could leave some stuff there so we wouldn't be lugging it all backwards and forwards.

The girls were all giddy with excitement; even Annie seemed less bothered by Felicity now, although I'd made a point of keeping a close eye on her and I think she knew it. Sometimes she would look round to see if anyone was watching and would catch my stare. I would raise my eyebrows – almost undetectable to anyone else, I hoped – as if to say, 'I'm watching, and I dare you.' I doubted even Felicity would have the brass neck to bully a child while her mother watched on, but I watched and waited. One wrong move and she'd wish she hadn't. I hadn't forgotten Annie's tears from two weeks earlier, but I also hadn't decided what to do about it yet.

We ran through the full show twice, so both teams would get the same opportunity. It went much smoother than Starstruck as there were long periods in between the girls' numbers for them to get changed, though of course we had all six mums backstage seeing to their own daughters – how this would work that night, when there were only three of us, was anyone's guess. After our run-through, we could settle in, relax and watch Team B take their turn. Sarah had to leave to get back to work for a couple of hours, so after tidying Annie's various shoes, tights and various other paraphernalia away, Annie and I made our way back to the auditorium.

The other mums were sitting on a line about a third of the way from the front, the girls also on a single line a couple of rows to the front of the mums. As the band had already started playing, I didn't want the curtain going up while we were still making our way to sit down, so we approached the lines from the outer walkway. Liz and Emma sat in the middle, flanked by other mums. *Great*, I thought. As I sat down, Diane made a point of turning her back to me and whispering something to Liz. I couldn't hear what was said over the music from the band, but I always considered myself pretty good at picking up on non-verbal cues, and whatever was said was almost certainly about me.

Annie took her seat next to Iris. She seemed like a nice enough kid, pretty quiet and in a class below Annie and her friends as she had started when she was five and had to catch up. I guessed she probably felt a little like a fish out of water too.

God, I wished Sarah hadn't had to leave. I felt like

such an outsider at that point. These mums all knew what they were doing, and I didn't. I had to depend on them for anything I needed to know about the theatre, or the cast, or etiquette, or a million other things, and yet I had the worst feeling that any one of them would throw me under the bus at the first opportunity. When I look back it seems ridiculous. What did I think they could do? I had no idea, but – not for the first time in a dancing-related situation – I felt like I was dealing with a pack of wolves.

It was great to watch the full show from start to finish, but I felt I just couldn't enjoy it as much as I wanted to. I was uneasy and felt very alone in the theatre that day. During a particularly long dialogue between the ugly sisters, I sent a text to Rob:

ANNIE WAS AMAZING IN THE DRESS REHEARSAL. LET ME KNOW WHEN YOU GET TO THE THEATRE LATER AND I'LL POP DOWN. I COULD REALLY DO WITH A HUG RIGHT NOW. THESE DANCE MUMS ARE ABSOLUTE BITCHES X

I knew Rob likely wouldn't respond until after work at 5pm, so was surprised when I felt the phone vibrate through my bag.

DON'T WHINE TO ME ABOUT IT. YOU WANTED HER TO DO IT. DON'T THINK I'LL BE THERE BEFORE 7PM. TELL ANNIE GOOD LUCK

Wow. I felt the prick of tears beginning to sting, so I quickly put my phone away and tried to focus on the show. I wasn't needy. Never had been. I didn't crave affection or validation the way some people do. But in that moment, I really felt I had needed Rob, and he had let me down. I was alone with this wolf pack and alone in our marriage. I had known it deep down for a few years, but that single text told me everything I had chosen to ignore about the pathetic state of our relationship. *Come January, we will need to have a serious talk about the future*, I thought sadly.

After Team B had left the building around 5pm, Annie, Holly, Felicity, Beatrice, Camilla and Iris headed back upstairs with just me and Diane, soon joined by Sarah. We were the opening night chaperones, and I was terrified. The kids chattered non-stop as they ate their sandwiches and crisps before we started thinking about make-up, hair and costumes.

"Okay," Diane shouted. "Girls, calm down a minute." She stood up with an air of authority and the girls duly paid attention.

"I think," she pronounced, "we should do presents now before it gets too chaotic." She produced a large bag from a cupboard in the dressing room, which I hadn't even noticed until then.

At the meeting, we had discussed buying gifts for 'opposites', so Annie and Phoebe bought for each other. There was a limit of £10, so we had chosen a small Cinderella ragdoll from the Disney Store and some sweets for Phoebe, wrapped in Cinderella wrapping paper.

As Diane gave the gifts out, there was a flurry of unwrapping and paper being thrown around.

"Mummy, look!" Annie squealed. "Look what I got!"

What the fuck...

Annie held up a beautiful white gold bracelet with a blue crystal slipper pendant on it. I could see from the packaging alone that this was not from a discount jeweller. It was stunning but must have cost £80... maybe more.

I looked at Sarah. Holly was showing her the exact same bracelet, bought for her by Belinda and Libby.

"Fuck..." Sarah mouthed to me.

"Yes, fuck..." I mouthed back. What would Jo and Belinda think when they opened our 'within the agreed price-range' gifts?

"Ah that's nice," Diane said, flatly, to Annie.

I looked up at her. "Was it not a £10 limit?" I asked.

"Well yeah, but we don't have to stick to it. We want the girls to have an amazing experience from start to finish, so we do tend to go overboard at times." She smiled broadly, seeming oblivious to my expression of horror. Or maybe she was enjoying my discomfort. An image flashed through my mind of me punching her and breaking those fucking smiling veneers.

Great. What I heard was 'we said £10 so you plebs would get some shitty cheap presents and then look like cheapskates to everyone else, highlighting your inadequacies as dance mums and showing us that you really have no place among us'.

I looked round the room and felt my heart sink deep into the pit of my belly. The Cinderella dolls we bought for Phoebe and Libby seemed laughable now. Pathetic. We should have known, but how could we? Yet Jo and Belinda knew. Sarah and I were definitely on the outer edge of this elite clique with no idea how to infiltrate.

It was too late to even go and buy something else – not that I could have afforded it. I'd only been told that afternoon that we had to buy the shoes and tights for the girls (silly me, assuming it was part of the costume so the theatre could have footed the cost). It was going to cost a small fortune in petrol and car parking fees, not to mention – this was the best one – while the girls were busy doing panto, and therefore unable to attend classes, we still had to pay for missed lessons. By this point, lessons were costing £65 a week. So, five weeks of panto was costing me £325 in fees for classes Annie could not attend as she was at the theatre, making money for the production company.

I had felt like such an idiot when Liz had told me. She smiled as she asked, "Didn't you know?" As always, my face said what my mouth didn't, so I asked anyway.

"Hang on, so we pay for lessons they can't possibly attend?"

"Yeah, it's always been that way, and who's going to argue?" She carried on smiling as she went back to turning her back in favour of someone far more interesting than me.

She was right, though. Who would argue? What could we do? Absolutely nothing. Nobody forced us to let our kids do panto. We could turn on our heels and march out in protest, but our places would be filled in a heartbeat – filled by kids and mums who don't complain, who happily hand over their hard-earned money to these leeches. We would never complain, and the teachers and Miss Victoria knew that. As long as our kids wanted to be part of these things, we would take whatever shit they threw our way – not only that but we would thank them for the amazing opportunity.

Why did this feel like one massive scam?

Once the girls were ready, they started getting more excited, filled with adrenaline and getting louder by the second.

"Girls, girls!" Diane shouted. "Show starts in twenty minutes. If you can quieten down, I'll take you down to the cast to give out your presents. Meet us down at the side of the stage," she instructed me and Sarah.

Give out our what now?...

Another message that had clearly been delivered when somehow neither Sarah nor I was there. And not just any old gifts… these were quality items. It seemed each of the girls had bought gifts for all eight members of the cast, the senior dancers, Miss Stacy and Miss Victoria. The 'Z list' celebrities who made up the cast were treated mainly to alcohol and expensive scented candles. The seniors received a variety of perfumes and expensive make-up palettes. Miss Stacy and Miss Victoria received jewellery (I expect it was probably engraved, lest they forget the little star who bought it), tickets to West End shows, spa days and memberships to a wine club.

This was insane. "What the fuck, Sarah?"

"I have no words" was her reply.

Yet another way to make us feel like crap. Shower everyone with extortionate gifts, no doubt trying to curry favour and buy their kids main parts in the next show or whatever… while we bought precisely nothing.

"Well, maybe we should get them something for the final show instead, then?" I asked Sarah.

"You think these ass-kissing bitches won't already have bought something for that? Jesus Christ, I don't think Stacy or Victoria received a single gift that cost less than £150."

"What could we possibly get to compete with that?" This question was more to myself than Sarah. "And actually, why do we want to? They can use our December class fees to buy themselves something nice. Fuck that. This has already cost about a million pounds. I'm fucked if I'm going to buy a present as well!"

"Quite right, now let's get down there and do this chaperone shit!"

11

Cliques

I'D SEEN HINTS OF it over the last few years, but panto showed me a level of bitching and cattiness I wasn't really prepared for. Mums would bitch about other mums, the B team girls, teachers, cast, any mutual acquaintances they may have... literally anyone. It seemed the point of their gossip was more about the story they told, and less about the person concerned. So basically, anyone was fair game.

And their daughters were learning from them. Felicity, Beatrice and Camilla would huddle together in the dressing room, whispering. Occasionally Iris would join them, though she didn't seem to be that interested in the gossiping, so would spend time with Holly and Annie as well.

They would look over at the younger girls, sneering. Sometimes one would catch my eye and notice that I was watching them. They would turn back to hide their face but then another one would peek out from the coven. There was no doubt in my mind that Annie was a regular topic for discussion. While Annie was (hopefully) oblivious, I was not, and I wanted these mini bitches to know that I saw what they were doing.

But I couldn't be there all the time.

Around a week or so into the show run, Sarah dropped Annie off after the evening performance. Annie's eyes were red and wet. "What happened?" I asked Sarah on the doorstep.

"I'm so fucking angry," Sarah whispered. "One of the coven tripped her as she came off stage from the finale. She was okay, and it wasn't on the stage, so the audience didn't see, but I think Beatrice said something to her when she picked her up. I asked Annie but she wouldn't tell me."

"Who tripped her?"

"I didn't see. I did ask them, but nobody seemed to know. I'm sure they did, but you know how crowded it gets when they're all coming off. It could have been an accident, I suppose, but I just don't think so."

My heart was racing, and I felt shaky. Fight or flight. Definitely fight.

"Okay, well let me know if you find out any more from Holly. But I'll speak to you tomorrow anyway. Thanks for dropping her off." I closed the door and leaned my head against it. It was late but Annie had gone into the living room. I guessed she wanted to talk.

"Did Sarah tell you what happened?" she asked, knees tucked up tight to her chest.

"Yes, she said you fell, but she thought you might have been tripped. Were you tripped, Annie?"

She looked at a spot on the carpet, nudging it with her toes. When she didn't answer, I asked again. "Annie, I need you to tell me what happened. Look at Mummy."

She looked up and our eyes locked. "Tell me," I pleaded.

The tears ran freely. "I don't know who tripped me up."

"Could it have been an accident, do you think? Is that possible?"

She shrugged and went back to studying the carpet. She didn't need to answer; I knew it wasn't an accident.

"So, what did Beatrice say when she helped you up?"

She looked up again, the emotional turmoil evident on her face. "I need you to tell me, Annie. You remember the other night when we talked about how sharing a problem can mean you're not having to carry it all on your own? This is the same. You have to tell me, so I can take on your problem and sort it. I want to help you."

The sobs became heavy and gut-wrenching. It broke my heart to see my baby like this, though again the sadness was almost outweighed by the anger, which was starting to eat away at me.

"Sh… she said… she said that… that Felicity was right and that next time it would be on the stage. And she said I should watch out because I would never know who was going to trip me up. She said it could be any of them… even Holly. And she said if I told anyone I would be sorry."

This was happening too often now. This was meant to be an incredible experience for Annie – not a scary ordeal at the hands of these bullies. My hands had clenched into tight fists. "Okay, thank you for telling me, sweetheart. So, this is what's going to happen. I am going to speak to Miss Victoria…" I grabbed her hands as she raised little fists to her mouth. Her eyes were wide with fear, and she shook her head. "No… no… listen, Annie. I don't want you to worry. I'll tell her it must not go any further, but I will tell her that because of this, I will be chaperoning at every show that Team A are doing. I'm down to do most of them anyway, so the girls won't know, and then I'll make an excuse to be there for the others. I will be with you at all times, and I will be watching from the side of the stage, like a hawk. I promise, Annie, if any of them even looks like they're going to do anything, I will catch it before it happens."

She nodded. "I don't know why they don't like me," she whispered, wiping the tears from her rosy cheeks.

"I promise you, Annie, if it wasn't you, it would be someone else. Those girls will always need to have someone to pick on because they're just horrible people and they enjoy it."

"But why me? What did I do?"

"Nothing, nothing at all. They probably see you as easy pickings because you're the youngest and the smallest. I can't imagine them doing this to someone who is thirteen or fourteen, or someone who is bigger than them. Can you?"

She shook her head.

"Remember, Annie, bullies are always... *always*... cowards. No exceptions. This is typical bully behaviour and it's horrible, but now you've told me about it, we can make sure they don't get the chance to do anything else."

It was gone midnight by the time Annie got to bed that night and gone 3am before I fell into a restless sleep, disturbed by dreams about high school, an uneven wooden theatre stage with loose boards, and little girls with pointy teeth and razorblade fingernails.

*

I expected some kind of push-back from Miss Victoria, something about health and safety and too many people at the side of the stage, but I was prepared, and maybe my tone alone told her that this was not negotiable.

"But they're normally such lovely, polite girls, I'm surprised that..."

"I dare say," I shot back, interrupting her. I didn't have enough restraint in me to listen to how good these little fuckers were, without losing it. "But be that as it may, I believe Annie, and I believe she feels intimidated by these girls, so if you want her to carry on doing panto..."

"Of course we do," she interrupted back. "We've had so much feedback from the director and production team about Annie. And the rest of the team backstage love her as well. She's got a real stage presence, and she's doing so well. I've had a lot of people asking about her, saying she's the one they..."

"That's nice to hear, but at this point I don't really care. I'm concerned, so I'm staying. I hope that's not going to be a problem."

"No... no, not at all. I'm sure it's not necessary, but as a mum I understand why you would feel that way."

"Good. And I do hope you'll be discussing these behaviours with the parents when panto season ends. I'm so disappointed that this has happened. This should be a safe environment. We're giving up Christmas for this, and I really hoped it would be a lovely experience, not a frightening one for a little girl."

I went back out of the stage door, where Sarah had been waiting with Annie and Holly. Annie didn't want to be there when I spoke to Miss Victoria, understandably, as she probably knew me well enough to know I wasn't about to take any shit.

"Come on," I said, taking Annie's hand and leading her in, followed by Sarah and Holly, past a speechless Miss Victoria.

It would have been an easy afternoon – only Sarah and I were on chaperoning duty – but we were on high alert. We watched the coven of bitches constantly. Any hint of them making a move and we would have been on them.

I wasn't sure whether Camilla was really on side with what they were doing or was trying to keep them happy. I could understand if she was. She had just turned ten, and so was younger than Beatrice and Felicity. Perhaps she felt it was better to be inside their circle than risk being outside it. I had some experience of 'better the devil you know...'

I watched all the girls constantly, and they knew it. They were waiting for an opportunity, and they weren't going to get it. So, they tried other tactics. While in their little huddle during the interval, they called Holly over.

"What?" she asked, not even looking up from the game she was playing with Annie on her iPad.

"Just come here."

"Wait a minute... I need to finish this round," she replied.

I wanted to step in, ask them what they wanted Holly for, what they whispered about, and what their fucking problem was. But I didn't. I observed. The buzzer went to indicate the second half was about to start. Thank God. Whatever they were scheming was not going to be happening for now.

Holly seemed oblivious to the situation, while Annie desperately tried to ignore it and focus on whatever she was doing, but I could see it. She was on edge, and she was unhappy, though she tried her best to hide it.

As the group trudged downstairs for the second number of the act, flanked by Sarah at the front and me at the back (I wanted to be able to watch them all), Beatrice doubled over on the stairs. *Is this it?* I wondered. Was she about to make her move? I was so paranoid; I was reading the worst into every move they made. I watched her reach out to Felicity, while her other hand grasped her throat.

"Oh my God... what's wrong with you?" Felicity asked her, sympathetic as ever. "Stop it, you're going to rip my sleeve!"

But something was very wrong.

Beatrice was struggling to breathe, and her face was swelling before our eyes. I pushed past the girls to get to her. Shit. I'd never come across anything like this. I picked her up and took her to the corridor opposite to give her some space. "Where's her EpiPen?" Sarah shouted.

Camilla started to panic. "What do we do? What's happening to her?"

"It's okay, love, don't worry. Felicity, please could you take the girls down to the stage and let Miss Victoria know what's happened. Annie, please could you go and get the EpiPen from her bag upstairs?" She stood there wide-eyed, not moving as she watched Beatrice transform from a pretty dancer to a hideous beast – her eyes now swollen shut, lips an ugly shade of purple and starting to blister.

"Annie, go now!" She ran back upstairs and was back and panting a minute later with the EpiPen. I snatched it off her and slammed it into Beatrice's thigh as we'd been instructed to at the meeting. I'd thought it so unlikely that this would happen, I wasn't sure I'd really been paying attention, and I was cursing myself for not taking more notice. Had I done it right? Would it do any damage if I got it wrong? My hands shook and sweat gathered around the back of my neck as I put Beatrice into the recovery position, having no idea whether this was the right thing to do in this situation. I sat back against the wall, gasping for breath myself.

Annie stood against the wall opposite me, her face pale, and eyes wide with fear. Sarah took her by the hand. "I'll take her down and have a word with Miss Victoria. You stay here."

"Don't leave her," I begged. Despite the chaos, I still had to make sure Annie was okay.

"I won't, I promise."

Miss Victoria must have crossed Sarah on the stairs. "I've called 999, and rang Gabby," she said. "Did anyone have nuts in their bags?"

"Not that I saw, although the older girls tend to separate themselves from the little ones. I didn't see what any of them were eating."

Miss Victoria gently laid a fleece jacket over Beatrice and stroked her face. "Don't worry, love, the ambulance is on its way, and your mum too." Her breathing had settled now but she looked like she'd been viciously attacked. Despite everything, I couldn't help feeling sorry for her. *It must be terrifying*, I thought, *to not be able to get any air into your lungs.* She had tried to open her mouth as she had been gasping, and I could see her tongue was swollen; I guessed her throat would be too.

"I think earlier they were playing that game with the jellybeans though," I pondered. "You know the one where some taste like marshmallows and others the same colour taste like vomit or hot chillies or something. I wonder if it could have been that…"

"Could be. They all know not to bring peanut butter, but Gabby checks everything for nut traces as well. I bet the girls never thought to check jellybeans."

Gabby was there in less than ten minutes, so I knew she had broken the speed limit, and no doubt parked right outside. Who would blame her, though? The ambulance came, and took her in. And Sarah and I went back to chaperoning kids doing panto. By the end of the second half, the girls talked about what had happened as though it were something they'd seen on television, not something terrifying that had happened in front of their very eyes, just an hour earlier. Felicity seemed to have actually enjoyed not only the drama but also her friend looking so grotesque.

We drove home that night, exhausted by the day's events. It had been a terrifying experience for everyone, but I was relieved that there would be at least a couple of days without Beatrice at the theatre. Maybe without her partner in crime, Felicity might be a little less bold. The threat had halved.

I was surprised a few days later, when Felicity seemed to have – almost overnight – developed a bad case of body odour. I think it surprised me mostly because she would have been so quick to tear someone else apart for such a crime. She was only eleven, so quite young to have started puberty, although I had noticed some tampons in her bag.

I almost felt sorry for Felicity when the other girls seemed to notice the smell and started to give her a bit more space. I watched as she tried using deodorants and body sprays in a futile attempt to mask the stench. Nothing worked, and the cast and crew had started to notice.

Shame, I thought one day, as I sat on top of a table, my feet on the chair in front of me. I bit into my apple, and I watched her, enjoying her panic and attempts to fight tears as she sniffed her costumes.

Sucks to be you right now, Felicity.

12

Competitions and
the Competition

ANNIE'S FIRST PANTO SERVED well in increasing her
stage confidence – so much so that when Miss Jessica
announced one afternoon that the new competition team
would be revealed later, we felt confident that some, if not
all, of the panto kids would be on the team. And of course,
they were.

Each child was expected to have a minimum of three
solo dances, duet or trio, and be part of the group dance
for their age category. They would attend private lessons
for each dance, at least once a week, with an extra lesson
before each competition. These lessons were compulsory,
and any failure to attend would result in not being able to
compete that week.

After two months of learning choreography and
rehearsing, team Energise was ready.

Sarah and Holly picked us up at 5am on a Saturday

morning, ready for the drive to North Wales. The girls were giddy with excitement on the drive, though they quietened as we approached the venue.

"Is this it?" Sarah asked. "Surely not."

I checked the address on the email we had received. "Yep, this is it, not what I expected for a town hall, but this is definitely it."

"This looks well scummy," Holly said.

"Hmm… it does a bit. Well, I'm sure it will be okay inside," I replied, admittedly not filled with confidence.

Belinda and Jo were just inside the doorway as we entered the shabby building. They, like us, were loaded up with costumes, food bags, make-up boxes, and various props and other paraphernalia.

"I think we have to sign in at that desk," said Belinda, taking charge as always.

We signed in and paid our fees. The entry fees had been paid weeks earlier – £10 per dancer per dance, and £5 each for the group dance. And now we were handing over another £10 admission fee. Part of me was hoping Annie would hate it, so we could leave this team – I wasn't sure how long I could afford to pay these fees, before Rob noticed. He still had no idea, but my overdraft was increasing every month.

In fairness, the building was cleaner and more modern inside. It was a listed building, so I supposed there was a limit on what could be achieved. We found a room with 'Energise', written on a sheet of A4, taped to the door. The room was more than big enough for us. Thankfully, the older girls were not performing until the following day, so we didn't have to contend with them. I was relieved, as

Annie still tensed up when she saw Felicity or Beatrice at the studio.

As we applied the required 'natural but pretty and noticeable' make-up, Nancy came through with Jemima. She was loaded up with Jemima's stuff, while Jemima didn't even carry her own rucksack.

The girls and mums chatted excitedly, but Jo – as always – was starting to feel sick with nerves.

"Get a grip, woman," Belinda said, expertly applying blush to Libby's already pink cheeks. "They'll be fine. They all know their dances."

"Yeah," I agreed, "and if they make a mistake they know just to carry on and improvise."

"I know," Jo said quietly, biting her nails. "I'm just worried that she won't win anything."

I looked down at the timetable we had paid an additional £5 for. "Jo, there are about twenty-five kids in each section. Twenty-four of them won't win. And we have no idea what those other dancers are like. Maybe, seeing as it's the first competition for them, we should just enjoy their performances and not worry too much about winning?"

"I know, but imagine if she doesn't even place in the top three…"

Was she serious? There were five girls here, just in our little group. So even if they were all on a par with each other, even if no other entries were at the same standard as them, two of them would not place in the top three.

"Well does it really matter?" Sarah asked. "What if she doesn't? And what if she does? What difference does it really make?"

"Well… none I suppose, I just really want her to win, or at least get placed, you know – for her confidence…"

Yeah right. For her confidence. Not for one-upsies with Belinda and Libby? Of course not.

Belinda, I noticed, was staying out of this. She probably felt the same as Jo but could hear how horribly self-absorbed it sounded when said out loud.

Jo was starting to grate on me. I understood her nerves – this was the first time they had performed in this environment, and they were doing solos. It was nerve-racking for us all, probably the mums as much, if not more than the girls. She was starting to make me anxious.

"Well, at least two of them won't place, so we need to make our peace with that," I snapped.

"I know, I just know she'll be so upset though," she went on, oblivious to the raised eyebrows and dropped jaws around her.

"Then I guess we all need to manage their expectations, don't we?"

"I'm just looking forward to watching them all dance," Nancy chipped in. "I haven't seen any of the other girls' solos, so it'll be nice to watch."

I was suddenly filled with a fear that rose in me from out of nowhere. Watching the other girls' solos. I'd seen Annie's a hundred times, both in the studio and at home, but none of the others. Not even Holly's.

"I'm just nipping to the loo," I said and left the room.

In the bathroom, I ran my hands under the cold tap, trying to distract myself from the anxiety that was building. I didn't want to watch the others. What if they were better than Annie? What if their choreography was better? Or their choice of music? Or even their costumes? I found myself aligning with Jo's ridiculous, self-centred worries. I would never show it. I would never let Annie know that it mattered whether she placed, or she didn't. But it did matter. And for the same reason as Jo was claiming. A win would increase her confidence. Not placing would erode it.

I suspected every mother in that place felt exactly the same, but only Jo was dim enough to say it out loud. The rest of us played at being supportive dance mums, but every one of us – if we dared to be honest – secretly hoped every competitor, except their kid, was rubbish. We pretended it didn't matter, but how could it not? How could a mother genuinely be thrilled if another child, even if they were one of our team, was judged 'better' than theirs?

The teachers had kindly allowed the girls to choose their own genres, so they could have done different groups and not been competing against each other. But they didn't want to. So, each of them had ballet, modern and lyrical dances.

As the girls lined up for their first section – ballet – I kissed Annie on the forehead.

"I'm fine, Mum, honestly. Just go and sit and watch." She appeared calm enough, but the dimple in her forehead told me otherwise.

"You'll be great. I love you," I said as I turned to walk away.

The Energise girls were the last five out of a section of over twenty. By the time Annie came on, Libby and Holly had already performed, but I hadn't really paid much attention. I had watched the first few performances from other schools and wasn't really concerned – they weren't as good as our girls. Granted, this was a 'novice' section – reserved for those who had not yet achieved a first, second or third place in any competition – but even so our girls were way better than the rest. In my opinion, at least.

While Holly performed, my thoughts were all negative. *What if Annie forgets her dance? What if she falls over? What if I gave the lady at the back the wrong CD? What if the CD is scratched? How will Annie react? Is she okay backstage? Does she feel as terrified as I do?* My usual fight response had transformed to flight.

I clapped for Holly and told Sarah how amazing she was. It was expected. And no doubt she was. I just hadn't taken any notice, as I was caught up in my own fears.

Annie walked beautifully onto the stage, and I gasped. She looked so confident, as though she'd done this a million times. Her shiny brown hair, scraped into an immaculate bun, seemed to pull her neck and spine higher than I'd ever seen. Her make-up was just enough for her delicate features to be seen from our seats halfway back, and she looked breathtaking. Her tutu had cost, as expected, as much as a holiday abroad, but seeing her up there, suddenly every penny seemed justified. Dark, forest green satin, with hand-sewn crystals adorning the boned bodice, with layers of stiff, black tulle complementing the lace appliques, which covered the join of the straps to the main body of the tutu, giving it a dark, gothic aesthetic.

Her music started and her performance began, quiet and slow at first, building into an emotive crescendo after around a minute and twenty seconds. If she was nervous (and I was sure she was) she didn't show it. Each movement was precise and graceful. Annie was ten years old, and she displayed more confidence than I could ever hope to have. As the final notes played and she landed her final position perfectly, I felt my heart was going to leave my chest. I hadn't noticed my own tears, until I looked at Sarah and she wiped them away for me.

She had done it. And she smashed it. At that point, I couldn't have been prouder. It wouldn't matter whether she placed or not; I couldn't have asked for more. I glanced to the side of the room, and noticed Miss Victoria and Miss Lorna, Annie's ballet teacher, both wiping tears away.

Phoebe and Jemima's performances were lovely to watch – not as good as Annie's, of course – but now my nerves were over, I was able to relax and enjoy it.

The girls all filed onto stage, holding their numbers in front of them. They took their places in a semi-circle, remembering to maintain a beautiful ballet position and a smile that was 'obvious, but not cheesy' – an instruction that had made no sense to me before today, but now I understood.

The judges whispered amongst themselves for a few minutes, and Sarah dug her nails into my arm. The silence felt thick and never-ending. Finally, the head judge stood up and the audience clapped, and she walked to the front of the stage. It was clear from her walk that she was a ballerina. I hoped Annie would benefit from that same posture later in life.

"Well, what can I say," she began, and she smiled. "We all know that ballet is a difficult discipline, and takes a lot of work, and hours and hours of practice, but I think it was evident today that every girl in this group has put in those hours. It takes effort, and sometimes we get corrections –

don't we, girls? – that can feel like criticism and a bit picky."
The girls nodded silently, their expressions unchanging.

"But as you move through your exam grades," she went on, "you'll be critiqued more and more, and you'll be better dancers for it, okay?" More nodding. "Overall, there were some beautiful performances today. Some of you need to work on your turn-out and there were a few other bits that could do with some work, but like I said, overall, a very enjoyable novice group."

My palms were wet, and I wiped them on my jeans. My tummy was churning, and my heart pounded so hard I could see each fast beat through my t-shirt. The nerves were back. I looked down the line and saw Jo looking pale and sweaty, leaning forwards in anticipation. Her little hands were clenched into tight fists, knuckles as white as her face.

"So, without further ado," the judge went on, "I'm going to give third place to number twelve."

We clapped, but felt our hearts sink. Not one of ours. That meant three of our team would be disappointed.

After number twelve had accepted her medal, curtsied, and returned to her place in the semi-circle, the judge continued.

"My second place goes to number twenty-one."

"Oh my God, that's Holly!" Sarah squealed, nearly drawing blood as she dug her nails deeper into my arm with excitement. "Oh my God, oh my God!"

I clapped loudly for Holly and felt Sarah's pride in her radiating.

"And finally, my first place goes to number twenty-two."

I looked at Annie, holding the twenty-two in front of her. I didn't dare believe it, and Annie looked down at her number, hesitating to step forwards and collect her medal. The judge approached her and said, "It's okay, it's you, sweetheart, well done," before handing the medal to an open-mouthed Annie.

I felt the tears welling in my eyes and grabbed my bag and dashed out of the door to see my daughter. I found her in the crowd of chattering girls, looking gob-smacked and confused. Her eyes were watery, but she was smiling.

"I'm so proud of you," I said, hugging her tightly. "You were beautiful up there."

I noticed Jemima and Libby to the side, whispering, but refused to let them steal our thunder. The mums gathered and congratulations were offered, somewhat reluctantly, I felt, from Belinda and Jo, though Nancy seemed genuine enough.

Phoebe stood with Holly and Annie, looking longingly at their medals, no doubt bracing herself for the disappointment that Jo would unleash on their journey home. I felt sad for Phoebe, but also a horrible part of me was glad Jo would have to cope with her worst fear. What did that say about me? I really didn't care. It could have easily been Annie that hadn't placed. None of them were really any better than each other. Of course, I thought Annie was better, but I was self-aware enough to know that was probably a mother's bias. I knew there would be disappointments ahead. Nobody could win everything. But I was ecstatic at that point, and didn't give a shit about Jo, Belinda, or any of the other mothers in the audience who were no doubt disappointed in their kids.

The lyrical section was next; a smaller group of only fifteen, of which ours were, again, the last five. After the first couple of performances, I was relieved that it was a smaller section. I found this to be mind-numbingly boring to watch, and knew that if Annie weren't in it, there was no way I could endure sitting through that. Again, our girls performed well – too close to call, Belinda said. And she was the expert.

Annie didn't place, and neither did Holly or Jemima. Phoebe came third and Libby got first. That was fine with me. At least, there couldn't be any bad feeling now. I hoped Jemima would at least place in the modern section, though I hoped harder that Annie would place above her.

Modern was an enormous section – thirty-four entries – and we were, as expected, the last five. It was torturous. Some performances were entertaining. Some were good – I hated those. I wanted them all to be rubbish. Some were rubbish – I felt sorry for those kids, and their parents, but more than that, I felt relief after each bad performance. I hadn't realised how much variety 'modern' covered – some performances were similar to lyrical, some were very (to my mind) old-fashioned: we're talking blue eyeshadow, jazz hands and winking at judges. Those ones made me feel ill. What teachers thought little kids winking seductively at judges was a good idea? Some were quite contemporary, and others, like Annie's, had a fair bit of acro content. One girl was made up to resemble a broken china doll. She wore a dirty, white, frilled dress, and had her long, dark hair arranged into two messy braids. Her act was creepy, but well-delivered, and I thought it was a likely winner.

I enjoyed the modern section more than the others, but still grew bored after about fifteen performances. I perked up a little when we finally got to number twenty-nine and Libby came on, as I knew Annie would be on soon, and then it would finally be over.

Libby had a powerful, lyrical dance, performed to, I think, something by Christina Perri or similar. She was good, but I wasn't a massive fan of ten-year-olds looking full of angst and heartbreak. They were too young to understand the story they were telling.

Jemima had a fairly bland number, I think danced to some song from the late seventies or early eighties, though I couldn't place it. Filled with a predictable combination of Miss Stacy's signature moves – skip, split-leap, drop, roll – there was little about it that was memorable, and it seemed Jemima had drawn the short straw when the dances were choreographed.

Then Jemima forgot her dance around forty seconds in – God knows how, as it was so basic and had been rehearsed about a million times. We watched in horror as she froze, seemed to consider her next move and then ran off stage. Nancy rushed out to console her granddaughter, who would likely blame Grandma for her forgetting.

Phoebe had a jazzy number. Cheesy, energetic and lots of pointing at judges while winking. Jo loved it. I wanted to vomit.

It didn't last long. Possibly unnerved by Jemima, Phoebe also froze.

"Come on, Phoebe!" Jo shouted. The rest of us watched on in shocked amusement, as Jo stood up in the aisle and started doing Phoebe's dance, hoping she could get her daughter back on track. "Come on!"

Phoebe remained rooted to the spot. I think by that

point the embarrassment her mother was causing was probably much greater than just forgetting her dance. I looked at Sarah, who was watching, open-mouthed in shock, as Jo refused to let up. She was absolutely determined that Phoebe could pull it back, but despite her daughter remaining statue-still on the stage, Jo went on to complete the entire dance, complete with something I think was meant to be a cartwheel done in an aisle space of around four feet across. God, I wished we were allowed to record in there. I'd have paid anything to have that on my phone. Nobody outside of that room would ever believe what happened without seeing it for themselves.

At the end, she calmly sat down and leafed through the programme as though she hadn't just attempted to do her daughter's competition dance, without any skill or training, and while wearing jeans and high-heeled boots with her coat on and cross-body bag still firmly attached to her. I didn't dare look at Sarah. She nudged me, but I couldn't look. I knew if I started laughing, I wouldn't be able to control it and would have to leave the room. I started thinking about serious things – the state of the global environment, politics, what I needed to add to my shopping list – anything to distract from the hysteria I knew I would struggle to rein in.

Annie was up next, so at least I could focus on her, though I doubt anyone else did – they would be reeling from Jo's performance for a while. I hoped Annie wouldn't be affected by the curse that seemed to have affected the previous dancers. I needn't have worried. She broke the curse and went on to deliver a flawless performance. Her acro tricks, which I had worried about, were delivered perfectly, and I could see from her expression, as she landed for her ending pose, that she was proud of herself.

Holly danced to a song from a film soundtrack – again I recognised it but wasn't sure where from. Maybe a Disney film? It was beautiful, and I looked at Sarah, who smiled all the way through it, tears in her eyes.

We were used to the routine by the time they all reappeared on stage. I noticed Phoebe's eyes were bloodshot and watery, while Jemima looked angry. Nothing new there…

In her summing up, the judge spoke about how all dancers would likely freeze on stage at some point in their careers, but the truly professional ones would carry on, improvise until either they remembered what to do or the music ended. She said improvisation, when done well, should be undetectable, though it was a skill that had to be practised. She spoke about how nerves can affect dancers, and the importance of being able to box off anything else outside of your own dance, to allow true focus.

Blah, blah, blah. Just get on with it, so we can go home, I thought.

"My third place goes to number seventeen…" Not our group.

"My second place goes to number six…" Not our group.

"And finally, my first place goes to number thirty-three!"

"Annie!" Sarah shrieked. Annie beamed as she stepped forwards to collect her second first-place medal of the day. Her eyes met mine and I mouthed 'well done' and made a heart sign with my hands.

The adrenaline left my body as we left the room, and I felt exhausted. In the makeshift dressing room, Jemima slammed her stuff into various bags. Nancy tried to help, but Jemima snatched hairbrushes and make-up items from Nancy, as though Nancy were the reason for all the wrongs in the world.

The rest of the girls were happy enough, and after Jemima had stomped out of the building, Nancy following with various costume bags and make-up boxes, the girls beamed as we took pictures of them with their medals. Miss Victoria, Miss Lorna and Miss Stacy came through to congratulate them. None of them even commented on Jemima's whereabouts or performance.

13

Getting Tougher

ANNIE'S FINAL YEAR OF primary school was when my eyes really opened, and I started to hate the world of dance.

Maybe it was her age – the cusp of puberty isn't easy for anyone – but Annie was incredibly sensitive. She had always been able to pick up on non-verbal cues, intuition developed from an early age, and I thought her instincts were strong.

She started getting upset about things that were brushed off by others, even by me, in an attempt to diffuse the negative emotions. But she noticed everything.

She noticed the times she would walk into the changing room at the studio and it would go quiet, and the girls would trail out, leaving her to get changed alone. The times she'd gone to a party and then been 'accidentally' sliced out of the pictures the mums posted on Facebook. The parties she wasn't invited to at all.

It cut me deep, and I knew it cut her deeper. If I could have wished for anything for Annie, it would not have been for the girls to treat her better – lots of people in life were horrible, and she would come across them sooner or later, regardless of how much I tried to protect her. I would have wished for her to become more resilient. Her strong instincts should not be ignored or down-played – we have them for a reason, and they can potentially save your life, right? I wanted her to be able to get through the tough times, knowing things may not always get better, but she would become better at dealing with them. Better at doing the hard stuff. Better at dealing with shitty people. Better at seeing people for who they were, and knowing their behaviour said more about them than it did about her. Better at rising above it all and seeing the bigger picture, and better at loving herself for who she was. I wanted Annie to be as proud of everything she had achieved as I was, and I wanted more than anything for her to be optimistic about her future and everything she would go on to achieve.

But I didn't know how to get her there.

I'd been deluded. Annie had performed for eight or nine years – shows, three years of panto, more competitions than I could count, most of which she had placed in the top three. She received distinctions in all her dance exams. She was adored by her family, and she was adored by the dance teachers. Praise was lavished on her. But I don't think she ever really believed it.

Once she reached high school, she could no longer do panto as a 'juvenile', and she couldn't be a 'senior' until she left high school, so there was a slight reduction in pressure after her last panto finished. And I was exhausted too.

Sarah and Holly had leaned into the dance world, as I tried to lean out, so we started to see less of them. Sarah took her role of dance mum more seriously than I did. She was lucky. Her husband was an entrepreneur in some kind of IT thing and seemed to travel overseas fairly regularly. This allowed Sarah to indulge in guilt-free time away from her home, be it at the studio for hours on end, or the long-distance competitions that became weekends away. There were no hard feelings. I loved Sarah, and Annie and Holly were still close.

I had just fallen out of love with the whole dance thing, and it was draining me.

Like any mother, I took my child's worries on as my own, and I had plenty of my own as well.

My marriage was hanging on by a thread, as was my sanity – yet I didn't really care about either. Rob continued to do his own thing. While we were at the studio, Rob would be at the pub, or on the PlayStation, or asleep. He never offered to take Annie anywhere other than school (how good of him), and I never asked him. I was too proud to ask him for help. I knew how he felt about it all. If ever I tried to speak to him, he would carry on with whatever he was doing while I spoke, then he would look at me and shrug. He didn't need to say the words. His face said them. 'I told you so'.

And he was right. He did tell me so. He griped and moaned a lot in the earlier years. Then I suppose he accepted the situation – not really being happy about it, but not wanting to cause an argument that he knew he wouldn't win. I had justified it all for so long, I had practically brainwashed myself into believing it all.

Annie enjoys it; it's an investment in her future; I'm working, so I should be able to afford it without Rob needing to know the full extent of the financial damage; she's good at it – this could be her career; it will help her make friends from outside school; it will give her confidence; she will learn other life lessons – poise, discipline, teamwork.

It was really starting to seem like I'd been lying to myself for a long time. One by one, my mantras started to laugh at me.

If she enjoyed this, why did she come out of every lesson either in tears or close to tears? I would ask, every time, if she really wanted to carry on doing this, and she would always say yes. "But why? Why do you want to do this when it upsets you so much?" I would ask.

"Because I love to dance." End of argument.

And I had to admit, I had an enormous amount of admiration and respect for my daughter. I felt humbled by her bravery and determination. I would have quit long before, if it were me. I knew I would. But to see this fragile, sensitive girl so determined to do what she loved, despite the shit that was embedded into the culture of the school, maybe even the rest of the dance world, was truly inspiring. Despite everything, my girl had grit.

Annie had become an outsider, and I knew how that felt. My instincts were to shield her, wrap her up and take her home, away from the nastiness and cruelty, but she wouldn't let me. She wouldn't be beaten.

Almost every week, there was at least one incident that boiled my blood. Mostly it was Annie being left out, being isolated. I would peer through the gap in the blinds into the studio and watch the lessons if I could. I would see the teacher ask them to pick a partner, and every time, Annie would be last – everyone else having pre-arranged who would partner who – or in the event of one girl being absent, Annie would be left without a partner.

They would do corner work, and I would watch and see them huddled closely – Libby would go first, followed by Jemima, then Phoebe, then Holly, then a few other girls, and Annie would be last – separated from her old group by another group of kids she barely knew, and didn't have the confidence to talk to. She became accustomed to isolation, and it would tear me apart to see it. They were all children. But I hated them.

Sometimes the incidents were more obvious. One time Annie slipped while landing an aerial. The girls – not all of them, but the ones she used to think of as her friends – laughed at her. She ran out in tears.

Another time she overheard a conversation about duets being choreographed – Phoebe and Libby were doing a contemporary one, and Holly and Jemima were doing a tap. I had to admit, that one pissed me off too. Sarah had never said anything. We might not have been as close as we used to be, but I still thought she might have mentioned it. The clique tightened.

And still Annie wouldn't quit.

I couldn't even pretend to give a shit when Jemima injured her toe quite badly at a competition, meaning the duet – and anything else for Jemima – might not be happening for a while. Tap shoes sometimes needed breaking in a bit, but Jemima's toe was a bloodied, mangled mess. Oh well. How awful for her.

But I was worried about Annie. She was spending more and more time at home alone in her room. We would still chat like we always had. I never felt she was being secretive – more that she was becoming withdrawn. She wasn't a little girl anymore – no longer a bright, giggly toddler – but she wasn't an adult yet either. Not even close. I saw less of her than I used to as she isolated herself in her bedroom. And I missed her. I desperately wanted to help but had no clue where to start.

My sister would say "take her away from that fucking dance school". It was easy for her to say. She had a three-year-old son, still too young to be involved in anything much beyond colouring in and feeding the ducks.

"It's not as easy as that," I would say. "She loves to dance. And she doesn't want to leave. I promise you, all she has to do is say the word, and we're out of there. But it has to be her decision."

And that's where my internal conflict grew and festered. It became mouldy and decayed and poisoned my soul.

I waited for Annie to make the decision. I reasoned that if she made the decision herself, it was the right thing and there would be no regrets for me and no resentment from Annie towards me. And we would wave goodbye to VCS, hang up the pointe shoes and tutus and never look back. Cloud cuckoo land.

She was eleven. She was a child. I should have been a better parent and made that decision for her. But I couldn't bear the thought of her hating me, so I let it carry on, despite seeing the damage being caused. I should have been stronger, done what was needed. It would have been for her own good. But I couldn't do it. Every day, I thought about that damn letter all those years ago. Would Annie be a different child now if we hadn't come down this road?

All the things I thought would help her – making new friends, growing her confidence – still eluded her. And here we were.

There was nothing good coming from this.

The Party

"ARE YOU SURE YOU *want to do this?" I checked with Sally as we walked up John Turner's street. I don't think I'd ever actually spoken to John before. He was in some of my classes, but there was something about him that unsettled me. He looked at me – maybe more staring than looking – a lot. I would catch him doing it and then I'd look away while he would just smile sheepishly. He seemed quiet, and quite studious. He wasn't as physically attractive as the rest of the boys in that group, and his personality didn't seem to fit in either, but somehow, he was cool by association. There must have been something about him that I couldn't see, but then who was I to question whether he was cool enough?*

"Yep." Sally looked excited and terrified in equal measures. We had left Sally's thinking we looked fantastic. Every step closer to John's house ate away at my confidence. By the time we arrived, I felt sick.

The door was opened by James before we could ring the bell.

Without speaking to us, James shouted through to the back, "Dylan! Guess who's here!" He turned back to us, well – to Sally. "Hey, sweetheart, why don't you come through and get a drink and then come and sit down with me?" Sally looked at me and I nodded my approval.

"Dylan!" *he shouted again as I stood in the hallway awkwardly. My mind raced. What would I say to him? I'm out of my depth here. I have no idea how to flirt or respond to flirting. I'm socially awkward, easily embarrassed, and I actually like this boy. Part of me wanted to turn and run, but the rest of me was curious. I was almost fourteen, and while I was a naïve fourteen-year-old, I heard the conversations at school and knew that not everyone was as innocent as I was. I had never thought about how I actually felt about that. Was fourteen too young to be fooling around with boys? My mum and dad would definitely think so, but I knew – if the rumours were true – that probably only I, Sally and a couple of others there tonight had yet to have their cherries popped. It seemed like something that had been way further ahead into my very distant future, but now, standing in John's porch, waiting for Dylan, I wondered what was on Dylan's mind. Did he like me? If he did, would my lack of experience put him off? I'd only kissed a couple of boys, nothing further than that. Why would Dylan want anything to do with me, when he could have one of the cool girls who (in my overactive imagination) were practically rampant Playboy bunnies?*

"Fucking hell, Dylan!" *James shouted a third time. He shook his head, and then turned. I looked up the stairs and saw Dylan coming down, tucking his immaculate white t-shirt into his jeans. He was barefoot and his hair was tousled. He grinned at me.* "Lydia, babe, glad you could make it." *He leaned in and kissed me gently on the cheek. The move took me by surprise as it seemed so respectful. Almost old-fashioned and gentlemanly. It seemed such a* natural, relaxed gesture for him, I wondered whether this was something he did to other girls.

"Where you been, bro?" James asked while slipping an arm around Sally's shoulders. Dylan did the same with me and we were guided through to the kitchen.

"Having a nap," Dylan replied, winking at James, not very discreetly. He had definitely not been having a nap. I didn't think I wanted to know, so I pretended I hadn't heard the conversation.

Music was loud in the kitchen – I think it might have been Technotronic or something like that. Loud and bassy. Not my cup of tea, but I wasn't about to request someone put on the latest Kylie album and be laughed out of the party before my first drink.

There were people standing around, most of whom I recognised from school. John was flitting around, mopping up spilled drinks. I knew his parents couldn't be home – what parents would allow this many teenagers in their home, playing music this loud, and drinking the alcohol I could see on every surface of the kitchen, including in the sink and three boxes of beer stacked on the floor.

"That's a lot of booze," I said to Sally.

"What you having, ladies?" Dylan asked us both.

"Not sure really. Sally?" I wasn't prepared for this either. I had the occasional glass of wine at family functions, but that was it. Sally had never had a drop.

"I'm not really a big drinker," she said. "Maybe a small glass of wine?"

James sniggered. "We don't have wine, how about cider? Same as wine but made with apples instead of grapes, so much sweeter."

"Sounds good, yes, we'll both have cider, then," I said before Sally could respond. James handed us each a can of cider. I expected it to be cold, but I guess it had been out of a fridge for a long time. The cider was delicious, though I would have preferred a glass rather than drinking straight out of a can. My grandmother had always said cans were left outside shops by delivery men, so dogs might have peed on them. I had no idea if this was true or not, but better to be safe.

"Come and sit down." Dylan took my hand, and led me back through the hall. As we walked into the front room, I caught a glimpse of one of the girls from school coming down the stairs. Lisa Harrison was probably the coolest of the cool girls, although she didn't look very cool at that point. Her mascara had run down her cheeks, a tell-tale sign that she'd been crying, and her hair was messy – far from the immaculately groomed and made-up Lisa from school. She wore a cute yellow baby-doll dress and had her shoes in her hands.

Dylan stopped briefly. Their eyes met and something passed between them. Lisa looked at me, at my hand in Dylan's hand, and walked straight out of the front door, still barefoot.

I looked at Dylan. "Don't worry about her. She's cool," he said.

"Is she okay?" I asked. "She didn't look okay?"

"Yeah, she's fine, probably just had too much to drink. Don't worry, she's fine. Let's grab that spot on the sofa before anyone else nabs it."

The spot on the sofa was not big enough for two. Tony Sandford and Christian Moyes, both in my French class, were already sat down, and were smoking what I knew to be a joint. Tony made a token effort to move up a bit, and Dylan swiftly sat down in the vacant spot.

"It's okay, babe, you can sit on my knee." He winked at me, pulling my hand so I sat on him. I was not comfortable at all – Dylan's knees were bony, and I felt self-conscious, like I was expected to do something, and I didn't know what that something was. I perched there, drinking my cider, and feeling awkward. Tony, Christian, Dylan and two girls passed the joint between them. One of the girls, Donna, offered it to me. "No thanks, I don't do that." I knew as soon as I said it how it sounded. Snooty. Fuck, I was not ready for any of this. Though the cider was definitely helping. Tony stood up just as I was draining the last few drops from the can.

"Just going for a beer," he said.

"Could you get Lydia another cider, mate?" Dylan must have noticed I was ready for another. The second one went down quicker than the first. After Tony had given up his seat, I had slid into it, and now that I felt less conspicuous and also slightly drunk, I was starting to relax. I had no idea where Sally and James were.

"Don't worry, they're in the back room," Dylan said, softly stroking the side of my face. "I promise, they're having a good time." Then he stroked and turned my face towards him in one smooth move and kissed me. His kiss was soft and gentle, everything I had hoped it would be. Despite the effects of the cider, I felt butterflies in my tummy, and something else – something I'd never felt before. This boy, who I'd been crushing on for over two years, was here with me, kissing me. There were other girls here – much cooler *than me – and yet he was here with me, kissing me like he meant it. I felt sure you couldn't kiss someone like that unless there was real feeling behind it. The other boys I'd kissed had been revolting sloppy experiences. I couldn't tell if the woozy feeling was alcohol or whatever this was with Dylan.*

He pulled my hair gently back from my ear. "Let's go upstairs," he whispered.

This is it, *I thought.* I'm going for it. *I'd had enough Dutch courage to think this was a good idea, and hell yes, I really liked Dylan.* I have to do this to prove I'm good enough to be one of them, *my tipsy brain convinced me.* I have to do it to show Dylan how I feel about him, and if I don't, he might just lose interest. *So, my mind was made up.*

As I stumbled up the stairs behind Dylan, Sally caught my eye from the kitchen. She didn't look happy, but I pretended not to notice. This was my opportunity to step outside of the nerd population, and become not only one of the cool kids, but possibly even Dylan's girlfriend. And I wasn't going to blow it.

Dylan led me through to what I assumed was John's parents' room, judging by the pale green and floral décor. He sat down and patted the bed beside him. As I sat, he pushed me onto my back and climbed on top of me.

"Hang on, Dylan," I gasped, as I felt the weight and the heat from him on top of me. "Let me at least take my jacket off."

"This?" he asked, and without waiting for a response, he pulled me back up and then pulled my jacket down my back, dragging it off roughly.

"Oww, you hurt my shoulder!" I yelped, feeling uneasy. I wasn't expecting this after he had been so tender just

moments earlier. The vibe had changed and now I felt out of my depth. Suddenly, I wanted nothing more than to go back downstairs, get Sally and go home.

Dylan pushed me back onto the bed and pinned me down aggressively. His leg clamped strongly between mine, leaving me no space to wiggle free.

I started to feel woozy. And scared. I had not had much to drink. Maybe it was because I wasn't used to it. I felt tired, so damn tired I could not keep my eyes open, let alone fight Dylan off. My vision started to blur. And then go black. And then come back but everything was fuzzy. Then back to black. And repeat.

Something was wrong, but I didn't know if this was how it felt to be drunk. All I knew was that I had no control over my body. I tried to lift an arm, not even to stop him – I knew I didn't have the strength – just to see if I could. But I couldn't. It was like watching a film, a horrible film, shown in a series of flashbacks that make no sense.

Hands under my dress. I could feel rough clammy hands on my stomach, grabbing at the fabric of my pants.

Blackness.

Then he was off me. Thank God. Was he going to let me sleep?

Blackness.

I was being pulled around, limbs being tugged, like a ragdoll, powerless to do anything to help myself.

Blackness.

Then Tony was there. I felt cold. Where was my dress?

Blackness.

"You're not having a go until after me, I'm not having your sloppy seconds..."

Blackness.

And then I knew. I was about to be raped, and I was unable to stop it. Even worse, I couldn't speak. I couldn't say no. Did that mean I was letting it happen? Did it mean I wanted it? I had wanted it. That was what I came upstairs for. I think. But I didn't think it would be like this. How is this happening?

I closed my eyes. I couldn't look at him. The only part of my body I could move was my eyes, and even they were failing me as images became more and more blurred.

I felt my bra rip as it was pulled down, exposing my barely formed breasts, and somehow the underwire must have come through the fabric and it stabbed sharply into my left breast. Not for long though, as it was pulled up and over my head, removed from me entirely without even undoing the hooks at the back.

The blackness continued to come in waves, alternating with brief flashes of boys, boys with no t-shirts on. Boys from my school. I couldn't see how many there were.

And then the pain below. I was a virgin, at least I had been until that point. The pain was excruciating. Like a searing white-hot knife slicing through not only my hymen, but also my dignity and the innocence I still had, less than an hour earlier.

I could hear Dylan's voice, no longer soft and seductive; now it was the most sickening sound I'd ever heard. He was laughing at me, encouraging his friends. "Go on, Tony, your turn."

I opened my eyes and saw the face of the boy who had gotten me a drink not long before. He leered down at me – drunk, stoned, I had no idea. But he was on top of me now, and the pain came back. With each violent thrust, Tony grunted like a filthy animal, his mouth open, dribbling on my breasts and stomach. He grabbed my breasts tightly, causing me to yelp.

Without warning, Tony slapped me. "Stop fucking looking at me, bitch." I tried to tell him I wasn't looking at him, but I couldn't form the words to tell him that. Another slap to the other side of my face. I could taste blood this time, and as my face stayed where the slap left me, I felt a trickle across my cheek from my nose.

"Fucking hell, Tone. What are you doin', mate?" Dylan suddenly seemed concerned.

"What's going on in here?" came John's slurred voice through the door. Maybe John would help me. He pushed Tony off me. Maybe this creepy boy from school would be my saviour.

"So sorry, mate," Dylan said. "I said he could have a go, and he got a bit carried away and started slapping her about."

"Fuck's sake..." John said. "Fucking blood everywhere!"

"Yeah, well about that... turned out she most definitely was a virgin, so you owe me a tenner for that, and another fiver as I was first to nail her."

I opened my eyes briefly and saw John's face, only inches from mine. "How the fuck am I going to get blood out of the bedding? They're back tomorrow night!"

Dylan's laid-back charm – the same charm that had got me into this bed – calmed the situation. "Don't worry, pal, I know how to sort it so they'll never know. Will do it in the morning. No problem. But seeing as you're here, and seeing as the bed's already a mess, you want a go?"

I could hear the laughter in John's reply. "Fucking right I do."

I thought the pain might have caused me to pass out, but I was only fortunate enough to experience temporary blackouts – likely no more than a few seconds. Worse than the pain was the humiliation as I listened to them all laughing at me, laughing at the nerd girl who turned out to be a complete whore. Could people downstairs not hear what was happening? Where was Sally?

I saw flashes of Christian's face too. Was that four of them? How many were here? Had every boy here raped me?

Eventually the sounds of laughter faded as I lost consciousness.

14

Auditions – Age Twelve

DESPITE GRADUALLY SLIPPING APART from the rest of the dance team, Annie remained determined to succeed. She wanted to be the best. Maybe she felt she had something to prove. If the girls were going to hate her, she might as well give them a reason – one that benefited her as well.

I overheard little snippets of conversations at the studio – mainly Miss Victoria, who had the tact and discretion of a bulldozer and struggled with confidentiality.

Libby and Jemima had been accepted to attend a prestigious and exclusive dance academy's summer school. Miss Victoria bragged as though she could take credit for this, but I googled it. The five-day residential was open to anyone willing to hand over almost four thousand pounds. It was exclusive all right – but only because most could not afford or justify the cost, not because attendees had any kind of talent setting them apart.

Holly and Libby were doing a photo shoot for a dancewear catalogue. Apparently, this had been arranged by Victoria when we were on holiday. So, you know, we probably shouldn't go away anymore if we didn't want to miss out.

And Phoebe's birthday was coming up. We hadn't heard anything about any plans, or at least I hadn't. This was unusual. Normally, Jo would be making sure everyone 'saved the date' months in advance. I guessed it was going on behind our backs. I didn't care, but I knew Annie did, and that hurt like hell.

They say being a parent is hard. People casually knock out anecdotes about sleepless nights, vaccination decisions, the cost. I had never worried about those things. Some might call me a masochist, but I had enjoyed the sleepless nights most of the time. Those quiet moments when the rest of the world (including my husband, who never stirred) was fast asleep, and it was just me and the child I adored and thought my womb would never carry. I cherished those times, knowing they would be short-lived as she grew.

Vaccinations caused a lot of conflict for other mums – not for me. Anything that could protect my daughter was my friend, and hers. It was a no-brainer.

Financially, we weren't well off, less so with each passing month's bill from the studio. But I justified it – I didn't drink, smoke, or gamble. I didn't buy expensive clothes – or many clothes at all – for myself. I had no expensive hobbies or habits. Annie was my life, and all my money went to her, one way or another. Well, mostly to Miss Victoria.

For me, the hardest part of parenting was the emotional agony of seeing your child in pain. Physical pain was bad, but grazed knees would heal. It was the emotional pain that cut the deepest.

I'd been there. I had dropped off my own emotional baggage many years ago, to clear space for a future for myself, and later for Annie. But I supposed even baggage had ghosts. Ghosts that lingered around – not adding weight in themselves, but more of a painful empathetic response. Pain that I thought I could bury away, deep, deep down, was resurfacing as I watched twelve-year-old kids chip away at my little girl.

I felt every slight she endured, as though it was my own, each one like an aggressive fist, clenching my heart. "I'm right here with you, Annie," I would say to her, and I was. "We'll get through this." She would nod in agreement, not believing a single word of it.

But she had opportunities – good opportunities. Some of which weren't offered to everyone. Each one filled me with dread, but she grabbed every one with both hands and put her heart and soul into it. And she did well.

Annie auditioned for a TV dance show, which would be aired on Saturday teatimes. She delivered a flawless acro solo and made it through to the next round, and then the next. As did Libby. The quarterfinals saw Libby eliminated, and Annie through. She didn't make it further than the semis, but I couldn't have been prouder. And she had come further than anyone else at VCS. She was sticking up two fingers at those who treated her as though she wasn't good enough. And I applauded her for that.

Another audition, this time held at the studio, for a local talent agency claiming to have links to soap operas,

West End shows, numerous commercials, and a host of modelling opportunities. As each child went through to the main studio to audition, I started tearing through the skin on my fingers until they bled. They were specifically looking for 'triple threats' – kids who could sing, dance, and act. Dancing was not a problem – singing and acting, though, might be. Annie was an introverted child, and the years at VCS really embedded that. I honestly thought she would freeze. I wished I could be in there with her. Or even better, at home with her. Away from this shit.

She came out looking hopeful. I was less hopeful, and I imagined her peers and their parents also didn't think she had what it would take. She had done what was required. Around seventy kids had been there to audition – varying levels of experience and talent, a variety of ages from around four to sixteen. Siblings of VCS students had been invited to audition too – I think Miss Victoria had seemed particularly keen to push forwards some boys as there weren't many male students.

As the day drew to a close, children and their parents were ushered through to the main studio, where they crammed in tightly, awaiting the results. Miss Victoria had envelopes in her hand.

"Okay, girls – and boys! So glad to see so many brothers and sisters here today!" She was twitching to walk up and down as she tended to do at these things – really drag out the suspense and drama – but thankfully there just wasn't room, so she would have to just crack on.

"Thank you to all of you for coming and spending your Sunday here at VCS. I'm sure you all had better things to do, so from the bottom of my heart, thank you." Bottom of her cash register, more like. Naturally, we had paid £25 per child for this experience.

Get on with it, for fuck's sake.

"I've been told by Sarah and Leigh who auditioned you that the standard today was amazing." *Amazing.* Why did that word seem so shallow and empty? Probably because it was so overused.

"But..." she went on. "There are only a few places available on the agency's books at this moment. Which is not to say they won't be back again, as they definitely saw talent they might be interested in in the future."

Yeah, I dare say. Come back in six months and spend another day of your life, plus twenty-five quid, to get your hopes up for nothing.

"I only have five envelopes, and these are for the five that Sarah and Leigh would like to take on and represent straight away. Like I said, they will be back for more, after seeing the amazing talent we have here at VCS."

Right.

"So, without further ado, I'll announce the names of the children getting an envelope. Please could anyone with an envelope have a look through all the information inside, and the parents will need to sign the contract before anything else goes ahead. You don't need to come up and collect them now – just come to reception afterwards. I don't want anyone getting trampled!

"Okay, please can the following kids come to reception for an envelope... George Greenhalgh, Jake Beckett, Jordan Beckett, Iris Walker, and Annie Moffatt."

My eyes widened in shock. *Jesus, Annie, you've done it!* She looked up at me and gave a little grin.

Nobody hung around. It had been a wasted day for them all. I heard the comments as people filed out past us in reception.

"*Well two of them are twins so that's why they got through...*"

"*Iris has Disney written all over her, not sure she can sing, though...*"

"*Three boys? Well, that doesn't seem fair...*"

"*Don't worry, sweetheart, there will be something better waiting for you soon...*"

"*Could have predicted that...*"

I didn't hear Annie's name. Though I picked up on the whispers.

"Well done, Annie!" Miss Victoria gushed from behind the reception desk, handing her the white envelope with her name on. "Make sure you have a read through it all and get it back to me as soon as you can. I know Sarah has something coming up in the next couple of weeks that she thinks you're perfect for."

"Okay," Annie replied quietly. "I will."

As we left the building, I squeezed Annie tight. "I'm so proud of you! I wonder what they're thinking of for you. Must get that contract back so you don't miss the boat."

"No need." As we walked past the rubbish bin on the edge of the car park, Annie deposited the envelope in. I stopped. Annie carried on walking to the car, and eventually I followed.

Once in and buckled up, I looked at her. "What... I don't understand."

"I don't want to do it, Mum." Her eyes were welling with tears.

"Okay... that's okay... I'm just a bit... confused, I suppose. So why did we come today?"

"I don't know really," she said, staring straight ahead, looking wistfully at nothing at all. "I think I wanted to know if I *could* do it. You know, the singing and stuff. But I didn't like it. And I didn't like reading the page out either. I don't want to do it, Mum, please."

No argument from me. "That's fine, no problem at all, Annie, as long as you're sure."

"I'm sure."

It gave me great pleasure the following week to tell Miss Victoria that we'd had a change of heart. Even more to see her expectant smile change to an expression of genuine disappointment. Maybe there had been a 'finder's fee' for her for those that signed contracts.

"Was it something in the contract?" she asked. "You know, they're always negotiable..."

I shrugged. "Nope. We haven't even seen the contract. She doesn't want to do it, so..."

"I mean, I'm sure we can negotiate a better deal for Annie. These things are really only a starting point." As expected, it was all about the money for Miss Victoria, so she assumed it was for us too.

"It's not about the money," I replied, though I was curious about what had been in the contract – even more so about what they would have agreed to following negotiations. "She's not interested. So maybe if you have a reserve list or something..."

Of course they had a reserve list. There was always a backup plan. After all, everyone's replaceable.

I felt oddly smug when I heard the news that Jemima

was going to be signing with the agency. There was something powerful about declining an opportunity and leaving it open for someone else. As much as Jemima and Nancy might go on to brag, I found it satisfying that she was only there because Annie had cast it aside. And I knew Annie felt the same way. Jemima was picking up crumbs dropped by Annie. I didn't think Annie had ever really wanted to be signed – she just wanted to prove she could do it, that no matter how the other girls treated her, she would not be deterred. She wanted to show them that these opportunities were just as likely to be hers as anyone else's. They weren't better dancers than her. They may or may not have been better at singing and acting. It really didn't matter. Annie had set out to quietly prove a point, and she had done it.

The Morning After

THE CREAM-COLOURED CURTAINS OFFERED *no protection from the summer sunshine.*

Sunshine is a universal symbol of hope and happiness, but it must have hated me. Intent on filling the room with not only a sickening heat, but a light so bright it caused me real pain as I slowly opened my eyes.

My face hurt. But not as much as between my legs.

Snippets of information invaded my brain. Short flashes of a horror film, sickening me to the core but inviting me to watch more. As if I had a choice. Did I have a choice now? Was I capable of deciding whether or not I wanted to see through my mind's eye the events that led to the pain I felt throughout my body? It would seem not. The human brain is an incredible, sometimes shitty piece of machinery. How was it I could forget everything Mr Hurst taught us in a history lesson as I turned over a test paper that very same day – despite desperately trying to recall the information – yet I could not actively switch off the images coming through now, no matter how much I wanted to? It was my brain, for God's sake. Why could I not control it?

Slowly, I raised my hand to touch my face. A flashback

of trying to lift my arm and being unable to. I could do it now. A bit late.

My left eye was the worst. It stung to touch the skin around it. And I knew without looking in a mirror that there was some swelling, though not as much as the pain told me there should be.

My lip had split. I felt dried blood crusted around the corner of my mouth. Not much. I remembered the feeling of it trickling down my face. Was that from my lip? Or was my nose busted too? I touched it gently. Some pain there. I dreaded looking in the mirror.

How had I got home?

I looked around the room and felt relieved that I was definitely here, in my own bed – fresh(ish) white cotton sheet beneath me, not pale green and sticky with blood.

I sat up slowly, and a tsunami of nausea came over me so quickly I only just managed to lift the bin from next to my bed in time. Thank God it had a bin liner in. I would be able to dispose of the evidence. Hot, tangy vomit. My stomach twisted and contorted with each painful retch. For a moment, I had to just sit and catch my breath.

I eventually stood up and looked in the full-length mirror on my wardrobe door. What a mess. I had on the pretty pink dress I went to the party in, but no underwear. Oh God, where was my underwear? Something so small and relatively insignificant as a pair of BHS lace knickers. But they were mine. They were an intimate belonging. They had been ripped from me and were no longer mine. Another violation. My bra... also gone...

My hair was a mess: sweaty, and the front strands matted together with the blood from my nose. Or mouth. I had no idea which.

It hurt to stand up. Even more to walk. But I needed to get to the bathroom.

Where were my parents? And my sister? The house was quiet, and I would normally have hated it. But not today. They must all be out or there would be the sound of a TV or something. Good. I wasn't ready to face them – or anyone else.

The pain from peeing brought tears to my eyes. Not just from the stinging, but from the humiliation that washed over me. I sat there – I don't know how long for – and I sobbed.

The insides of the top of my thighs were bruised badly, and for some reason my stomach too. I couldn't explain that one, but I remembered the pressure from the weight of the boys' legs and hips as they each pinned me down. I had a feeling, though no clear picture, that they helped each other. Like they needed to. I had been completely paralysed by – I assume – fear. I couldn't lift a limb to help myself, so they really had no need for backup.

The shower was hot – as hot as it would go. Normally I preferred a cool shower. Good for closing pores, or opening them, or something. But I needed to scald. I needed to burn the filth from my flesh. I could smell them on me. Beer, sweat and cum. I had been aware that at least one of them had ejaculated on my stomach, but I had no idea which one.

I grabbed my mum's loofah and scrubbed maniacally. The abrasive texture of the loofah and the scalding temperature of the water felt cleansing, but not enough. I scrubbed and scrubbed until my skin started to bleed, little dots of crimson needing to escape my body as though they carried with them the relief and healing that I needed but would not be allowed. Then I stopped. I couldn't do anything that might invite questions.

It was almost 4pm. The fragments of memory still hadn't shed any light on how I got home. I put on some fresh PJs. Fluffy. Laundry-scented. Comforting, ordinarily. Knickers underneath with one of my mum's maxi pads. I had no idea if my period had started or if this was a serious injury. I convinced myself it was a period, because the alternative was too scary to contemplate.

My legs shook as I walked through to the kitchen. On the back of a chair at the breakfast bar was my denim jacket. So at least I had brought that home with me.

My mum had left a note.

Lydia,

We've gone to Liverpool today to see Aunty Gem, and she's booked a table at a pub there for 8pm, so it's probably going to be late when we get back. I've left you some dinner in the fridge. If you need us, Aunty Gem's number is in the address book, and the restaurant is called La Piazza, on Robert Street, but I'm not sure of the number.

I know you were home very late last night. We'll discuss that later. Hope you had a good night with Sally.

Don't wait up.
Love you
Mum x

That was good. She'd heard but not seen me. And I could make sure she didn't see me until tomorrow.

My front door key was next to the kettle. I must have let myself in. I wished I could remember.

I picked up the jacket to throw it in the washing machine. No, the bin. I would never wear it again. The pink dress would go in the bin too. I checked the pockets for any loose change and pulled out a business card. Fab Cabs – local taxi company. This must have been how I got home. I couldn't have called them. Even if I'd known the number (which I didn't), I don't think I'd have been able to speak, or even hold a phone up.

I flipped the card over and there was a message scribbled in blue biro.

Hope your ok. Dropped you off 7.42am. you weren't in a good way. James helped you. If you need anything, I'm driver 4082. Take care.

That answered one question at least.

15

More of the Same...

ONCE YOUR EYES HAVE been opened, it's hard not to see things for what they are. You become highly tuned to whatever it is you've been thinking about.

Like if you're thinking about buying a red Mini Cooper, suddenly you see them everywhere. Or when I desperately wanted a baby and assumed my broken uterus would make it impossible for me, so everywhere I went there were pregnant women and babies.

Even your feelings. Once somebody starts to irritate you, just with one little habit, you notice every time they do it. I used to work with a man who had psoriasis and would not only scratch his head constantly, but would go on to tip his head forwards and ruffle his hair, allowing the flakes of dead skin to land on his desk.

Then some other things they do start to bug you. Then everything they do bugs you.

It was like that with dancing.

In the earlier years it had been easy to ignore those

niggles, because the opportunities outnumbered them. I could just about get on board with annual uniform changes, with no reason I could see other than having to replace perfectly good leotards with brand new ones. It also meant they couldn't be sold on to younger girls as they would all be changed. In my mind, this was VCS showing attention to detail, high standards and expecting all students (and their families) to get on board. It was about discipline. And I bought into that. I liked structure. I liked rules.

But over time, the bads start to outweigh the good. I became resentful. Everything about that place, especially the teachers, started to irritate the fuck out of me.

I would listen to Miss Victoria giving the same spiel she had given us, to the little ones and their mums. Drawing them in. Making them believe their kid was a star of the future and they *must* attend as many classes as possible to develop that talent. Filling their heads with ideas of becoming a world-class ballerina, or some other such rubbish. And some would go on to become career dancers. But not many. And of those who did, I suspected they had pushy parents with large bank accounts. Dancing was an elite sport. No poor people here.

I watched the teachers' interactions with the parents of the younger kids, recognising their dialogue almost word for word. I had been so gullible. And I certainly wasn't the only one.

The kids were (and this was to my mind, not something ever said out loud by anyone, of course) categorised into one of three groups.

The genuine talent. VCS would latch on to this and nurture the hell out of it. They would flatter the girls and the parents, and brag about them to anyone and everyone who would listen. It was nauseating. These kids were pure gold. They made the school look good, and they were a good source of income. Category 1 kids were the rarest group at VCS. I thought Annie probably fitted into this category.

The less talented but rich kids. These girls – and the occasional boy – were not natural dancers. They were not bad but didn't have what it would take to make it big in such a competitive field. What they did have, though, were parents with huge amounts of disposable income. Category 2 kids would usually receive the same level of attention, praise and flattery as category 1. They were unlikely to become professional dancers, but they were willing cash cows, eager to be milked, so the school would do exactly that. There was a shelf life for these kids, so it was worth a few gushing words every now and then to cash in while the going was good.

Category 3 covered everyone else. They would be praised and flattered only as part of a group – 'didn't they all do amazing?' and such like. Never a bad word about them would be said – after all, category 3s were large in number, and therefore made up the foundation of the school. Their 'bread and butter', so to speak. These kids would not be overtly excluded – opportunities might be open to everyone, but they came with a cost that made them exclusive. Miss Victoria would say lovely things about these kids to their parents, but only if asked; she would not actively seek them out to lavish praise or suck up in the same way she might with category 1 or 2 parents. And category 3 kids would never be on the front row of the shows. Ever. It just didn't make good business sense, to be fair about it – much better to showcase the real stars and play to the egos of the wealthy.

Over time, little pieces of information would leak out. The mark-up (and therefore profit for Miss Victoria) on the show costumes. Some of the teachers not being paid regularly – not Miss Stacy, of course, but others lower down on the food chain. Suspicions about why some fees would always need to be paid in cash.

And the gossip. As I was part of that inner circle of competition team and panto mums, Miss Victoria would confide in me. She would tell me stories about other kids and their parents. Nothing of any major significance, and usually something I had zero interest in. But often she would tap the side of her nose and say "keep that one to yourself". Who would I tell? I had distanced myself from other mums, and nobody outside of the studio would give a shit.

One story bothered me a little. A category 2 kid had lost a hoodie after leaving it in the changing rooms. Then Miss Victoria had noticed a child wearing the exact same hoody – a category 3 child. Why was she telling me this? She even gave me the names of those involved.

"Maybe she just has the same hoodie?" I offered.

"Don't think so," she whispered. "Those are like seventy quid at least. I don't think her mum would be able to afford that."

She was probably right. It probably had been taken by the category 3. But there was no proof of that whatsoever, so I felt uncomfortable at being on the receiving end of such an explicit piece of gossip.

A piece of advice from my grandmother years ago sprang to mind – if they talk *to* you like this about others, imagine what they say *about* you to others. Miss Victoria (and increasingly Miss Stacy and Miss Jessica too) had seemingly little understanding of confidentiality.

'Don't say anything as it's not common knowledge, but X got a part in X.'

'X has a lot going on you know, with her mum having cancer.'

'Didn't know if you knew, but X's mum and dad are splitting up. Turns out dad has been seeing someone else.'

I'd never liked gossip. I knew how it felt to be discussed behind your back. And it erodes trust. I knew, as sure as night meets day, that I would be gossiped about too. Everyone else was, so why would I be any different? The danger was that much of the gossip seemed to be hearsay, and more than likely, complete bullshit.

I started hating the place, and every visit just affirmed that for me. It affected my sanity, and it was affecting Annie's confidence in a negative way. We were starting to suffer the long-term effects of spending too much time in such a toxic environment.

I prayed to a God I didn't believe in that Annie would just make the decision. The agency contract had given me hope that it might happen, but she still hung on, desperate to dance, while being slowly destroyed by it.

Back to School

MY LIFE BECAME A *living hell.*

Sally had left the party when someone told her I was upstairs shagging Dylan and 'might be a while'. By the time the rumours had spread across the school – the tales being that of a gang bang instigated by the slutty nerd girl – my old friends couldn't look me in the eye. They saw me as dirty, though nowhere near as dirty as I saw myself. No amount of bleach or scrubbing or vomiting or my mother's diazepam would make that night disappear.

I couldn't remember every detail, but I remembered enough. Every so often, without warning, another image would appear like a swift jab to my gut.

The faces. The pain as the boys took turns on me. The sickening feeling of being fully exposed for everyone to see. And worst of all, the laughter. I could hear it constantly, like a stuck record – each of their voices distinctive enough to be able to just about identify where in the room they were, and who was on top of me. I couldn't get away from that sound. I had my Walkman on from the moment I woke up until I finally drifted into a nightmare-filled sleep, just to drown out the laughter that haunted me.

As I sat one lunchtime in the school library, desperately trying to focus on my history homework, a bag was dropped loudly onto the table next to me. I jumped and looked up to see Lisa Harrison flop down into a chair. Donna – the girl from the party who had been smoking weed with the boys – was also with her. I had no idea what to expect. All I had wanted was to be one of these girls, and now I wanted to be as far away from them as I could. But I had no friends left. I had become something else on the night of that party, so I would have to take whatever friendships I could find.

"You walk home my way, don't you?" Lisa asked, leaning back on her chair and smacking chewing gum as she spoke.

"Er... I don't know... I walk... er..." I had no idea where this was going.

"You walk down Bethnel and then Woodlands and then Smithy, same as I do, but then I turn left at the bottom, and you turn right."

"Yeah, I do..." I replied suspiciously.

"Cool." She smiled. "We should walk home together. Donna's getting picked up tonight, so I'll be all on my own." Lisa and Donna both wiped away imaginary tears. "I have food tech last lesson, so meet me outside block A." It was not a request. It was an instruction. I nodded and she picked up her bag and left, Donna following closely behind, giggling as they went.

I had no idea what to expect. But as instructed I rushed to block A after my history lesson – eager to get out of there as quickly as possible to avoid the stares and whispers from the boys at the party, and anyone in the lesson who had heard the rumours.

As the food tech students filed out, Lisa filed out among them. She saw me and came straight over. "Are you ready?" she asked, linking my arm, as though we were the best of friends. Caught up in the exodus of students, I felt relieved to not be alone, and suspicious at the same time. Why did Lisa, most popular girl in the school, want to walk home with me? I had only appeared on her radar at the party – before that she had no idea who I was. And I didn't speak to her at the party. We only crossed paths as she had come down the stairs and left.

"Let's go to the shop and you can buy me a Mr Freeze," she said cheerfully. The shop across the road from school was always packed at this time of day, and Mr Freeze was the most popular purchase – mostly as the weather was hot, but also because even the larger ice pops were only ten pence. I paid for two – a raspberry and a cola. Lisa took the cola, without discussion, and linked my arm again as we set off.

"It was good to see you at the party," she said. "Nice to see you making better friends now." I felt bile rising. I missed my old friends desperately. "I know your old nerd mates aren't being very nice to you at the moment, chick, so I want you to know, we'll look after you – me, Donna, Paula and Carly."

As I processed this statement, I felt increasingly like I was in trouble. Donna was Dylan's cousin. Paula Howarth was John Turner's long-term girlfriend. Carly, I knew from primary school, was a nasty piece of work, and I strongly suspected that Lisa had a thing for Dylan. Every one of those girls had a reason to not like me, and yet here was the leader of the pack, inviting me in. There had to be an ulterior motive. But I was short of options. And maybe if

I was inside their circle, I could become part of it and one day they might see me as one of them. I didn't feel like one of them, but I didn't feel like I belonged anywhere at all.

It didn't matter anyway. Lisa had decreed that they would look after me, so there was little I could do. I couldn't very well turn down her invitation. And who else could I turn to? I had to opt in and ride the wave.

16

Under Pressure

THE PRESSURE CAME AT us from all sides – like some poor wilderness babies separated from their family and now surrounded by a pack of hungry wolves. There was no easy way out. The summer that Annie turned fourteen, I wanted to test the water. I wanted to know if saying 'no' would really be as bad as I expected.

Miss Victoria had scheduled eight workshops across July and August for Annie's age group. There was, of course, a full programme of back-to-back workshops to cater for all genres and all ages – after all, summer holidays meant the kids were available all day, every day, and I imagined the pound signs in Miss Victoria's eyes. Ker-ching…

"You can't do all of them," I told Annie. "They're £25 each, and I need to save money over summer so I can afford dancing the rest of the year." We had arrived early at the studio, and were sitting in the car, waiting for someone to turn up and let us in.

She looked disappointed. But she knew. Even at her young age, she knew there was no bottomless pit of money. Her school friends had started getting 'allowances'. As soon as the subject was raised, I squashed it, telling her if she wanted an allowance, that was fine, but she would have to pay for dancing and all associated costs out of said allowance, which would likely leave her with a huge deficit. She was a bright kid. She knew this was a battle she didn't really want to win.

"So, how many can I do?"

"Four, maybe five if you put your birthday money towards one."

She pondered. She didn't have much money. For birthdays and Christmas, family and friends would gift her things she needed, or wanted, usually dance related – a new leotard, warm-up boots, light-up vanity box. She spent so much time dancing, she never really had time to do anything else like other kids her age, so had no real need for cash.

"I think I only have about twenty quid, though…"

"Well, that's okay. I'll put the other five in. So, you need to pick the five and put your name on the lists in reception. And ask them whether it needs paying up front and whether I can bank transfer."

She got out of the car, blew me a kiss and made her way into the studio. I had stopped going into the building by then, other than when absolutely necessary.

As expected, Miss Victoria wanted workshops to be paid 'cash only' on the day of the workshop.

The choice for Annie was tough, but in the end, she decided to leave out tap, street dance and commercial. It made no difference to me. Each class was as toxic as the next, as far as I could see.

She came out of the studio with tears in her eyes. This was now a regular occurrence: at least four times a week, I would have guessed. Anyone else might have thought it was her age, but I knew there was more to it. "Just say the word, Annie," I would tell her every time, and every time she would say, "Well, I'll see how it goes before I decide." Her grit and determination were both inspiring, and terrifyingly masochistic. I knew I couldn't have put myself through this when I was her age. Having the option to walk away from something causing so much distress and choosing not to.

Annie had a fight inside her, and she was not ready to surrender. I just wasn't sure what the point of it all was. What did she need to prove? And to who – those nasty bitches?

"Everyone else is doing all of them," she said quietly on the way home.

I focused on the road. "I'm sure they are, sweetheart. I'm sure they are. But I think maybe they feel they have to… like to make sure they're not missing out on anything." I glanced over, and she nodded as silent tears fell. I pulled over.

"Annie, why do you want this so bad? Every day almost, you come out of there crying. You can't honestly tell me you're enjoying this anymore." I wiped a tear from her soft cheek and tried to force a smile. "This is not the face of someone having fun, is it?"

"But I don't want to give up, Mum. I can't. What else would I do? And I like it. I like dancing. I just hate everything else."

"Do you want to be a dancer, Annie? I mean when you're older. Is this something you want to do as a career?"

"I think so, but I'm not sure." How could she be? She was fourteen.

"So, maybe have a think about what that might look like if it was the route you chose to go down. You'd need to get a job to pay your way while you do the auditions, at least until you get something. I honestly don't know what kind of job that would be, but I suppose it would need to be flexible hours. Auditions are going to be tough… way tougher than anything else you've done so far. And once you have a part in something… how long will it last? One season? Maybe two? Maybe even ten? But then what?"

Annie looked at me.

"I don't want to talk you out of this if it's what you want to do. You know, Annie, I've got your back, and I'll do anything I can to help you. But I can only imagine how hard it is. And I don't think it's for everyone."

I brushed a stray hair from her face as she let out a small sob. I knew she wouldn't survive a career in dance. Not because she wasn't good enough. I knew she was an incredible dancer. But so were thousands of others. And it was a dog-eat-dog world out there that we'd only scratched the surface of so far. Annie was sensitive. Too sensitive for a life as competitive as this. It would destroy her. I wanted it to be her decision, and I meant it when I said I would support whichever decision she made, but I needed her to be able to make an informed decision. And nobody at VCS was going to tell her – or any of the other girls – about some of the pitfalls. I had read stories online, watched documentaries, and was hoping as hard as I could that she would not choose this path.

My suspicions were right. Those girls who attended all of the workshops were elevated way above those who didn't. I wondered whether they did these things as a test to see who had a limit and who didn't. Like a cult, loyalty should be absolute, and it should be given without questioning. Those who showed loyalty were rewarded – better solos, better costumes, better music, better positions on the stage when shows came around.

I got it. I could totally understand why a mum who had demonstrated an unwavering commitment to VCS would expect preferential treatment. There was definitely an argument that the more you did, the better you would be. I'd probably argued that point myself over the years as I tried to justify my own willingness to dance to the VCS tune.

This was a new perspective, deepening the hatred growing inside me. As soon as you said 'no', your card was marked. Miss Victoria would no doubt be gossiping about Annie – or me, more than likely. I imagined her telling Belinda and Jo that Annie's heart was just not in it anymore. Though the truth was that she had realised there was a limit as to how much this particular cash cow could be milked. She, and the teachers at VCS, would start to focus on other kids – those with 'more commitment'.

They overlooked the vile behaviour, which must have gone on under their noses.

On one of the rare occasions I went into the studio to pay Annie's fees, I was greeted by Miss Victoria. "Annie's having another drama today," she told me, rolling her eyes.

I was taken aback. Having a drama? What the fuck did that mean?

"Oh no, she's upset? What happened?"

"I have no idea." She shrugged. "She's so sensitive, isn't she?"

The lack of caring shown was shocking. Maybe if they bothered to ask her what was up, they might have been able to help. But they didn't give a shit. And they didn't want to hear about the snipy comments made by the likes of Jemima and Libby. Those girls were helping enormously with Miss Victoria's retirement fund, so she adopted tunnel vision, conveniently blocking out anything she should probably address.

There was an additional pressure for me. Unlike many of the other mums, I didn't have a supportive husband. Rob had never understood why Annie danced and why she would put herself through it if it made her so unhappy. And – though I would never admit it – he had seen Miss Victoria for what she was a long time ago. The standards produced at VCS were high, there was no questioning that, but Miss Victoria was a grifter. Any opportunity to cash in was exploited to the max. And cash was preferred.

My pride stopped me from sharing any dance-related concerns with Rob. Nobody likes to hear 'I told you so', do they?

So, I kept the costs secret. I worked overtime when I could to help with the costs, but it would never be enough. I thought about getting a second job, but if I did that, I'd have to ask Rob to sometimes take Annie to the studio. It would only be a matter of time before Rob discovered the real cost of dancing – in financial terms, at least.

Real Friends?

THE MONTHS THAT FOLLOWED *were clouded with fear and uncertainty for me. I had become the runt of the litter of cool kids. Every day at break times, we would gather behind the science block. I had started smoking at their insistence and would often be asked to 'crash us a fag?' by the boys who had seen the most intimate parts of me, and now acted as though nothing had happened.*

Dylan paid me no more or less attention than he had before the party. He would flirt with me in classes, his hand lingering a little longer than necessary when it touched mine as he passed handouts to me. Then at breaktimes he would show the same level of interest as he did with any of the other girls.

I started to wonder if I had imagined the whole thing. Maybe it had been a terrifyingly visual dream. I would spend a few peaceful moments imagining that to be the case, but reality would eventually set in. A dream would not have caused the horrific bruising on my thighs and stomach that was so difficult to hide that I had to forge notes to get out of PE classes for almost six weeks. A dream would not have caused an injury to my breast that had looked like it was infected at one point – I remembered this to be the wire from my bra. And a dream would not influence the way other people behaved towards me. Sally, Angela and Amanda would not avert their eyes when I approached because of a dream.

For I while I had felt paranoid, like everyone was whispering wherever I went. I wasn't sure if the whispering eventually stopped as people moved on to other gossipy news, or whether I had simply become used to it.

I never discussed what had happened with anyone. Not my family, not teachers, and definitely not the popular girls who seemed to have (at least on the surface) accepted me as one of their own, albeit an inferior member of their club.

Each night I would meet Lisa, and sometimes Donna, after school, rushing across the grounds to be outside their classroom doors before they came out. I would dutifully take their heavy school bags without being asked, and I would buy them each a Mr Freeze from the shop before we walked home together. One day I bought them both a bag of Space Raiders as well, just so I could say "my treat", as I handed over the goods that I'd gone without lunch to pay for. They hadn't asked me to, and though I realised later this was a major attempt to suck up, at the time I resolved it in my mind by telling myself I had treated my friends without them asking because I wanted to. Not because they asked (or told) me to. Because I was a nice person, and because they were my friends. Nobody could say I was a mug if I did something without it being asked for, right?

Once home, I would get my headphones back on and listen to whichever Now That's What I Call Music! *album my dad had bought recently on double cassette. To block out the sound of the laughter.*

After dinner, I would meet up with Kelly and we'd go for a walk or hang out in one of our houses. Jackie *magazine* was becoming too babyish, so Kelly's mum had changed her subscription to Just Seventeen, *and later she would change it to* Mizz. *I was surprised at Chrissy allowing Kelly to read these, as there were so many features and articles on sex, relationships and other topics, and I thought Chrissy was actually quite prudish.*

I hadn't told Kelly about the party. She went to another school, so she hadn't heard about it, and I wanted to keep it that way. She was the only person who really knew me and saw me for who I was. Not some filthy slut who gang-banged the cool kids at a party. Not a pathetic mug who trailed round in the shadows of the popular girls like a servant. I could be me with Kelly.

"Did you read this article yet about when the right time is?" she asked me one day, as we pored through magazines.

"No." I didn't even look up. I was looking at the autumn fashion shoot in Mizz. Fashion was safe. I could look at the models and imagine what it would be like to be them. Physically perfect, with physically perfect boyfriends who appeared to adore them. These girls would never allow themselves to be raped. They wouldn't attend stupid parties just because they wanted to be popular, and they would drink coffee, not cider. They would do only wholesome activities, such as hill-walking, watching movies, reading, and they would look perfect while doing them. At night they would sleep soundly, dreaming of wardrobes filled with the latest trends, not grunting boys, thrusting and dribbling.

"It says here that you should do it when you're ready, but what does that even mean?" she went on. "Like, do you *think you're ready now? How would you know when you're ready?"*

"I'll never be ready. I'm not doing it."

Kelly rolled her magazine up and whacked me with it, giggling. "Yeah right."

"I'm serious, Kell. I'm not. I don't get it. Why would anyone want to do that?"

"Well I didn't mean right now obviously," she said, rolling her eyes, "but surely at some point in the next couple of years you will."

"Nope. Not me."

She laughed. "Yeah, you will. You'll be the biggest tart going once you start. I know what you're like."

I sat up and crossed my arms defensively. "What do you mean by that?"

"Nothing," she grinned, "other than you're saying that now, but once you've done it the first time, I bet you'll be like a porn star."

I ran from Kelly's room to the bathroom and vomited.

Kelly didn't know what had happened. I knew she didn't because we shared everything. Usually. And if she'd heard a rumour, she would have asked me about it, I knew she would.

Kelly knew me better than anyone else in the world, and now she was saying she could see me for what I really was. She was seeing me the way others, people from school, saw me. At least, that's the way I heard it. I opened the bathroom door to see Kelly looking concerned. "You okay?" she asked.

"Yeah, I think maybe my tea didn't agree with me. I'm going home. Will call you tomorrow."

But I didn't. And when she called me, I asked my mother to tell her I was out.

The next night I asked my mother to tell her I was out again. I told her I didn't want to be disturbed as I was studying, as I knew my mum would need a good reason to conspire with me in lying to Kelly.

For the next two weeks, Kelly called every night, and every night my mum would cover for me. I eventually told my mum that Kelly and I had fallen out. She wasn't happy about lying for me but said from now on she just wouldn't answer the phone if the caller ID showed Kelly's number. She wasn't going to lie for me anymore. She didn't ask for details of the fallout, and I didn't offer any.

Eventually Kelly stopped calling. I felt bad. I didn't want her to think she had done anything wrong, but I desperately wanted to be alone and away from the judgements, and whispers, and talk about sex and anything else. It was hard enough getting through the school day; I couldn't keep up the façade outside of school. I was pretending. But I wasn't sure what I was pretending. Was the real me actually a normal kid who was pretending to be cool to fit in? Or was I really a complete whore pretending to be something else?

I felt so confused about who I was, who I wanted to be, who people thought I was. It was too much. I withdrew into myself and coasted through school days with a passive acceptance that this was the way things were, and I just needed to go along with it, just get through the day. Every day was a day closer to the end of school. It just seemed so far away. Still almost two years of this shit, and every day was a struggle. I wasn't sure I had it in me to survive high school anymore.

17

Star of the Week

I SAT IN THE car one Thursday night, waiting for Annie to come out of her ballet lesson. I watched the other girls troop out together. Laughing and joking. No sign of Annie.

She appeared a couple of minutes later. She didn't need to tell me. I understood her behaviour. It was like watching myself – hanging back before leaving, so she didn't have to walk out with them. Walking out alone was better than walking out with a crowd but being somehow separate from it. Everyone was alone sometimes, but being alone while being around other people – that really hammered home the feeling of isolation.

As she got in the car, I saw the tears. This was nothing new but was still painful to see.

You would think you'd get used to a specific type of pain when you feel it so often. Like period pain – when you first experience it, you think you're going to die. But you don't. Every month, even though it hurts like hell, you adapt. You prepare for it. You expect it. You stock up on painkillers, have your hot water bottle at the ready, plenty of chocolate on hand. You feel it, but you get used to it. You learn to live with it – after all, is there a choice?

But every time Annie came out of the studio, shoulders hunched over, and I saw the tears – either ready to come, or already free-flowing – I wondered whether the ripping sensation in my gut might actually kill me. There was no physical reason it would. But to see your child – your baby, the centre of your universe – in pain hurts worse than anything else you can imagine. And I had known pain.

"We do 'Star of the Week' now," she said, smiling through her tears, almost laughing. But not quite.

"What do you mean, you do star of the week? I don't understand."

"Miss Stacy has brought it in but wants all the other teachers to do it too. A trophy for whoever has worked the hardest or done the best in that lesson."

"Jesus Christ, you're fourteen! What the hell…" I was confused. Surely not.

"And guess who got it this week?" I couldn't answer. I shook my head and gestured for her to continue. I was still trying to process the idea of a 'good behaviour' reward being given to teenagers. It would be justified by the teachers as being something to work towards, dangling the proverbial carrot. But it wasn't really. It wouldn't matter who had really earned it; it would come down to whose parents had toed the line. Parents were not immune from having to do better.

"Jemima." No surprises there. "She didn't even do anything amazing. She wasn't even sweating like everyone else. I don't know why they chose her."

I hated these things when Annie was at primary school. Merit awards. A child per class every week chosen for some ridiculously banal reason to receive a trophy and certificate, for nice handwriting, or helping someone on their table, or using nice manners. Said trophy would do the rounds until everyone had received it, and then it would start again. It meant nothing. It didn't really reward the kids who did well or put in extra effort. Why make the effort, when you only had to sit back and wait for it to be your turn? It pissed me off when she was in primary school, and it pissed me off more now she was older.

"I don't even know what to say, Annie. I'm lost for words." I needed to think about how to voice this without going batshit crazy. Treating them like little kids was too petty to get upset about, but it was the controlling and wielding of power that grated on me. Anyone outside of VCS would have laughed – firstly at the teachers for doing something so bizarre, and secondly at me for giving a shit. But I knew the coveted trophy would be used as another stick to beat the kids with, just in a sneakier way. And another way to 'encourage' the mums to play nicely.

"I know." Annie giggled through gentle sobs. "I know I'll never get it. I don't even know why I care." She wasn't stupid. She could see it for what it was. But it still had the desired effect. Annie didn't need a bloody trophy; she'd managed perfectly well up to then without being 'star of the sodding week', but now it was there, it was something else to want, to strive for. Another layer of competition, when none was needed.

"Rise above it, kid." I tried to sound calm. "You know how good you are at dancing. You don't need a trophy to tell you that. I assume you only get the trophy for a week?" She nodded. "So, every week the baton gets passed. It's no achievement, Annie, you know that, right? So, when it goes to someone who you know doesn't deserve it, who has done nothing to earn it, you see how ridiculous the whole concept is, right?" She nodded in agreement. "And you must remember when Thomas Baxter got the merit that time for washing his hands after using the toilet?"

She laughed out loud, really laughed. And it was a sound I had missed for such a long time. It wouldn't stop her wanting that fucking trophy though.

The following week brought a new low – one I didn't think even VCS could stoop to.

Annie's version of events and Miss Victoria's were very different. The way Annie told it, the trophy had been given to Libby for something she had done as part of an improvised routine. Annie had tried not to show her disappointment in not receiving the award (though I imagined the tears were there, fighting for their release). Miss Stacy had made a comment along the lines of... 'today's star of the week award is going to Libby Bickerstaffe for mastering something she's been struggling with for a while.' The girls, including Annie, had clapped and said well done. Miss Stacy went on to say that it was a close call between Libby and Annie. Annie had perked up at hearing this (to me irrelevant and pointless) comment, but Miss Stacy elaborated. What influenced her decision was that Libby had been lighter on her feet, and that the girls were at an age where their bodies were changing and lots of girls put weight on, but as dancers they needed to make sure they were in tip-top condition. They might have to be lifted in a routine, and that would be difficult if someone was heavier. She had looked at Annie directly, and smiled as she suggested they might all want to think about whether that chocolate bar or piece of cake was really a good idea.

As Annie recounted this, I felt every bit of her humiliation. Her teacher had (in a roundabout way) called her fat. In front of her peers. She had not won the trophy. That was fine. But why go on to single her out to tell everyone why Annie hadn't won it? She didn't do that for anyone else. Fifteen or sixteen other kids in that class also didn't win the trophy, but they were left alone. So why pick on Annie?

Thankfully, we were at home before she told me the story. The red mist descended quickly, and I wouldn't have been able to drive if she had told me earlier. I wondered if that was why she waited.

Fury was building within me, and I started shaking. A numbness crept up my face, starting at my neck and gradually taking away all feeling. The familiar black and white haze in my vision told me it was a panic attack, and I think I felt some kind of relief that I wasn't having a stress-induced stroke. This would pass. I sat on the sofa, feeling like my body was made of lead. It was hard to ignore the physical symptoms, even though I knew what they were – I'd been here many times before – but my brain needed to focus on the cause. Miss Stacy.

After a few minutes, the fog lifted, and my body became my own again. But the shaking remained. I felt my head might explode as the anger in my brain grew. I had a shot of whisky before dialling the number – not something I did often, but I needed to calm my fury, or risk becoming incoherent.

Annie put her hand out to stop me. "Wait! Before you ring, there's something else I should probably tell you." Oh God. What else?

I ended the call before it connected. "Go on…"

Annie sat down at the kitchen table. "At the start of the lesson, Miss Victoria came in and asked us to put our hands up if we wanted to go to dance college after we leave school." She took a deep breath. "Everyone in the class put their hands up, except me."

I sat down across from her. "She asked me why, and I said I just wasn't sure yet what I wanted to do, and she said she was surprised at me. Then Miss Stacy was weird with me after that."

Ah… and there it was. Annie was not a 'sure thing' anymore. They wanted to focus on those who would prove to be advantageous one way or another and cut loose those who had no value. She had the talent – she had proved that time and again – but she didn't have the desire to do it. Who could blame her? Her years at VCS had shown her how nasty girls could be, especially competitive girls.

I composed myself before calling Miss Victoria, my hands still shaking as I found the number again.

"Hiya, Lydia," she said. "You all right, love?" Her scratchy voice sounded upbeat, friendly.

"No, actually, I'm not." I surprised myself with the level of stoicism I was portraying, especially as it was so far from the emotions bubbling away inside me. "I'm not sure if you're aware of some of the comments made in Annie's class tonight, but I'm absolutely furious." I didn't sound furious. And that was good. *Keep a lid on it, Lydia. You can release the monkeys at any time. Just make your point first.*

I relayed the story Annie had told me, including my suspicion that her not committing to a dance career may be behind it. Miss Victoria tried to interrupt a few times, but I wasn't having any of it. I raised my voice slightly and continued. I'd seen her do this before: commandeering discussions until the other person/people were so exasperated/short of time/confused, they wanted a quick ending to said discussion. And she would have the last word. She would end the conversation with something upbeat – maybe a little joke, or a compliment even – but it was clear the conversation had ended. That was not going to happen on this occasion, and she resorted to only 'hmm hmm's'. She was probably bored with listening to me, undoubtedly frustrated at not being able to get a word in, and I didn't give a single gram of shit.

After I relayed my understanding of the events, I asked her "so what was that all about?" and waited for her response. She didn't have one. "I'll speak to Miss Stacy and call you back."

"Fine." I ended the call abruptly. My days of politeness and ass-kissing were over.

It was over three hours later that she eventually called me back. During that time, I had mulled it all over and taken myself on an emotional rollercoaster – working myself into a dangerous frenzy, and then calming down, likely through exhaustion, and repeating this several times. Whether she would get Mental Lydia, or Disturbingly Calm Lydia, really depended on the time she called. As it happened, she spoke to the latter. Anyone with half a brain cell would recognise a calm before a storm, but Miss Victoria was oblivious. She mistook my quieter tone to mean I had calmed down and would therefore be easier to placate. It did not mean that. But I let her speak. I found sometimes that staying silent could be quite unnerving, and I wanted her to experience that.

Her voice was softer than usual, gentler. I knew this not to be the voice of atonement, but that of someone who knew the damage done, but needed to make light of it and distance themselves from any potential fallout.

"Hiya, love," she sang. "I've spoken to Miss Stacy, and I think it was just a misunderstanding from what she said. You know how much we all love Annie, and Miss Stacy was so upset that she might have upset her. She definitely didn't mean to. She wanted to give Annie some encouragement, which was why she spoke about her. Like saying she was almost as good as Libby in that lesson. She said the comments about weight were aimed at the whole class, not just Annie. And it was more about keeping healthy and making sure they are strong and have the stamina to do their best. Annie's a beautiful girl, and to be honest we're all gutted that she doesn't want to go to dance college, 'cos she's such a natural. But I understand and support her whole-heartedly with any decision she makes, whether or not that includes dancing. She's like part of the family, and we just want her to be happy. We know how sensitive Annie is, so we do try and give her positive feedback. I think that's why Miss Stacy mentioned her and not any of the others…" Blah, blah, blah…

I'd seen Miss Victoria spin her bullshit enough times to know when she was reading from a script.

So many lies.

They must have been sitting together for those three hours, drafting this response. She couldn't deny any of it; there had been a class full of witnesses. The only response was to control the damage. Make light of the comments. Change the wording ever so slightly – so if anyone were to be asked, this would not be an incorrect version of the truth, it would just be a different interpretation, and with Annie being so sensitive, maybe she had just taken it to heart.

No bullying here, just an incredibly sensitive kid who had her feelings hurt. Yeah right.

18

Just the Two of Us

WE HADN'T HAD SEX for over five years. I wasn't bothered. I was too busy, and too tired and had zero interest in it. I was preoccupied with dance-related issues of one kind or another and had been for years. Rob's lack of interest in dancing was not only irritating, and I imagined hurtful to Annie, but it drove a real wedge between us.

We had nothing in common anymore. I could never commit to weekends away or holidays, or even the odd night out, because we might be needed at the studio or some competition or other.

I would sometimes see other dads either at the studio or at the theatre during show weeks or panto. They were so excited for their kids, so proud of them. Some would watch every show, even though their kid might only be on stage for less than two minutes.

Rob wasn't like that. He'd come to one show – be it Starstruck or panto. And it always felt a little begrudging. He'd never watched Annie in a competition either. Not a single one.

Before Annie was born, we'd go on nice holidays when we could afford it, less extravagant ones when money was tight. We'd have nights out together – just going out for dinner or a couple of beers, or maybe the cinema every now and then. Even when Annie was a baby, and then a toddler, we'd do city breaks, and have days out at the beach or the zoo... the location didn't really matter – everything was exciting to Annie and we were both infatuated with her.

I'd known what I was getting into. The never-ending demands and the never-ending costs. Rob could never understand why I couldn't just say no. He'd played football as a kid, and expected dancing would require pretty much the same level of commitment from parents. Football kits might have been more expensive than leotards, but he didn't need a new kit every year, or whenever those in charge fancied a different colour. He didn't need a different kit for every night of the week, and he didn't need multiple hand-made bespoke kits for competitions. As far as I knew, there were no exams in football. No bullshit costs like pianist fees for imaginary pianists.

Football and dancing were not comparable.

And we grew apart. I felt resentful that he didn't pay more attention to Annie, not that she seemed to care much. I was also envious of his free time, of his peaceful, stress-free life without bitching and back-stabbing, while simultaneously feeling guilty for being a terrible wife.

As we moved further and further away from each other, we became more like housemates than husband and wife – our arrangement more practical than romantic.

So, it was no real surprise when we came back from the studio late one Tuesday night to discover Rob gone.

Annie went straight up to bed, exhausted after three hours of stretch and ballet classes, and I made a cup of tea before sitting down with the envelope I'd picked up off the hall table as we came through the door. My hands shook as I took out the letter, written in Rob's unmistakeable scribble…

Lydia

I'm so sorry it's come to this, but I think its time we were honest with ourselves. Our marriage has been over for a long time, whether or not we wanted to admit it. I hoped that once Annie got a bit older and maybe left dancing, things would get better and back to how they used to be — like we were just on pause for a while. I thought if nothing else we were at least honest with each other and could trust each other but it's not the case is it?

I accidentally opened your bank statement today. I swear it was an accident. I never thought there was any reason to worry about money, or to check up on you. I hope you believe that. But what I saw on there shocked me. I had no idea how much you were spending on dancing. I worked out how much you'd have left each month — not much at all — and then I started to wonder why I hadn't seen a credit card statement for such a long time. I called the credit card company, and they told me you asked for them to be done online only. So, after I answered their security questions, I got the balance.

What the fuck happened Lydia?

£27,343.92 is the current outstanding balance, in case you wondered.

I don't understand why. Why are you spending all this money on something that makes Annie cry? How could you get us into debt like this behind my back? You have to know we have no way of paying that back in the next 30 years. The house will have to be remortgaged – there's no alternative. I hope it's been worth it, though I don't think so.

I can't trust you any more Lydia.

I'll be at my mum's until I figure out what to do and what I can afford, given the mess you've got us into.

For now, I'll keep paying the bills. I don't want Annie to suffer because of what you've done, and I'll get some advice on the debt, but you need to know I'm not paying all of it. You got us into this so you'll have to make some decisions, maybe start saying no every now and then at that fucking studio.

I'd like to see Annie whenever I can (or whenever she's not at dancing) but I know she would want to stay with you. After all, you give her everything she wants, or maybe it's everything Miss Victoria wants.

I don't want this to be any more difficult than it needs to be. At some point, we need to sit down and figure out the practicalities. But make no mistake, this marriage is over.

If you need me, you have my mum's number.
I'll come and pick up the rest of my stuff at the
weekend, and then you can have my key.
    Rob

I put the letter down and sipped my tea. I should have been devastated. But instead of feeling my heart breaking, I felt a warm wave of relief wash over me – relief that I didn't need to hide our financial situation from Rob anymore. I knew how mad he would be, and I didn't blame him for that, but once a dark secret comes out, it can lose its potency. A secret's power lies in it *being* a secret – not always the secret itself. Take that power away and you're left with only the bad thing, not the bad thing and the worry of being caught out. So, yes, I was relieved he knew.

But even more than that, I felt relieved that I didn't need to even think about him anymore. I had no hard feelings towards Rob, no real feelings of anything at all towards him. But I always had to at least consider him. And I was too tired to consider anyone other than Annie. As much as I hated it, dancing remained all-consuming, and it didn't look like that would change any time soon.

At least with Rob gone, I could focus on Annie. She needed me, and I needed to be there for her.

As long as Rob would continue to pay the bills, we'd be just fine.

19

Why Are We Doing This?

"I'M SO SORRY, ANNIE." I hugged her tight, stroking her hair as she sobbed.

"But I don't understand why..." She looked up at me, her big brown eyes bloodshot and puffy from the tears.

"I guess... we just grew apart, that's all." I wasn't going to tell her about the debt. She didn't need to know about that. "It happens sometimes. When you get married in your twenties, you can be completely different people by the time you're forty. Different interests, different directions. Not always one person or the other to blame."

"Is Dad having an affair?"

I winced. I hadn't even considered that.

"No, love. He's not." In truth, he could have been. It could have gone on for years. It could have gone on in my own home – Annie and I were rarely there. Would I even have been bothered? Probably not. "And we haven't fallen out, so in some ways things won't change too much. We'll still do what we do, and you can see Dad whenever you want to. We both love you more than anything else in the world, and that will never change."

She drew her knees up tightly to her chest and huddled in the corner of the sofa. She looked so small, so vulnerable.

In trying to do the best for her, I had wrecked all of our lives.

My phone pinged to advise a notification had landed. From dancing.

Now what?... I opened it and had to adjust my eyes to read it. It had been typed angrily, I guessed – all in capitals and lots of exclamation marks. Miss Jessica.

EVERYONE IN MY 6PM CLASS NEEDS TO BE IN STUDIO 4 BY 5.55 READY FOR 6PM START!!! NO EXCUSES!!! AND I EXPECT HAIR TO BE IMMACULATE AND ALL IN FULL CORRECT UNIFORM. THERE HAVE BEEN MANY TIMES RECENTLY WHEN GIRLS ARE LETTING STANDARDS SLIP AND THIS JUST LOOKS SLOPPY!!!

What the fuck?... Who the hell did she think she was talking to? I didn't think she meant Annie. We were always early, and unless there had been any uniform changes (which wouldn't surprise me), she was always in correct uniform. Even so, the tone of the email made my heart race so fast and hard I could hear my blood pumping round my body.

My fingers jabbed the keypad on my phone as I replied before I could think it through and talk myself out of it.

I assume you don't mean Annie, but perhaps it would be helpful if you were to send these rather curt messages to those they are aimed at, just so they know. Otherwise, you risk gaslighting people who are not the issue, and those you're really aiming it at, don't think you mean them. And just a suggestion – you might want to go easy on the exclamation marks and use less capitalisation. You just look angry and silly.

I added a smiley face emoji and hit 'send', and immediately felt my tummy flip. Should I have done that? I saw Miss Jessica's picture pop up underneath my message. There was no way of recalling it. But I didn't really want to, anyway. Little dots indicating an imminent response, and more faces popping in to show they had seen it. I imagined all of the dance mums reading it, open-mouthed, and showing it to their kids. 'I can't believe she's just spoken to Miss Jessica like that' they would say. And then they'd settle in with some popcorn to watch the war of words about to unfold. They all agreed with me. I knew they did. They just didn't have the balls to say it. Frightened that any backchat from parents might mean their kid being relegated to the back row come the next show. Or not being given a main part in something or other.

Well, fuck that. I'd had enough. I was sick to death of biting my tongue, of toeing the party line, however ridiculous the demands may be. I wouldn't make Annie leave VCS – I was still adamant that it had to be her decision – but I sure as hell wasn't being spoken to like this, especially on a message. At least have the bottle to say it to people's faces. Little madam on a power trip.

Oh Christ, I'd really started something now. Tiny profile pictures popped up underneath my message, each one accompanied by a notifying 'ping', to let me know who was in the audience for the shit show that was about to start. *Hope you've got plenty of popcorn…* They were here for this and would be glued to their phones.

Adrenaline flooded through me as I relished the idea of the fight ahead. I'd been spoiling for this for a long time, and now I was enjoying goading her.

AS PER SCHOOL RULES, ALL CHILDREN MUST BE IN FULL UNIFORM, OR THEY WILL NOT BE ABLE TO TAKE PART!! ALSO, THERE ARE SOME CHILDREN WHO HAVE NOT YET SIGNED UP FOR THE LANCASTER FESTIVAL. AS PER COMPETITION CONTRACTS, YOU MUST CONFIRM AVAILABILITY AT LEAST 2 WEEKS BEFORE THE EVENT! IF YOU HAVEN'T ALREADY ADDED YOUR CHILD'S NAME TO THE LIST IN RECEPTION, PLEASE DO SO TONIGHT OR YOU WILL BE IN BREACH OF CONTRACT!!!

Jesus, this was escalating, and I was loving every second. I was calmer for my response to this one…

As per my previous message, it would help if your rants messages were directed at those who need them. Please can I just ask…where on the contract does it say availability should be confirmed 2 weeks before the event? I don't think ours says that. Please can you also clarify the consequences of breaching the contract. Thank you

I smiled as I pictured her reading it, imagining her face reddening, steam coming out of her ears, and her stamping her feet.

Nothing for almost twenty minutes. Then an email notification. From Miss Victoria.

Hi ladies, please can you all make sure you have signed one of the up-to-date contracts. You can either print off the attachment or we'll have some at the studio if you pop in. These must be signed before the end of this week, or your children will no longer be able to compete. Thanks. Miss V. xxxxxxx

The smug satisfaction I felt a few minutes earlier now muddled with a crushing, claustrophobic sensation in my chest. The contracts were worthless. As soon as VCS wanted something different, a new contract would be created. Failure to sign a new one would mean exclusion from the competition team. They had us all – the mums just as much as the kids – dancing to their tune.

I threw my phone across the room, my jaw clenched. Annie sat bolt upright.

"What is it? What happened?"

"Nothing, sweetheart." I could have kicked myself for losing control in front of her. She had enough to deal with, without her mother causing problems. "Honestly, nothing to worry about. Just a bad day, I guess. And now I need to go into the studio to sign a new contract. Nothing major, just an inconvenience, that's all." I forced a smile, which I hoped would reassure her. I started to worry about the consequences of my insubordination. "We'll be fine, Annie, I promise you. I'm here for you, if you want to talk. Or if you don't want to talk, I'm here if and when you change your mind."

A few days later I bumped into one of the mums rushing to get into her top-of-the-range Range Rover, holding her Jigsaw jacket over her head to prevent the rain from ruining her freshly styled hair. She stopped when she saw me. "Bloody hell, you were brave, weren't you? You know, on the messages."

"Oh... er... well, I don't know about that..." Any bravery I had in that moment had long gone and been replaced with something akin to nervous dread. Not for me. I could handle any kind of argument that came my way. But I knew it wouldn't work out that way. Best way to silence the mums was to show them who was in charge. Put the kids in their place, to keep the mums in their place. "I'm sure I'll feel the wrath of Miss Jessica sometime soon."

"No, I don't think so. She's a pussy cat, really." She laughed. How could anyone find any humour in this? Maybe I should add 'sense of humour' to the growing list of things I seemed to have lost.

"Yeah right... a pussy cat who likes sending shouty messages."

"Oh God yeah, I know what you mean. Bit rude, isn't she?" She nudged my arm with her elbow. Like we were friends. Or co-conspirators. "Yeah, we all said you were totally right in what you said. They do overstep the mark sometimes, don't they?"

I wanted to say 'yeah they do, but none of you lot say a bloody word about it, just sitting and watching, letting them get away with it.'

But I didn't.

Instead, I smiled as sweetly as I could. "I'll let you go anyway and get out of this horrible weather." I watched as she climbed into her enormous car and reapplied her lipstick. These bitches would never stick up for their own daughters, never mind backing me up. How could they carry on like this? Being spoken down to by dance teachers, young enough almost to be our daughters. They would watch on, letting someone else take on the argument, in full agreement with me, but never letting the teachers know that.

The following week's competition rehearsal included the group dance. And this was when I came to learn the error of my ways. Despite this particular dance being almost two years old, Miss Jessica and Miss Stacy had decided it was time to switch it up a bit, and Annie was moved from the front row to the back.

Hatred boiled within me, threatening to spew out like an uncontrollable volcano. None of the teachers – except Miss Victoria, of course – had children yet. Still, they knew the best way to hurt a mother was to hurt their child. And it did.

This time, Annie's pain was on me. Entirely my fault. I couldn't keep my trap shut and Annie would pay the price. I hated myself almost as much as I hated them.

20

A Different Child

"WHOSE IS THAT SWEATSHIRT?" I asked Annie as she came into the kitchen where I was folding laundry before the nightly trip to the studio. "It's about twenty sizes too big for you."

"It's Dad's. He said I could have it. It was freezing at Nana's." I was relieved that Rob's mum didn't have a third bedroom. Selfish as it was, I didn't want Annie to stay there.

"Freezing? That'd be a first, its normally hotter than hell at Nana's. Is there a problem with the heating or something?"

"Dunno. Dad reckoned it wasn't cold, but it was."

"I hope you're not sickening for something." I felt her forehead – it didn't feel particularly warm. "You've been feeling the cold a lot recently. Hope it's not a fever starting."

"I'm fine."

"Well, let me give you some paracetamol anyway. It won't do any harm."

"Mum, I said I'm fine! Just back off, will you!"

I stood open-mouthed and watched as she left the kitchen and slammed the door behind her. Had I been pushy with her? I didn't think so, but it was so unlike her to snap like that.

I left it a few minutes before going up to her room. As I opened the door, she jumped off the bed. "What's going on, Annie?" An enormous ball of dread appeared in my stomach.

"Nothing! Just get out!" She'd never raised her voice to anyone before. Could it be her age? Fourteen wasn't easy. Maybe Rob moving out was hitting her harder than I thought. Did she blame me for it?

"Annie, please. I just want to help. I need to know you're okay."

"I already said I'm fine. What else do you want from me?" she snapped.

"Annie, you're scaring me. Please tell me what's going on."

She glowered at me.

"Okay, okay, I'm going," I said, backing out of the door. "Assuming you're still going to dancing tonight, you need to have something to eat soon, so come down as soon as you're ready."

"I'm not hungry." The volatile teen of a few moments ago had been replaced by a different one. Quieter. Sadder?

"Well, at least have a bit of soup or something before you go."

She nodded and I left the room. Something was wrong. Really wrong. This wasn't just teenage stroppiness. Something about the way she had dived off the bed had unsettled me. Such an odd thing to do. But then I realised… she was hiding something. I didn't think we had any secrets. I knew teenagers usually did – God knows I had an enormous one at her age – but I always thought we were closer than that. What could be so bad that she didn't want to tell me?

Oh God…was it drugs? Surely, she knew better. Maybe a boyfriend? That needn't be a secret, unless it was someone that she knew I wouldn't approve of. Maybe the boyfriend was on drugs…

After dropping her at the studio, I broke the speed limit driving home. She was only there for an hour and a half that night, so I needed to be quick. I ran up to her room and started to search; first round the side of the bed she had jumped to. I frantically cast aside the array of clothing littering the floor. Nothing. I checked her bedside cabinet. Nothing there of any concern.

There had to be something. She hadn't taken a bag to dancing that night, so whatever she was hiding had to be in her room.

I checked her drawers, her wardrobe, even the pockets in her clothes, careful not to move anything that would hint at her room being searched. I finally found what I was looking for under her bed. Hidden behind a couple of old stuffed toys, some items of scrunched up clothing and a few books, I saw the box. I'd bought it to keep under her bed, to help her keep her room organised. It clearly hadn't worked, but the box was still there – the shiny grey plastic so non-descript, it would never draw attention. But it had mine now.

I dragged it out and took a deep breath before opening it. When I saw the contents, I felt a heavy weight behind my ribs, as though my heart was literally breaking, and I grasped at my chest as though I could somehow keep my heart whole. The toolkit of a child in real despair. As I touched each item, I understood the story they were telling me.

I counted twelve boxes of laxatives (various brands and strengths), four boxes (one almost empty) of diuretics, a sharp knife from the kitchen drawer, some old flannels heavily stained with blood. My baby's blood.

Salt. What was she doing with salt? Surely not rubbing it into her own wounds.

I found a possible alternative explanation... wrapped in a carrier bag were around seven or eight smaller bags – the ones we used in the bathroom bin. As I pulled one out, I didn't need to open it. It had been knotted at the top to keep the contents from spilling, but the smell was unmistakeable, and holding the bag in my hand, I knew. Vomit.

My beautiful daughter had an eating disorder.

Many years ago, I'd done a lot of reading on the topic. It was almost impossible to understand why anyone would do this to themselves, but the psychology around anorexia and bulimia was complex. This had been my worst nightmare. I'd never said it out loud, for fear of giving power to the words, but as I sat on Annie's bedroom floor, it all started to fit.

I hadn't seen her in anything other than baggy clothes for a long time. She had been complaining a lot about the cold. Annie had always been sensitive – some might say 'oversensitive'. And she had struggled to fit in. She was a perfectionist. She wanted to be the best, at everything she did. I'd thought I could smell sick a few days earlier, but Annie said she couldn't smell anything. Rob leaving. Was that the start? How long had it been going on?

A montage of memories – things that I hadn't even picked up on at the time – flashed through my mind, in no particular order, my brain flitting from one thought to another. It all made perfect sense.

She had lost weight. Quite a bit of weight. But I'd put it down to the amount of exercise, and maybe she was shifting a bit of 'puppy fat'. I'd never commented on it, though.

And the blood. I could think of no other explanation for the knife and blood-soaked cloths. She had to be cutting herself.

But how could I question her? A cold trickle of fear ran down my spine as my mind filled with horrific images. I would risk losing any trust she had in me if she knew I had searched her room. But how else could I raise the subject? Other than asking her to remove some of her clothing, and I wouldn't expect anyone to strip on demand – least of all a teenager with such a secret.

Kelly

"HAVE YOU SEEN KELLY recently?" my mum asked, unpacking the shopping.

I was doing homework at the kitchen table, with headphones in as always. "What?" I asked, switching my Walkman off.

"I said, have you seen anything of Kelly?"

"Nothing at all, not for months now, not since we fell out."

"Well, I thought I saw her walk past the house the other day, but I wasn't sure if it was her. She looks so thin."

I was taken aback. I hadn't even seen Kelly from a distance since that night. I desperately missed her but couldn't bring myself to get in touch. Either I would have to keep my secret from her, which felt like lying, or I could tell her and risk the same reaction I'd had from everyone at school. So, I chose to bury my head in the sand and avoid either scenario. We'd never had any secrets between us, and this was a big one. But I knew I couldn't tell her.

God, I hoped she was okay. I knew her brother had a cancer scare the year before, turned out to be nothing, but it was scary for the family as a cousin had died of ovarian *cancer, I think in her twenties. Surely that couldn't be happening to Kelly.*

"Yeah," my mother continued. "Well, I bumped into Beryl that lives next door to them when I was shopping, and she was telling me. Apparently, she hardly eats anything, and she's started going to dancing a lot more, and she started running as well. Looks like her legs could barely hold her up from what I saw. Beryl thought she had that anorexia thing that Karen Carpenter had."

Jesus. I'd heard of it before, but it was something I'd never actually come across. I imagined it to be some weird illness that only about four or five people in the world happened to have. I'd seen a documentary about Karen Carpenter. My parents watched it as they loved the Carpenters, and I remembered it fascinating me that someone so beautiful and talented would do that to herself. It was desperately sad.

"Do you think I should ring her?" I asked my mum.

"Not sure you'd even be able to," she said, putting the salad vegetables in the fridge. "Beryl spoke to Chrissy and she told her Kelly is always out doing one activity or another. I guess she maybe had to find new friends after you two fell out."

Was it my fault? She was fine the last time I saw her. She looked strong and toned as she always did. I hadn't noticed any change in her appearance, but maybe it was because I was so wrapped up in myself and what happened to me, too selfish to think anyone else could have anything going on. I hated myself more than ever.

21

Darker Times

"PLEASE TELL ME WHY," I begged her. "I can't help you if I don't know what's going on in your mind. Sweetheart..."

"I already told you, like a million times, I don't know!" We were past the stage of denials. The first four or five months from discovering the secret box under the bed had been rough. Annie had dismissed all of it, excuses for everything. The cuts on her leg were from when she fell into a bush. The baggy clothes were comfy and that's what everyone was wearing. The weight loss wasn't much – and she was fine. She was cold because the weather was cold.

She still didn't know I'd found the box. I needed her to trust me, and there was no chance of that if she knew I'd invaded her privacy.

Sometimes I'd pretend, just for a moment, that I could believe her. I'd suspend reality and indulge in the lie, just for a minute. But then I'd remember what I'd found in her room and would slam back to reality like a car crash.

So, we'd danced around the issue for a while, until

I'd accidentally walked in her room one day as she was getting dressed. I'd stopped abruptly. I hadn't known she was in her room. And I certainly wasn't prepared for what I saw. She was getting ready for dancing. I only usually saw her as she was ready to leave the house, so she'd be covered up, wearing joggers and a hoodie, and she would come out of the studio in that same attire, going straight up to her room when we got home.

I'd wanted to see what she looked like since the day I found out. I felt to blame for all of it and wanted to see what I had caused. I wanted to feel the pain that Annie was feeling. But more than anything, I needed to see how serious this was. I didn't know how I would know, but I expected that there would come a point where the weight loss could not be ignored or brushed off, and we would have to have the conversation. I knew exactly what she was doing – I just needed to find a way to open the door to speak to her about it.

I'd left her room and gone back downstairs. I sat at the kitchen table, head in my hands, and felt completely overwhelmed. I was out of my depth. My child was sick, and I had no idea how to help her. She was doing this to herself; there wasn't any medicine I could give her to make it go away.

"Why did you come in my room?" she demanded from the doorway.

"I… I didn't know you were in there. I was just bringing your clothes up."

She glared at me.

"Annie, we need to talk about this. Please come and sit down with me."

"But I'll be late for dancing…"

"Annie, this won't take long, and you won't be late. But I'm not taking you to dancing until we talk about this." She sat across from me and I watched as her shoulders slumped in defeat. Her face looked so small, so child-like. Beautiful, but so very delicate. Fragile.

"Look, I'm just going to say what I need to say for now, and then we can talk later." She looked up at me, eyes watery. "I need you to know that no matter what you say, no matter what excuses you come up with, I know what you're doing." She opened her mouth to protest, but I lifted my hand to cut her off.

"I know what you're doing," I repeated. "And I really hope that if nothing else for now, you can be honest with me. You don't need to tell me everything, but please know I'm here whenever and wherever you need me, whenever you want to talk."

She nodded.

"And I want you to remember back to the times when you were little, and you would share your problems and worries with me, so I could take half of it from you." She nodded sadly, silent tears landing on the table in front of her. "Sweetheart, I want to take this from you again. I want to be able to help. But I need you to talk to me so I can do that."

She sat back in a gesture I read as not wanting to go there. Not now.

"We'll come back to this," I said as I stood and grabbed my car keys. "Like I said, I know what's going on, and I'm here for you. Always."

It had taken a while to get past the denials, but

eventually she came to understand that it was just a waste of energy she didn't have. Annie's eating disorder became an elephant in the room. She didn't discuss it, and I was scared to push her on it – scared she would close up altogether, and I desperately wanted her to let me in. I needed her to.

I started reading books about anorexia and bulimia. Some of what I read, I could relate to. Some mentioned sufferers feeling 'in control'. Others suggested the illness became like a friend – and God knew Annie had struggled with friendships over the years. The more I read, the more difficult it became to understand – so many factors linked to the causes, so many differing opinions on how to deal with it as a parent, so many differing medical opinions.

I understood it was a mental illness and should be treated as such. The answer was not going to be to sit her at the table and keep her there until she ate something.

Mealtimes were tricky. I started serving smaller portions, trying not to overwhelm her, but even then, she would push food around her plate, trying different ways of spreading it out, or stacking it up, to make it look like she'd eaten something. I'd find chewed-up food, wrapped in kitchen roll, in the kitchen bin.

After meals she would go upstairs, and I'd hear the music going on as she attempted to hide the sounds of retching and heaving as she brought back up the tiny morsels she'd consumed. I wasn't sure if she knew that I could hear the vomiting. Even if I'd not been able to hear it, I would find evidence under the toilet seat. I never mentioned it. I figured I could use that toilet seat as an indicator, should it be needed. Later, it would become a way of being able to see whether she was getting better.

I had initially been surprised that she still had the energy to dance, but I learned that sometimes it was as though the illness itself almost gives you the energy to push harder, to keep going. Like a voice in her head, spurring her on, telling her she could do more.

Shortly before Annie's fifteenth birthday, I received a call from school. She had collapsed and an ambulance had been called. I made it to the school in record time, giving not a single thought to the speeding tickets I was accruing. I flung the doors open, terrified, to see Annie on a stretcher in the reception area, surrounded by paramedics, teachers and office staff. She saw me and lifted a hand weakly to wave. I ran over to her and kissed her head. I couldn't hug her as she was lying down, so instead I held her hand. Her face was pale and clammy. As I held her hand, I noticed how bony it was – like a Halloween prop with skin stretched over it.

"It's okay, Mum, we're just doing a few tests here so we can see what's going on," said one of the paramedics cheerily. He was a gentle-looking middle-aged man with a reassuring manner.

"Mrs Moffatt, please could I have a word in my office?" asked Mrs Nolan, the headteacher.

"I'll be right back," I said to Annie and kissed her hand. She nodded and tried to smile, though I could see the fear in her eyes. I closed the door behind me.

She launched right into it. "We've noticed Annie looks like she's lost a lot of weight over the past few months. Is there anything we need to be aware of?"

I sat down and was unable to control the tears as I figured out where to start. Mrs Nolan passed me a tissue. She was not as sympathetic a character as you'd hope for in one who was responsible for your child for several hours a day.

"She won't eat," I blubbed. "I can't get her to eat anything, and when she does, she throws it back up." I couldn't catch my breath. She nodded, as though she expected this to be the case. Not that I needed her to tell me something I already knew, but I thought these people had safeguarding policies.

I sat, head in hands, and sobbed. Months and months of worrying had built up and had now broken the floodgates. She patted my shoulder. "It's okay," she said, as there was a knock of the door. The paramedic opened it a crack, and I stood quickly to leave the office.

"We're going to take her in," he said. "I think she's probably stable now, but it might be worth doing some tests." *No need*, I thought. *We know what the issue is.*

The Accident & Emergency department was unusually quiet, and I was grateful for that. A curtain was drawn around us, as a doctor came in and introduced himself. "Hello, Annie, I'm Dr Hussein. I understand you collapsed at school?" She nodded, nervously. "Can you tell me what happened?"

Annie was sitting upright on the trolley she'd been helped onto when we arrived. "Erm... I don't really know," she said, quietly. "I just went a bit dizzy and then I think I fainted, but I can't really remember."

"Oh, okay," he said, putting the tips of his stethoscope into his ears. "Do you mind if I have a quick listen to your chest?" Annie looked at me, fear in her eyes. Thankfully, Dr Hussein picked up on that. "Don't worry, you can keep all your clothes on. I know it's not very warm in here today. Is that okay?"

"Erm… yes."

He lifted the back of her polo shirt, and I winced. Her spine and ribs were pushing against her skin, no flesh to protect them from the bruises that were evident on each of her vertebrae. "Jesus, Annie, how did you get the bruises on your spine?"

She jumped as Dr Hussein put the cold stethoscope plate on her skin, and goosebumps appeared.

"I think it was at dancing when we were doing floor work," she said, twisting to look, as if she could see her own back.

"Did you not use a mat?"

"No! Mum, nobody uses a mat, so I'm not gonna ask for one, am I?"

"Well, I think you might need to from now on. Annie your bruises have bruises." She rolled her eyes and Dr Hussein gave her a conspiratorial smile, as if to say 'Mums, eh? What are they like?'

"Okay, well everything sounds fine in your chest, but we need to take some blood. Are you okay with that?"

I felt her grip tighten as he inserted a cannula into a vein in her arm. Then I felt it loosen. I watched as her eyes rolled back and her head slumped forwards. She was sliding off the trolley.

"Oh my God, what's happening?" I shouted, as I scooped her up from under her arms. As I guided her to the floor, she began to twitch and convulse violently. I kneeled, cradling her head to stop it from smashing into the hard, tiled floor. Dr Hussein had gone to get help.

I stroked her face, as I waited for the doctor to return, each second feeling like an eternity. The convulsions slowed eventually, and as Dr Hussein returned with a nurse, Annie's expression changed, and she was back in the room. "What happened?" she asked.

"You just fainted, that's all," Dr Hussein replied. "Maybe because I was about to take blood?"

"It doesn't normally bother her, I don't think," I interrupted, "and why was her body jerking like that?"

My concerns were ignored as the doctor and nurse lifted Annie back onto the trolley and fussed around her, taking her blood pressure and heart rate, shining a torch into her eyes, and eventually reinserting the cannula, which had dislodged during her so-called fainting episode. She watched the nurse as she did this, as if to prove a point that she would not faint just because she was squeamish.

"Was that what happened at school? Did it feel the same?" I asked her.

"I think so, I'm not really sure... Mum, what's happening? What's wrong with me?" Her worry dimple appeared, a sure giveaway that she was concerned, maybe even frightened.

I squeezed her hand. "Annie, you know this will be because you don't eat. You know that don't you?" She shrugged. "There's only so long your body can continue without fuel before it starts to let you know, right?" I clocked the doctor and nurse looking at each other. I was sure they knew before – her appearance was not that of someone in good health.

Why had I not made her see a doctor earlier? If I were on the outside, looking in at this situation, I would be judging this as nothing short of child neglect.

"Right, we'll get this sent up to the lab. You'll need to wait for the results, I'm afraid. We need to be sure you're okay to go home. Is that okay?"

As they left, I kissed Annie on the forehead. "We're going to be here a while, I think. Why don't you try and have a snooze?" She lay down and turned away from me, to face the wall, but she kept tight hold of my hand.

She was scared, I knew she was. I stood beside her, stroking her head, just like I did when she was a baby, and then a toddler, and then a child. Now a teenager and yet still my baby. I desperately hoped this would be the wake-up call she needed. I hoped all would be well with her blood test, and we could leave the hospital that day, Annie having learned a valuable, albeit terrifying, lesson, and we could pick up our lives without this horrible illness. Maybe not even pick back up… maybe we could start fresh somewhere new, with no bitchy girls, no blood-sucking dance school, no pressure. Maybe I could homeschool the last couple of years, get high school over with, and then we could think about what to do with the rest of our lives.

But these were just fantasies. I knew deep down that this was not something you can just 'snap out of'. There would be some tough times ahead.

It was several hours before the blood results came back. My back was throwing agonising spasms from sitting on the hard plastic chair in a horribly unnatural position as I didn't want to take my hand from Annie's grasp. I nudged her gently as the doctor came into the cubicle.

"Okay, Annie, so, your blood tests are showing low iron levels, which we can sort pretty easily with some iron tablets." I watched a subtle change in his expression – something about the lines around his eyes told me some concerning news would follow. He looked at me this time. "But it's the potassium level that worries me. Normal levels are usually 3.5 to around 5.2ish. Annie's is 2.5. Anything below 2.5 can be considered critical, so we need to put her on a potassium drip to get that number back up. Then we'll take another blood test and go from there."

"Critical?" My palms were sweating, and my heart was beating furiously against my ribcage. "What do you mean critical?"

"Look, Mrs Moffatt, I don't think there's any point in sugar-coating this. Annie's condition is serious. We've not taken her weight yet, but I can clearly see she's underweight. I'm assuming she has an eating disorder?"

I looked at Annie, wanting her approval before I disclosed her most guarded secret. She didn't protest. "Nothing diagnosed," I said, looking down as I felt a wave of shame wash over me. "But yes, I think so. She's been losing weight for a few months." I still wasn't ready to disclose that I knew about the vomiting. In truth, I knew there was probably a lot more I wasn't aware of. Anorexia thrives on secrets, and I knew I was aiding and abetting by keeping quiet.

Annie was moved on to the children's ward overnight. Her drip would take a couple of hours, and then depending on the results of the next test, she may need another one. I was given a hard, uncomfortable fold-down bed so I could stay with her, but as she fell asleep, I watched her. I could see the goosebumps on her arm and she was shivering as she tried to pull the worn, yellow hospital blanket higher.

I climbed onto the top of the bed beside her, hoping she could benefit from my body heat. I tucked my own blanket around her. I definitely didn't need it. The ward was hot and stuffy, and I was sweating in my clothes. Rob had brought Annie some PJs, but nothing for me. Cheers, Rob.

I didn't sleep a wink. I tried to cuddle her to keep her warm, but was terrified of breaking her. She was so tiny, so fragile, I worried if I leaned into her too hard, I would crush her bones.

This was the first of many sleepless nights.

Hospital

IT WAS THE WEEK *before Christmas during my last year of high school. We would be breaking up for the holidays in a couple of days, and I couldn't wait. It was a year and a half since the party that ruined my life. The physical wounds had healed eventually, but the nightmares, flashbacks and depression that resulted from them continued to linger. But school would be over in a few months. I had survived this long – a few months more and then I could start a new life without the cool kids I had come to despise. I was starting to see light at the end of the tunnel.*

As always, I had my Walkman on, so hadn't heard the doorbell or my mum knocking on my bedroom door. I jumped when I caught her out of the corner of my eye. She gestured for me to take my headphones off, and I noticed how sad she looked.

"What's up?" I asked, sitting up on my bed.

"It's Kelly, love." She sat down next to me. A chill passed through my body. My mum's face alone told me this was bad news. "She's in bad shape. You know how poorly she's been for the last year or so..." I suddenly regretted not going round, not calling her back, just removing myself from her

life. All because I didn't want to share a secret that she didn't even know I had. How fucking selfish I'd been. Was it too late?

I shook my head and felt the sting of tears welling up. "It's not that..." my mum said, knowing exactly the conclusion I'd jumped to. "But she's really poorly, Lydia, and you should go and see her before it's too late."

"Noooo! What do you mean before it's too late?" My mouth was dry. I tried to swallow but my throat had tightened.

"Sweetheart." She grabbed my hand in hers and looked down. "Kelly's been starving herself for a long time now, and there's only so long you can carry on like that." She paused. "Kelly's organs are shutting down. She's been in and out of hospital for a few months, but it's looking unlikely she'll come home now. She's not responded to treatment, and she's slipped into a coma. Chrissy thought you might want to go and see her before it's too late."

By the time we arrived at the hospital ward, my coat was damp with tears, which had flown freely.

Regret was a word I thought I knew, thought I understood its meaning, but only now could I really understand how devastating an emotion it really was. My chest felt heavy, like someone was sitting on top of me, unwilling to budge even slightly to give me the chance to help myself. My lungs were unable to fill with the air I needed, and I began to feel light-headed. What the fuck was wrong with me? How could I be so selfish? Kelly was seriously ill in hospital, more than likely because of me, and I was the one having a panic attack? I deserved way worse than a panic attack. It should be me in that hospital bed. I wished it was. Kelly should have had every opportunity the world could offer, and I loathed myself for letting this happen. I wanted nothing more than to swap places with her. No, not that. Nobody should live through the hell I was living. I wouldn't wish that on anyone. I just wished I could have been the one so close to death. For as much as I desperately wanted Kelly to live, to give me a chance to help her, and make this right, I felt a twinge of envy that she would probably be relieved of her time on earth.

Kelly had done nothing wrong. She had brought up a subject I didn't want to discuss. That was it. And for that, I had cut her out of my life without explanation. She had no idea what she had done. I tried to imagine how that must have felt for her, and the realisation of my own behaviour sickened me to the core.

If I had told her what happened, maybe she could have helped me through it. Maybe I'd been unfair to assume I knew how she would react. I had assumed she would judge me, and who knows? Maybe she would.

But maybe she wouldn't. I'd never given her the chance to prove me wrong. Or prove me right. I'd been so selfish. I'd never stopped loving my friend, but was so caught up in my own trauma, I just couldn't let her in. And now it was too late. I needed to rewind time, to go back and do things differently. If the Gods of Time would only take me back to the rape, if they could transport me right now back to John's parents' bed, to the absolute worst time of my life, I would take it. I would go through every second again just to do things differently – better – with Kelly. To do what I could to stop this happening to her.

I approached her bed, and gasped. She was unrecognisable. Even without the tubes and machinery that surrounded her, I would have struggled to recognise her. Her head looked so small and skeletal. Her eyes were deeply sunken into their sockets, and cheekbones were sharp. Her hair – once so thick and shiny – now hung around her face in limp, unloved strands, so thin I could see large patches of her scalp.

Her arms were by her sides over the top of the sheet, everything tucked neatly and tight around her tiny body. There was barely anything left of her. Her once elegant hands now looked like they belonged to an old lady, bones and veins visible through papery skin. Her arms, shoulders and collarbone, all nothing more than skin wrapped tightly around her skeleton with nothing to pad in between. I couldn't see her legs under the sheet, but I could see how little space they took up in the bed.

I wanted to crawl into the bed beside her, hold her close and wish her better. But I could do none of these things. The equipment keeping her alive acted as a barrier, though she couldn't have been held – not without breaking her fragile body.

My heart was breaking as I sat beside my best friend, who I hadn't seen for such a long time. I held her hand. I told her I was there and, through tears, asked her to forgive me. There was no response. I didn't know if Kelly could hear me, but I had to try. It was the only thing left at that point – to seek forgiveness.

The call came the following morning. Kelly had passed away peacefully during the night.

22

A New Routine

A THOUGHT HAD BEEN niggling for a while. It wasn't like I hadn't considered it – more that my attention was so focused on Annie that I didn't really have the headspace for much else.

Had the teachers at VCS not noticed the change in Annie?

Surely, they would have told me if they'd noticed anything of any concern. They had a duty, right? It was a 'safeguarding' thing, wasn't it? I started to question everything I knew, thought I knew. Would they tell me? Or would they help her keep a secret, even if it could harm her?

Annie dozed off one afternoon after school, so I got in the car and headed to VCS.

"Jesus, are you okay?" Gladys asked, as I came through the reception door. "You don't look well."

"Is Victoria here?" I asked, trying to catch my breath. My heart had been pounding so quickly and so heavily, I was struggling to breathe. Miss Victoria had been in her office and must have heard me. She stuck her head out of the door; she was on the phone, but gestured for me to come in. I closed the door behind me. I didn't want this becoming fodder for the gossips.

She ended the call and sat down across from me. Her office was little more than a storage cupboard. Unorganised paperwork, random bits of costumes and uniforms hung from a small rail in one corner, and a metal filing cabinet was in another. I wondered what was in the filing cabinet. Were there records about the students? What was on Annie's?

"I haven't seen you for a while, love, is everything okay?"

"No, it's not. It's definitely not okay." I tried to control my emotions – there would be time for that later – but I couldn't do it. I had no control over my voice cracking, or the tears that flowed freely. As I sobbed, she moved her chair closer and put her arm around my shaking shoulders in the most motherly gesture I had known her to make. She passed me a tissue.

"I know, I know…" she said, soothingly.

I straightened up. "What do you mean? What do you know?" I sniffled.

"We know Annie's been struggling, finding things hard at the moment, that's all."

"Has she spoken to you? Or any of the teachers?" I sniffled, needing another tissue, but not wanting to derail the conversation by asking for one.

"No, not at all. You know what she's like, Lydia. She's like a quiet little mouse." She tried to smile sympathetically, but

I doubted she was capable of sympathy. "But Miss Stacy and Miss Heather have seen the marks on her arms and legs."

I felt myself recoil, needing to move away from this woman. They knew.

They knew and they hadn't told me.

"When did they see them? When did they notice? I need to know how long it's been going on." Blood pounded in my ears as I suppressed my anger. I needed information, and that wouldn't be forthcoming if she became defensive. I couldn't suggest that I blamed her, or any of the others. Not yet. For now, I needed the details.

"I'm not sure, love. I think it was probably before the summer holidays last year that Stacy asked me to come and have a look at Annie... not because of the cutting, but Stacy thought she was looking really thin. I didn't have time to check on her, though, 'cos I needed to get home early that night 'cos I was off out with my sister." She hesitated. I thought she must have realised in that moment how bad this looked for her. "So, I only knew a few weeks ago. Miss Heather came out of ballet and asked me to go in and watch the girls do their exam piece. To be honest, she's not the only one – there were three or four girls in that class alone with marks on their bodies. Similar marks. I must admit I was quite shocked at Annie, though. She's definitely lost a lot of weight..."

I took a moment to process what I had heard before responding.

"So, what you're saying is that back in July... possibly earlier, Miss Stacy asked you to come and have a look at Annie because she was concerned, but you didn't. And nobody thought to express any of these concerns to me?"

"Well, no, because at the time, you see, I don't think she had the marks on her arms and legs, although I'd have to check with Stacy."

"But she must have looked in a pretty bad way if Miss Stacy had asked you to come and have a look at her?"

"Hmm, I suppose she must have, although Stacy didn't mention it again after that, and then we broke up for summer, and then when we came back it was like they'd all started doing it – not the dieting, but the cutting. It must be a new trend. You know, I blame social media for a lot of these things. You know even Daisy Morgan is doing it, and her mother is a nurse! You'd think she'd know better, wouldn't you?"

I was unable to speak. Completely gob-smacked. Was this woman for real?

We were now in May. She – or at least VCS – had been aware of Annie losing weight for almost a year. Ten months ago, it was noticeable enough that Miss Stacy had voiced a concern, but it had been ignored. And now this fucking idiot of a woman was telling me not only the name of another child who was cutting herself, but she was actually dismissing it as a social media trend.

"So, were you not going to tell me?" I asked.

"Well, I wasn't sure how to go about it. We talked about it in our staff meeting last month…" Great. So, all VCS staff knew about this before I did. "But we weren't sure whether it was a breach of confidentiality and whether we'd get in bother if we discussed it with you."

I raised my eyebrows. Unfuckingbelievable.

I stood up. "I can't hear any more right now. I need to leave." Before she could dig any deeper, I was out of the studio, and back in the car. I sat quietly, contemplating. The shock of discovering the contents of the grey box had been like a punch to my gut. But to discover the entire staff of VCS knew about this, and said nothing, was a knock-out blow.

There was no way I could sit back and let this be brushed under the rug, but for now I needed to focus on Annie. She was in turmoil, and I needed to be there for her and her needs took priority.

No More

KELLY'S DEATH HIT ME *harder than I could have ever imagined, and I spiralled into a deep, black depression. My mother got some tablets from the doctor when she told him I was only getting out of bed to use the bathroom. He said I would be fine on them. Maybe I would have, if I'd bothered to take them.*

I hated this – the way I felt with all the regret and sadness building every day. But I deserved to suffer. I was responsible. If I hadn't cut her off, this wouldn't have happened. I understood it to be a complex illness, but in my mind, our friendship – at least before the party – was stronger than anything else, including anorexia. I could have saved her, if I'd known. And she would have been there for me, if she'd known. I'd been so fucking selfish, so caught up in myself, that I'd not even thought about how my actions might affect other people. I refused to take my medication because I wanted to hate myself. I fucking deserved it. I deserved to live a life of torment.

Every thought I had led back to the night of that fucking party, as though I had lived two completely separate existences – before the party, and after.

I didn't go back to high school after Kelly's death. I couldn't care less about the cool kids anymore, one way or another. I didn't care about my exams either, though I did make an effort to at least go in and sit them, even though I knew I would fail them all.

I wanted to see them all one last time. I was carrying an unshakeable grudge and the months I spent in bed gave me time and space to think clearly.

23

Now They Were Concerned

"IT'LL DESTROY HER, VICTORIA," I said, as calmly as I could, doing my best to push down the anger so I could try to reason with her.

"I'm sorry, Lydia, but we have to think of her health, as well as the safeguarding aspect..."

"That's fucking rich! Safeguarding? Don't make me laugh. If you gave a shit about safeguarding, you'd have told me about the weight loss and the cuts when you saw them, instead of gossiping to anyone and everyone else!"

Victoria stepped back, hands up defensively as though I would attack at any moment. To be fair, it was not an unfair assumption. "Lydia, please don't swear at me. I know you're upset, but we also have to think about the school's reputation... we don't want people to see her and think that we're encouraging girls to become unhealthy..."

I froze, open-mouthed. My brain filled with a million responses, none of them coherent. I sat down on the scratty chair in Victoria's office. I saw her wince slightly, as she saw me sit on top of a costume. *I dare you*, I thought. *I just dare you to ask me to get off it.*

"So, despite her coming here since she was two years old, despite the blood, sweat and tears – of which there have been a lot – and despite the thousands and thousands of pounds you've drained from me, you're cutting her loose because her appearance might reflect badly on you? I don't believe I'm hearing this!"

"I… I didn't mean it like that… I just meant that we have to put her health first and the teachers are all worried about her… that's all."

"And you think I'm not! You think I want her to come here? You think I don't blame myself for letting this happen… for letting her come here even though she cried nearly every time? Do you honestly think I want her to dance at all?"

"Sorry… I don't understand… I thought you…"

"I should have pulled her out of here years ago. But I didn't. You and all the other teachers brainwashed me into thinking it would be good for her. Do you still think that, Victoria? Do you think she's thriving?" Victoria stared at me, blank-faced. She didn't know how to respond, and she was right not to try – there was no suitable response, nothing she could say that wouldn't fan the flames of my fury.

I clenched my knuckles and used my thumbs to push back my cuticles so hard that one of my fingers started to bleed. I felt nothing. I took a deep breath, knowing that, ultimately, she had control over who could or couldn't dance here. I needed to play this carefully.

"Look, nobody knows better than me what Annie's health is like. I'm the one taking her to her appointments and looking after her. I also know that right now she needs to feel like she has control of something, anything, and by stopping her from coming here, I'm scared it will push her harder to take control of something else."

I didn't think she was bright enough to read between the lines, but maybe she did. Or maybe she just thought it was an argument she was unlikely to win. She took a moment to consider her options.

"All right, how about this, then? If you can get a doctor's note saying she's fit to dance, we'll accept that. But she must eat something before she comes, and you have to stay on the premises. Does that sound reasonable?"

It did sound reasonable. But the doctor refused. He said her repeatedly low potassium levels were already putting her at risk of cardiac arrest. I understood that.

I didn't want her to dance either. But Annie had become so depressed, and she had already hinted that if she couldn't dance, she had nothing else. I hadn't pushed her on what that meant. I couldn't bear to hear it.

This was a lose-lose situation. If she danced, her life could be at stake, as she risked possible cardiac arrest. If she didn't dance, her life could still be at stake, though through her own determination to level-up in the game she was playing with her health, and her life.

The reality sickened me.

I considered which unthinkable scenario was worse. No parent should ever have to think about which death would be best for their child. But that was the reality. Annie might die suddenly, doing what she loved – no warning, no come-back. Or she could stay at home, depressed, determined to die from a slow suicide by starvation. There was no good option.

I knew how it would look to the teachers, to the other parents... even my family. Rob – in particular – thought I was insane. What mother would want her anorexic daughter to push herself beyond her limits physically and risk possible death? They saw me as an uncaring, pushy mum who didn't care about her kid. I got it – I'd think that way too if I were just an observer to this horrific situation.

But the rock and the hard place I was caught between were equally grim. And I made the decision to support Annie. I reasoned that if she felt she had at least some control left, there was a chance we could make it through. I was terrified that taking that decision away from her might lead to... I couldn't think about it.

We came to an agreement that none of us were really happy with, but it was the only option available. Annie would go to classes, only if she had eaten something, and she would not be able to take part in anything other than slow stretches. No cardiac stress.

It seemed to work for a while.

But as her condition continued to deteriorate, she had less and less energy, struggling even to make the effort to get to the studio, so the frequency reduced.

It wasn't long before a new routine would also take over.

School became an ad-hoc activity. Annie had a standing appointment at the GP surgery every Wednesday. Each week they would carry out a blood test, and ECG, check her blood pressure and take her weight. Each week

her weight would drop – 44 kilograms, 43.7 kilograms...
43.2... 42.9... 42.5... 41.8... 39.8... 39.4... 38.2... 36.4.
How much more could she lose and still exist?

But the blood results were the bigger concern. Every week a Thursday phone call to tell me what that week's potassium level was. Every week it was in the serious to critical range. So, every Thursday we would trek up to A&E, where Annie would be hooked up to an IV – sometimes twice depending on whether the levels had increased enough. This would often turn into an overnight stay. We even had a bag packed, kept in the car, for these occasions.

Eventually a meeting took place between me, Rob, Annie, her schoolteachers and a nurse. It was decided that Annie was too poorly to attend school, and that she had to use all her energy to focus on recovery.

I asked my doctor to sign me off work, which she did – surprisingly for three months. As I got home from the appointment with her, I burst into tears. I wasn't sure where the tears came from, but I felt light with relief. I hadn't realised how hard it had been, trying to juggle everything – working, school, dancing – while worrying constantly and not really being able to focus properly on anything. My work suffered, the house was a tip, and I could never think about anything other than where we were on any given day. I had lived for months in constant fight or flight mode, unable to relax, always waiting for the phone call from the surgery or school or hospital. Rob had helped with the odd hospital trip, but he mostly left it to me. It was a mess of my making, as far as he was concerned, so I should be the one to deal with it.

So, our new routine continued, but it felt softer, calmer, less chaotic than before. I was grateful for the chance to focus – guilt-free – on Annie, on taking care of her. However this ended – and I had read enough about anorexia to know the reality – I could at least take this time to be with her. To look after, and nurture, her as I had when she had been a baby.

But that didn't mean it was easier. Far from it.

Every morning, I'd wake after a feverish sleep, filled with nightmares about bones, and food, and Annie being dragged away from me by some unseen force, reaching out for me as I tried and failed to pull her to safety. And Kelly. It wasn't surprising, I supposed, that my unconscious thoughts – and some conscious ones – had turned to Kelly. I hadn't been there for her. But I was damn well here for Annie, no matter what.

I'd listen out for any sounds from Annie's room, and every morning, there was silence. The all-too-familiar fear, building and growing every day. I was so caught up in Annie, I barely registered the signs of my own anxiety anymore. But they were still there – the nausea, the feeling of dread in the pit of my stomach. Every morning, preparing for the worst, yet still hoping for the best – whatever the best looked like.

Would today be the day?

Each morning I'd open her bedroom door tentatively, hardly daring to see – like watching a particularly scary horror film and clutching a cushion in front to cover my eyes. Not wanting to see, but knowing I had to. The fear would be released, temporarily, as I would see a tiny arm lift from under the duvet. A brief moment of relief at seeing her moving, soon replaced by the shock of seeing just how sharp an angle can be made by a bent arm with almost no flesh on it, her elbow now a knife-like point.

And the dread would be back.

How is she still alive? There's barely anything left of her. Please, Annie, why won't you eat?

24

Building Resentment

UNDER THE CLOSE SUPERVISION of eating disorder specialists, Annie eventually plateaued. Her weight still dangerously low, fluctuating between 34.5 and 36kg, her potassium levels showed no improvement.

As weeks turned into months, we watched the seasons pass with no sign of recovery.

Annie still showed up at the studio every now and then when she had the energy. Miss Victoria would make a fuss, telling her how pleased she was to see her. Sometimes she would tell her she was looking better, looking well even. I would recoil. Why say it? By what standards did my child look well? She could no longer take part in lessons, but I thought maybe she still needed the connection to something… a buoyancy aid to stop her drowning. Despite not actually dancing, she would come home bruised after just sitting on the floor or a hard chair for over an hour, bruised by her own bones pressing fleshless skin against a hard surface.

For the most part she would sleep. Fifteen or sixteen hours a day, sometimes more. I encouraged her to stick to a bedtime and getting-up time, just for some level of normality. Each morning, she would come downstairs, have a cup of black tea and maybe a couple of mouthfuls of cereal. Then she would start to watch a film on the sofa before falling back asleep way before the end.

When she was awake in the afternoons, we would chat, watch crap on TV, sometimes read or play board games, but her concentration was poor – her brain unable to function properly on the amount of fuel it received.

As she slept on the sofa, her head on my lap, wrapped in two or three blankets, I had time to think. And I was tortured by my own thoughts: a mishmash of horror – real and imagined, scenes from the last few years, and some from long ago.

Every day I thought of Kelly. I wondered whether she was looking down, and what she would say to me... to Annie... Would she say I was failing Annie, as I'd failed her?

Memories of high school drew parallels in my mind – Annie and Kelly were (to my mind) perfect human beings, both of whom I adored, both of whom were destroyed by this evil illness. I hated anorexia as though it were a person.

I felt the weight of guilt both for Kelly back then, and for Annie now.

And I blamed others as well as myself. Back at high school, I could trace everything that went wrong for me back to the night of the party and the events that unfolded following the brutal rape. Somehow it made sense to me that the boys who assaulted me were indirectly responsible for Kelly's death.

Now, I blamed VCS – mostly, but not exclusively, Miss Victoria. She was responsible for the culture of bullying, criticism, belittling, and creating conflict between students. I replayed the times Annie came out of the studio in tears, and the reasons why she would be so upset. The devastating comments hadn't been directed at me. They were directed at my daughter. They hurt me, only because they hurt Annie. I was big enough, old enough and tough enough to brush off insults, and to see the situations for what they were – most of the time. But Annie wasn't. She didn't have the life experience to see the bigger picture or to see how different things could be if she removed herself from VCS. She knew only this.

From the age of two, an age she couldn't even remember, this had been all she'd known. It had been naïve to think she could just leave. It was too big an ask. She could no easier leave VCS than I could pack up and move to a different country. This was what she knew, and even though it made her miserable, there was some degree of comfort in familiarity. She knew there could be a different way of living, but it was nothing more than an abstract concept.

I had no idea what I was doing. I didn't know whether my approach of giving her some control was helping or harming her. I wanted clear answers and firm directions from the specialists, but they couldn't give me either. There could be so many root causes, so many health implications, so many ways of keeping secrets and nurturing the illness, and so many potential outcomes. There were inpatient centres dealing purely with eating disorders, but reviews were mixed. Annie's GP didn't recommend them, and felt they could do more harm than good.

So, we existed in a state of limbo – not getting any better, but still managing a day at a time. Not living, but existing.

I would spend hours thinking back to when Annie was little, reliving happier times... how bright she'd been at school, enthusiastic about everything, so eager to learn. I missed the times when I would cuddle her at bedtime, reading her one of her favourite stories until she drifted off. The times I could keep her safe.

Some days my mind wouldn't allow passage there. Instead, I'd be diverted to much darker places, an inner masochism hell-bent on reliving times I'd sooner forget. The focus might change. Sometimes I'd indulge in a metaphorical self-harm session where I'd deliberately raise the memories that had been buried deep down. Memories of sitting on a boy's knee at a party, his intentions so obvious, yet ignored. Clothes ripping. Unimaginable pain and humiliation. And so much blood. I'd replay the scenes on a continuous repetitive loop, until I could stand no more.

Sometimes it would be that last time I spoke to Kelly. The look of hurt and confusion as I walked away from her, leaving her with no idea of what she could have done to deserve that. Other times, I'd recall the last time I saw her, wired up to machinery keeping her alive in a hospital bed. I could visualise the texture of her skin – so thin and papery, veins not only clearly visible, but protruding, as though they had nowhere beneath the skin to hide.

Those visions would often morph into more recent memories of Annie.

I would think about all the times I had felt pain on Annie's behalf, and I would torture myself further by putting myself in her pink satin ballet shoes, wanting to feel the pain she felt. My own was not enough. I had to engorge on hers. It was selfishly indulgent, and horribly self-destructive at the same time. As though somehow, like a leech, I could suck out the pain my baby was feeling and draw it into myself. I wanted, so badly, to take it all away from her. I could handle it – however bad it was.

I recalled all the comments from the teachers at VCS, the comparisons, the unhelpful criticisms not just of the techniques, but of their appearances. The gut-wrenching anxiety of walking into a noisy room, only for it to go quiet. Of hearing whispers about parties and days out, competitions and auditions that had been kept secret. Nothing cut quite so deep as deliberate exclusion. Despite my feelings towards them, I could almost forgive the parents for their part – after all, they just wanted the best for their girls. Rightly or wrongly, their intentions might have been based on something loosely connected to the love for their child. And I could understand that. Who amongst us wouldn't do whatever they felt was necessary for their child?

But the teachers… supposedly professional adults – women – who should have damn well known better. Had they never experienced what it was like to feel hurt by another person's words?

I always liked the analogy about the piece of paper screwed up into a tiny ball. When flattened out, the damage done could still be seen. No amount of stroking it flat, apologising to it, or trying to bend the creases back in the opposite direction could turn back time and make that piece of paper what it once was.

No matter the outcome for Annie, the damage had been done. She might recover physically, but it seemed the emotional damage would take much more time to heal.

Hatred and anger festered within me, growing every day, and threatening to consume me from within.

I needed to take action. I needed to let Victoria know the extent of the damage she had caused.

Aftermath

I OPENED MY ENVELOPE *in the school hall. I looked at the first sheet – History E, Geography F, Religious Studies F – then shoved the papers back inside. There was no need to see any more. I caught sight of Lisa heading my way – the usual crowd behind her.*

"Long time no see," she said, looking me up and down. "You walking home after this?"

"Yep," I said with more confidence than usual.

"Thank God for that. I can't be arsed carrying my own bag anymore after doing it for the last seven months." Her idiot friends laughed. "Here you go." She slung her bag at me.

"Fuck off, Lisa. Carry your own shit." I threw her bag down on the floor and headed out of the door. I knew they were behind me, just far enough not to draw the attention of any teachers, but close enough that I knew they would catch me up soon. Barely a few feet outside of the school I never wanted to see again, I was spun around violently.

"Who the fuck do you think you are?" I was surprised this came from Donna, and not Lisa. Lisa was busy delving in her bag.

"I'll tell you who I'm not, and that's your little bitch. Not anymore. I'm done with your shit, all of you. You've pushed me around for years, humiliated me, and I'm not having it anymore. I don't need to see you; I don't want to see you and I can't tell you how fucking relieved I am to never have to have anything to do with you ever again." I could see the looks of shock across their faces, turning into confusion, and then into amazement that the runt had finally stood up for herself.

"Come with me, chick," Lisa said, linking her arm with mine in a way she'd done many times – usually when she wanted something. "Let's have a talk, just you and me."

I had no reason not to. What could be done to me now that hadn't been done already? Nothing. And that gave me a sense of control and power I'd never had before. They can't hurt you if you don't feel anything, and I hadn't felt much at all since Kelly died. They could try to hurt me physically. I had so much anger inside, I wanted them to do it. I wanted to fight back. I had no idea if I could, but I wanted an excuse to try. They could call me names – slut, whore, dirty bitch – nothing I hadn't heard before, and certainly nothing I hadn't said to myself. I was ready for a fight, in whatever form that took.

"You lot wait here," Lisa instructed her followers. "We won't be long." Ever faithful, they did as they were told.

We walked, arms linked, looking to anyone who saw us like the best of mates. Lisa grinned like a Cheshire cat as she spoke. But I grinned too. Whatever she had, it wouldn't faze me. I was so far past giving a shit about this nasty bitch that it was an effort to humour her. But I liked that she still thought she could intimidate me.

To my surprise, once we rounded the corner and were out of sight of her friends, Lisa softened. "Look, I know we've been horrible to you at times..."

I stopped walking and looked at her blankly. "And..."

"Well, I know you've really liked Dylan for such a long time, and he told me he was your first. He was my first too, same night actually, which is probably why I hated you so much. I was pissed off that he just abandoned me as soon as you rocked up."

"Hang on, you've dragged me down the street to tell me you were jealous? Am I understanding you?"

She sighed and looked at the ground. "Yes, that, but there's something else..." She sounded hesitant. This should be good. "I thought that as your friend I should be the one to tell you, well show you anyway..." She dropped my arm and rummaged in her bag again.

"That night, the night of the party when you... well, you know... the whole gang-bang thing..."

I looked at her, refusing to rise to it, refusing to react in anyway. "Well..." She pulled out a carrier bag from inside the bag I'd been forced to carry home for her so many times. "You should know, chick, because it's only fair that you do, that the boys, all of them, had kept these and they've been passing them between each other ever since."

I looked in the bag. Sheets – pale green and heavily blood-stained. Stains so old they had lost their shade of crimson in favour of a muted brown. Anyone else wouldn't even recognise it as what it was, but I did. I felt dizzy and hot, a wave of nausea rooting me to the spot as I looked in the bag and saw the evidence of what had happened to me so long ago.

"It's all in there," she went on. "They kept all of it. They kept it and would get it out every so often but wouldn't let anyone else see. I think they thought of it as a bag of souvenirs, or trophies or something." Her expression said it all. She'd had no idea. She'd really believed that I'd willingly participated that night. "Anyways, this one time, I found the bag at Dylan's. I wanted to know the big secret they'd been passing round. I took it all home without him knowing. He asked me about it, but I denied it, said I had no idea what he was talking about. I broke up with him a few weeks later. I was so scared of what he could do, so I needed him to think the breakup was nothing to do with me finding the bag. I didn't tell anyone else, not even Donna."

I'd never seen this Lisa before. Her shoulders slumped, and she looked at the floor, kicking some imaginary stone around. "Anyways, for what it's worth, and I know it's not much, but I'm so sorry." She squeezed my shoulder – a gesture of solidarity, pointless though it was – and she gave me a sad smile. "You do what you see fit, chick. Good luck, babe." She ran back to her friends, and that was the last I saw of her.

I grabbed a lamppost to steady myself and slid down it onto the pavement. I waited for the dizziness to pass, and then slowly opened the bag again. I found my lace pants, ripped at both sides and damaged at the back from the force of being pulled off so roughly. My bra was in there, still fastened, and missing one of the wires. I wondered for a moment what had happened to the wire. Had John's mum found it? Or had the boys done a crime scene clean-up before they got home?

At the bottom of the bag was a yellow packet, with an unmistakeable label. Kodak.

I hesitated before opening it. I knew I was about to be confronted with images I either wouldn't remember or had tried for years to forget.

It was hard to look – even harder to keep down the vomit I could feel needing to be let out. But I had to. My memory of that night was so patchy. Even the times I thought I had been conscious didn't feel real. I needed to see what had happened. I needed closure, however painful it might be.

It seemed odd that I'd never been aware of the camera, but it seemed it had been passed around just as much as I had. Thirty-six prints. Standard size. Matte finish. Negatives there too. God knows how they had had these developed without questions being asked.

And there it was. I sat on that pavement looking at the exact moments my life had changed, and I'd changed, and I'd unknowingly started to change Kelly's path.

The first picture was a close-up of a can of cider. I guessed this was setting the scene. Just looking at the picture, I felt as though I could taste it – I taste I'd never forget but would never drink again. The second was a picture of Tony holding the can while pouring something into it, grinning at the camera. So, I'd been drugged. It seemed so obvious.

The next one was taken from the bottom of the stairs – me being led upstairs by Dylan.

The pictures that followed were like those a police officer might take at a crime scene. Young, naked female sprawled on a bed, her face bloodied and hair matted into a dark crimson mess. I remember telling my parents I'd fallen over and landed on my face. Looking at these pictures, I'm amazed they believed me, but they must have. I don't remember much more about the days after it happened.

And then the trophy shots.

Dylan's slim but muscular body on top of me, face curled into a snarl. He had his jeans on, but they were down to his knees.

The pool of blood between my legs.

John's turn. He looked like he thought this was romantic. He cradled my bloody face softly as he raped me.

Then Tony. Tony was as naked as I was. His flabby body repulsed me, and I could no longer hold it in. I leaned over to the street and vomited down a grid. When my stomach was empty, I carried on. There were more pictures of Tony than the others. Tony's expression was mocking, and then laughing, and then hate-filled fury. The pictures showed me facing one way, then the other as he rained blows down on me. One picture showed his fist pulled back, knuckles white, ready to strike.

Christian had a starring role too. I got the impression he had been pressured into taking part. But I didn't care. He still did it.

It was all here. The final snaps were intimate close-ups of my entire battered body. The last one was my face, close up. I had one eye partially open, but unseeing. It must have been taken less than ten inches from my face. For reasons I could never explain, this seemed like one of the worst violations – that one of them had been both a participant and witness to my horrific ordeal, and then, within such close proximity, seen my suffering and my humiliation and wanted to preserve that particular moment in time.

25

Obsession

DAYS, NIGHTS, WEEKS AND months all started to blur together. It was hard to keep any kind of routine. Annie slept almost round the clock anyway, and my nights were long and torturous. Sleep for me was intermittent – usually broken by nightmares. I'd get up in the early hours, when the rest of the world slept, oblivious. Ghosts from the past haunted my days and nights, and it became more and more difficult to box off my emotions. I was filled with hatred.

And I recognised that hatred. It was like an old enemy who had reappeared to torment me. All those years ago, I'd hated so many people. Dylan. Tony. John. Christian. Lisa. Donna. Sally. It was impossible to rate them in order of who I hated the most, though if I had to pick, Dylan would likely be up there with Tony, probably closely followed by Sally.

But I didn't hate them anymore. I'd taken back my life. I'd done what I needed to do to make sure I'd had the last laugh.

So, as I sat at home, unable to help Annie, I pondered…
no… obsessed… on what became glaringly obvious. I
would never be able to forgive Victoria. I would have to
confront my demons for there to be an end to the pain I
was feeling.

A Dish Served Cold

I HELD ON TO *those photos for years. I didn't know what to do with them. I could burn them, ceremonially destroying the evidence and effectively cleansing myself in a way I couldn't do with bleach and a rough loofah.*

I could take them to the police. I still had the sheet and the underwear as well – all hidden in the carrier bag Lisa gave them to me in, inside an old handbag at the back of my wardrobe. It would surely be an easy win for the CPS – fully evidenced with an actual picture book. But what would happen then? I'd have to go to court and face those bastards again. I might be cross-examined by a barrister, about something that happened so long ago. How would that work? They would surely ask me why I hadn't reported it. Why was I reporting it now? How could we be sure the photos weren't staged? Was the blood on the sheets still evidence or would it have somehow changed into something else in the years that had passed?

And what would it do to my family? They would be devastated. It would crush them to know this happened and I went through it alone. I couldn't put them through it.

And I didn't want it made public. I couldn't bear the thought of Chrissy knowing, putting two and two together and realising it was not long before Kelly and I stopped speaking. I still blamed myself for Kelly's death. Every single day I felt both sorrow and guilt, for what I'd done, or not done to help her. I didn't need that guilt to spread out any further.

And so, I hung on to them: preserved them with tissue paper I took out of my parents' wedding album. Even though I didn't know what to do with them at that point, I knew they were valuable, priceless even. There may come a point when I needed these photos more than anything else, so I had to take care of them. There was no rush. After this amount of time, I could afford to spend as long as necessary. I needed revenge. But it had to be right. I needed to hurt those boys so badly, but it had to be done properly. If I waited, I knew eventually the idea would come to me.

In the end it wasn't so much an idea that I came up with. The world moves ever forwards and holding off had been the best way after all. The explosion of social media into our lives came at the perfect time for me – somewhere in those years between receiving the photos and starting my new life with Rob.

Myspace pretty much passed me by. I was nervous about it all. Friends Reunited terrified me. I had no interest in reuniting with anyone. Facebook somehow seemed softer, more anonymous, yet gathering traction every day as more and more people joined. I wasn't interested in 'likes' or 'followers', and I certainly did not want to be contactable. So, I created a fake profile under the name Lisa Harison – spelt just wrongly enough that I hoped people would assume I meant Harrison and accept my friend requests. I guessed there may be people who were already friends with the real

Lisa who might not accept, but that didn't matter. I only needed a few to accept.

I sent friend requests to every name I could remember from my year group, including the girls I'd been friends with before it happened. Except Sally. I could get everything I needed without needing to feel a knife twist in my soul every time I would see a post. I'd grown resentful towards Sally. She treated me like a leper, turning her back on me when I desperately needed a friend to turn to. She had been there. If she'd only come to check on me. If she'd only wondered why suddenly most of the boys had come upstairs. She could have stopped it.

Over the following days, the magic of Facebook did its thing and started suggesting 'people I might know'. So, I started sending them all requests too. Some I knew, and some I didn't. But as the acceptances started coming in, I began harvesting information. Who was still in touch with who. Who had moved away and who still lived in our hometown. Who was doing well and who wasn't.

And still I was in no rush.

Every night for almost six months I scrolled and scrolled, making sure I didn't miss a single post, being careful not to 'like' anything, even by accident. I didn't want to draw any attention to myself. I needed to lurk in the social media shadows, and it could all be over if someone noticed an extra Lisa Harrison on everyone's friend lists.

And then I spotted it. I didn't know what I'd been waiting for until I found it.

The four boys who had raped me had all accepted my friend requests. None of them posted much. The odd football-related video, occasionally pictures from a night out. I knew *from hours and hours of scrolling that Dylan was still local and working as a solicitor in town. Tony seemed to be doing very little. His photos suggested no job, no education beyond high school, no sign of a girlfriend, and his photos suggested he could well be addicted to meth. It was hard to figure out where he was living, as there wasn't much to work with. I couldn't find anything to suggest he was in touch with anyone from school.*

John had moved to Manchester. He had a fancy job with an IT company. His posts gave the impression of a nice, clean-cut young man. Someone you'd like your daughter to date. Unless you knew him the way I did.

Christian had also moved away and was now living in Kent. I wondered what had drawn him to Kent. He could not have gotten further away from Lancashire without leaving the country. I hoped he was running away from his past. And I was grateful that the internet – in particular, social media – was making the world suddenly a much smaller place. It wasn't as easy to run away anymore.

It was Christian who first came to my attention. A sweet post about his mum and dad's silver wedding anniversary, looking forward to their party tonight 'on my old stomping ground'. He tagged in both of his parents, his brother (I assumed) and the local football club function room. Perfect. I could do this. And it wouldn't even be difficult. I was a little disappointed I wouldn't be there to see it, but I hummed happily as I put three incriminating photos inside a pretty card with doves and hearts or some other such shit on the front. In my best calligraphy, I carefully wrote his parents' names on the envelope. I took my battered old Walkman – years out of date, practically a relic, but somehow it still worked – and I caught the bus to the stop nearest the football club. It was only 11am. I wasn't sure if anyone would be there at that time and was relieved to see no cars in the car park. I didn't knock to check. I simply pulled my hood up – just in case there was any CCTV – walked up to the door and posted it through the letterbox. It was as easy as that. One down, three to go.

I decided I should probably deal with John pretty soon after Christian. I didn't want to leave too much time in between if I could help it. Better if they don't get the chance to talk to each other – although, of course, I knew I had set in motion a chain of events I would have limited control over, especially now I knew everyone concerned was connected through the power of social media.

John was easy. His parents still lived in the house that haunted my dreams. It wasn't far from where I lived. I could have been there and back in less than an hour, but I had no desire to revisit the scene. I didn't want to walk up the street that I'd not been near since that fateful night, so long ago. I could confront my demons from a distance.

John's parents would receive a package in the mail – recorded delivery – in the next forty-eight hours. The package contained not only the photos of John violating me, but one of the more intimate close-ups leaving no doubt as to how the sheets had become so heavily stained with blood. And for good measure, I carefully folded the pale green sheet and wrapped it with string. The photos were placed in a sealed envelope, tucked under the string and then wrapped in pretty pink tissue paper before going into a large envelope. I had no idea what John's parents were called, so it was simply addressed to Mr and Mrs Turner.

I was halfway to reaching the closure I craved.

I knew the boys – now men – would be talking about it. My only regret was that I wouldn't get to see the carnage I'd caused.

I wanted to wait for a while before tackling Tony. Partly because I wasn't sure how to approach it. He didn't seem to have any family or friends I could send pictures to – certainly nobody on his Facebook pictures who didn't look smacked off their tits. If people didn't care about him, and he didn't care about anyone else, it was going to be harder to hurt him. But I also wanted them to be lulled into a false sense of security. Or ongoing terror and anxiety, not knowing when their turn would come.

I put a marker on my calendar for six months ahead. That would give me enough time to figure out a plan, and – I hoped – six months of fear for both him and Dylan. I needed them to suffer emotionally. To feel real fear. To feel scared of something they wouldn't see coming and would be powerless to stop. I prayed they were still in contact with each other and had heard from Christian and John.

Fate stepped in and took any decision out of my hands. Although I was incredibly pissed off that I didn't get my revenge, it turned out Tony died a horrible, and very deserving, death. There were a few RIP-type comments on his page. Why? I wondered. He wasn't going to read them.

I put his name into Google a couple of days later and found the news story – well, not much of a story, just a few lines in the local paper. More than he deserved, but I was grateful for the few details provided. He had been discovered in a derelict building, likely used as a crack den. A post-mortem would be carried out, but it appeared as though the cause of death may have been an opioid overdose. However, further investigations were being done as there was evidence of sexual assault.

Perfect. I only hoped the opioids didn't numb the pain or humiliation for him. I hoped he had been gang-raped to death. Maybe karma was a real thing.

26

Consume

Definition of con·sume [kənˈsjuːm]

Verb – eat, drink, or ingest (food or drink): "my daughter could no longer consume a meal"

Similar: eat, eat up, devour, ingest, swallow, gobble

(of a fire) completely destroy: "VCS consumed my daughter"

Similar: destroy, demolish, wipe out, annihilate

use up (a resource): "our time, energy, finances, and sanity had been completely consumed"

Similar: use, use up, utilise, expend, deplete, exhaust

One to Go...

Again, I would bide my time. Savour the planning process. He was the last one, so there was no rush. For the next year and a half, my dreams were filled with violence, bloody massacres. My daydreams were calmer – more civil – yet equally destructive. Was public exposure the finale I wanted? What about something more insidious? Drip-feeding little blackmail titbits from time to time. More than pain, I wanted Dylan to feel real, overwhelming fear and devastation.

I followed his life – or the life he presented – and made notes. Who was in his life. Where he went on holiday. His favourite restaurants. Nothing that really inspired me. He was living the life of a million other twenty-somethings. He seemed to have a good job with a firm of solicitors, though in what capacity, I wasn't sure. He certainly seemed to be well-paid. Nothing on his Facebook feed gave away the monster hiding beneath the façade.

One night in late November, I sat scrolling idly with a glass of wine in hand, when my attention was grabbed by a relationship status update. *Dylan Woods is engaged.*

This came out of nowhere. There had been one picture that he'd been tagged in showing him with a girl, looked like in a nightclub. I'd assumed it was just someone he'd hooked up with on a drunken night out. I scrolled back and found the picture.

Fucking hell.

I hadn't recognised her before, but it was Sally. No longer a mousy, bland, nerdy girl. She was stunning. Her hair was slicked back dramatically, emphasising her features. Either she had spent a lot of time practising her make-up application skills or she'd had it done professionally. Her eyes stood out despite only light make-up on them. Her lipstick was dark red and gave her mouth a full, vampy look. She was almost unrecognisable. Almost.

She was known on Facebook as Sal Jay. Chances were I wouldn't have found her even if I'd tried.

I had won the Facebook lottery. She had no restrictions on who could view her page. I couldn't believe my luck. It was meant to be.

I followed their wedding plans with great interest. An autumn wedding the following year. Local. Expensive. Sally's excitement about their upcoming nuptials was the gift that kept on giving for me. Every aspect of planning the big day was posted online.

'Cake booked!'

'Cars booked!'

'Venue booked!'

It went on and on. Sally was an only child, and her parents had good jobs (I had no idea what they did, but back when we were at school, they always had expensive cars, exotic holidays, and a beautiful home, so I'd always *assumed they were loaded). There would be no expense spared on this wedding, and I couldn't believe my luck when she tagged in each company providing some aspect of goods or services. I started keeping detailed notes. Their wedding became my wedding. I knew who each bridesmaid was (I was surprised Angela and Amanda were not among them), what style and colour they would be wearing (teal, Grecian style), the colour scheme (teal and burnt orange with lots of greenery threaded through), the cars (vintage), Sally's shoes (Jimmy Choo), rings (Harry Winston, Los Angeles). And most importantly, I knew the date and the venue. September 18th, Ashforth House. It was no more than I expected.*

Ashforth House was a listed Georgian-style building on a privately owned estate. If the house was impressive, the gardens were definitely more so. Zoned into different areas, each one had its own distinct style – immaculately manicured contemporary, English country garden, Japanese garden – though it was best known for the rose garden. September might have been out of season for the roses (I didn't know this to be true – I'd always thought of them more as summer flowers), but when in full bloom, visitors would flock from all over the world to see over 120 varieties in every hue and colour imaginable. A beautiful backdrop for a perfect wedding. Not this wedding, though.

It was less than an hour's drive for me, so I took a trip there a few weeks before the wedding.

27

Never Again

THE COOL AUTUMN AIR felt thick with tension as I marched across the empty car park. I'd been driving past late every night for weeks, just waiting for the right time. That night, I figured the school would be closed for half term, so as I drove past, I expected the car park to be empty. But it wasn't. There was a single white Mercedes – Victoria's – parked in the spot closest to the reception door. This was the chance I'd been waiting for.

Every step on the neglected gravel car park echoed, magnifying my suppressed rage. My daughter had been left bruised and broken by the woman who waited inside. Her tiny body now bruised from the slightest touch, her heart like a ticking timebomb, and the damage to her soul was unquantifiable. The cruel, competitive culture of VCS, combined with Victoria's greed and lack of empathy, her calculating nature, and the manipulative ways she had sucked in not just the kids but the parents too, was unforgiveable.

I pushed open the door, and the wind picked it up, slamming it back against the reception desk.

"I'm up here." Victoria's coarse voice came from the loft. "Just come up." I knew she wasn't expecting it to be me – even I hadn't been sure I would be there until two minutes earlier. But I was invited upstairs, so I wouldn't want to be rude.

She must have been having a clear-out. I'd never been up into the loft at the studio, but the main reception floor was covered with costumes and props from (I guessed) at least twenty years of shows, competitions and festivals. The reception area was filled with the musty smell of clothing long since forgotten about. As I looked around, the brainwashed part of me still had some respect for the costumes. Mustn't stand on them. Mustn't get them dirty.

But I didn't want to touch anything either.

I tiptoed between the mountains of nylon and polyester, anticipating the electric shocks from the shitty fabrics, careful not to stand on any of the props. I wondered what they had been used for. There was a small metal bucket, several plastic flower arrangements – some hand-tied, one in a basket – a giant sequinned apple, a clam shell made of polystyrene, a red metal stool, hats and canes aplenty.

She must have been chucking it down to get rid of it, without any care, so it seemed ironic that I would take so much care around the pile of rubbish. But I knew there were stories behind each prop, a little girl behind each of the costumes. I wondered what those stories were. Would those girls have gone on to become world-class dancers? Or did they forget about dance as soon as they became interested in boys? Did they go on to follow the career path of their dreams? Or did the effects of this environment destroy their confidence, like it had for Annie?

I climbed towards the loft cautiously, the soft gloves tight around my fingers, and making it difficult to grasp each rung of the ladder. As I reached the top, I was surprised at how enormous and light the loft was. Clinical, florescent lights buzzed in the eaves, and as I stood up, I saw Victoria, her back to me, going through one of several long rails of costumes.

She glanced over her shoulder, clearly expecting someone else, and jumped at the sight of me. I understood how shocking it must be – frightening even – to be in somewhere you considered home, somewhere safe, and to be cornered by a figure dressed head to toe in black. I knew the scarf wouldn't hide my identity from her. It didn't need to. It was merely a precaution. I'd spent enough time in the studio over the years to be confident that there were no security cameras, but I wasn't going to take any chances. Once up in the rafters, there was no need for that precaution anyway, so I pulled it down.

I wanted her to see me.

As she realised who it was, I watched as her expression changed from friendly and relaxed, to uncertain. Afraid, even. She should be.

"Oh… hi, Lydia… I didn't expect to see you… how's Annie doing? Is everything okay?" Her voice trembled a little. Good. "I was wondering how she'd been the other day. We miss her so much, you know."

"Really?" I picked up a prop close to where I stood – an umbrella – and through my gloves, I ran my fingertips

273

over the spike end. "You haven't called." This prop was heavier than I'd expected. How much damage could it do?

"To be honest, I wasn't sure you'd want me to call…"

"You hurt my daughter," I spat, hands clenched into fists at my sides, while holding tight to that umbrella. My pulse roared in my ears, and I fought my anger, pushing it down deep into my gut. I needed to stay calm. I needed her to hear what I had to say. "You know, I always thought you would be her safety net. Did you know that? That you and your teachers would be the ones to notice if anything was wrong. Physically, I mean. Like I know you noticed one of the older girls had something wrong with her spine, right? Something her mum didn't know about? I remember thinking how amazing it was that you'd been so observant, and how lucky we were to have you looking out for them. I mean, let's face it, once they get to a certain age, they can be a little secretive… so I felt reassured that if any of the worries I had were a reality – drugs, self-harm, weight loss… I'd know about it before it became a problem."

I tipped my head to the side and smiled sweetly. "Because I had you. I had you and the rest of your staff seeing her nearly every day, wearing nothing more than a leotard. If there was anything going on, she might hide it from me, but she could never hide it from you, right?"

"Lydia, I'm so sorry about that. I've apologised already, and I know how angry you are with me. If it makes you feel any better, I'll never forgive myself for not stepping in when I could have…"

I almost laughed. "No, no, it doesn't make me feel better, and I'm way fucking angrier than you know about. You were in a position to help, to get this nipped in the bud. You should have told me as soon as you saw it, but you didn't. You robbed me of the chance to address it before it got to this point. You were never sorry. You only got concerned when you worried it might affect your reputation."

As I spoke, I couldn't help looking at the umbrella tip. I imagined driving it hard into her skull, through an eye perhaps, for dramatic effect. I imagined the pop of her eyeball, and the horrible image gave me a glimpse of inner peace. "Did you honestly think you'd get away with it, Victoria? That there would be no repercussions for you? That I'd be able to watch my daughter slowly fading away from me, knowing you could have stopped it, and I'd just become a memory to you? Old news. 'The mother of a kid that used to go here'?"

Victoria walked slowly towards me, hands open as though to embrace me. But she stopped short. "Get away with it? I did her a favour. She was a good dancer, no doubt about that, but she wasn't strong enough to live that life. I showed her how cruel the dance world can be."

The words hit me like a slap, and without thinking, I had crossed the room, grabbing Victoria by the collar of her shirt. "You think the dance world can be cruel? You have no fucking idea what I'm capable of," I hissed, my voice shaking with barely controlled rage. I'd dropped the umbrella, but I didn't need it. The fury inside me making me capable of anything.

But Victoria was quick. Way quicker than I expected for someone of advancing years, and suffering from arthritis. She twisted out of my grasp, shoving me back hard enough that I stumbled into a nearby table. The hair accessories and other paraphernalia that had been carefully laid out clattered to the floor, but neither of us cared. I regained my balance, my heart pounding with adrenaline. This wasn't going to end with just a fight. I had come for closure, and I wasn't leaving without it.

Victoria corrected her posture and brushed the dust from the scuffle from her clothes. I could see her wince in pain – the arthritis no doubt – but, like a predator sizing up its prey, unwilling to show any sign of weakness or vulnerability, she paced up and down. "You really think you can come here and scare me?" she sneered. "This is my studio, and you need to get out. Now!"

By then I was steady on my feet, and I reached inside my jacket, pulling out a small, yellow-handled switch blade. Victoria saw it and stepped back. "You can't believe you can hurt me with that and not get into trouble, Lydia." She raised her hands in a move I'd already seen once that night and no longer trusted.

Before I had time to think about the consequences, I lunged at her, hearing a primal scream and not knowing which of us it belonged to. As I got within less than a foot of reaching her, Victoria sidestepped. In the chaos of movement, her foot caught on the raised wooden slats that edged the loft door, throwing her off balance. She flailed for something to hold on to but found nothing. Her body twisted awkwardly, her arms windmilling as she crashed through the loft door.

I heard the sickening thud. And then nothing. Silence.

For a moment, everything was still. I froze, breath coming in ragged gasps, my rage still simmering beneath the surface, but reducing.

I glanced around the loft, checking for anything that might indicate I'd been there. I wasn't worried; there would be the DNA of hundreds of people up here. I was leaving nothing recent. The blood I'd intended to spill had not been spilled.

I edged, hesitantly, towards the loft door and looked down.

Victoria lay in a twisted heap, eyes wide, her mouth opening and closing in silent gasps. Something jutted from her neck, blood already soaking through her shirt, and her head was at an angle that could only result from a broken neck.

I descended the steps as carefully as I'd ascended them, only minutes earlier.

I watched, silently, as Victoria's hands fumbled uselessly at the wound. One leg of the little, upturned milking stool was a different shade of red to the others as it glistened with the blood of the woman who I hated more than anyone else in the world. Her head was cradled by the other legs. If her neck hadn't twisted and broken, it looked as though one of the other legs might have pierced her skull.

But somehow, she was still alive. Impaled by a prop, head at an unnatural angle to the rest of her body.

The arrogant expression as she'd paced in front of me a few moments ago was gone, replaced by one of disbelief and fear. "No... no..." she stammered, her voice weak as her blood pumped from the wound. I crouched beside her and smiled as I listened to the beautiful sounds of blood bubbling in her throat and choking her.

"Hmm... what to do? What to do?" I whispered.

I mean, technically I hadn't done anything wrong here –
she'd tripped over and fallen through the loft door. I hadn't
even pushed her. I could do the right thing – *should* do the
right thing and call 999. I was no doctor, but I was fairly
convinced she was bleeding out, and coupled with the
broken neck, there seemed little point in being dramatic and
calling for an ambulance. There would be so much hassle –
police questioning, paperwork, an inquest maybe…

This was the second 'sliding door' moment I'd had –
only a few yards from the first one so long ago. Call for
help, and deal with the fallout? Or walk away, let her bleed
out?

Nobody knew I was there. She had fallen through the
door and landed on a prop. Simple. I hoped it wouldn't be
a child who found her like that.

I stood over her and watched as her chest movements
became quicker, more panicked, and that soothed me. I
felt my anger slowly ebbing away. I hadn't intended this.
I didn't know what I'd been expecting as I'd dressed in
black and slipped the switch blade into my pocket. I'd had
no definite plan in mind – though I was clearly open to
anything that came my way. The fall – well, not so much
the fall as the landing – was out of my hands. Perhaps
karma was stepping in for once.

Victoria's breathing grew laboured, shallow. Her face
paled, and her hands were stained red as they slipped
away from the wound. Her gaze found mine, a flicker of
pleading in her eyes now. But I remained still, unmoved,
unconcerned, for a moment.

"You could have helped Annie. Just like I could help
you right now. Just one call, that's all it would take. All you

needed to do was call me and I could have saved Annie from the hell she's in right now. One call. Just one fucking phone call, Victoria. Well... I mean... I could call an ambulance, but I'm going out with my sister tonight, so..."
I bent down, close to her bloodied face. "You're in fate's hands now," I whispered as I stood up and left the building for the last time.

The Wedding

WHEN THE BIG DAY arrived, my plan was in place. I was disappointed I wouldn't see the moment of impact, but I sat in my car just outside the estate. Only with binoculars could I see the building itself. I had a vague idea of the timings.

It was 2pm. The ceremony was done and dusted, and Sally would now be Mrs Woods. I wanted to make sure that bit went ahead without issue – it had to be too late for her to back out. I pictured it clearly – Sally's Facebook page had been like a vision board, so it was not hard to imagine the details. I knew from speaking to the venue (they weren't great at confidentiality) that the wedding breakfast was at 1.30 and speeches were at 2pm.

This was it.

I had visited the venue, heavily disguised, just the day before. I told the event coordinator that I had booked a surprise break for the newly-weds – four nights in New York – and the envelopes contained all required information. I knew they were heading to Boston a few days after the wedding, so my lie was believable – a few nights tagged onto the start of their honeymoon from a (wealthy) relative. Unfortunately, the relative was not quietly generous, and requested the surprise be presented after the best man's speech, but before the bride's father. I asked for an envelope each to be given to Sally and Dylan, and one for the father of the bride – to be opened at the same time.

They would be opening those envelopes around now. Sally and Dylan's envelopes both contained the rest of the photographs – all of them spread between the two envelopes. Dylans contained a little extra – the ripped, bloody, lace pants. They were a last-minute addition, just to make sure those watching would pay attention. I couldn't risk them being able to put on a poker face and bluff their way through it.

I imagined Sally's dad – always so formal and strait-laced. If he read my letter first – and I knew he would – he would not read it out loud. That didn't matter. It wasn't ideal, but I had to be realistic. In my mind's eye, he had stood up to open his envelope. The guests were eager to know what the surprise was – it would have to be something incredible for the wedding running order to be sabotaged like this. Brides could be notoriously neurotic about their big day, so it would have to be worth risking the wrath.

I could see it all unfolding in my mind. Brian (I had eventually found his name through my research), cautious as predicted, was reading the contents before delivering them as part of his speech. He would be sitting down now, looking across at Sally and Dylan. The colour would have drained from three faces almost simultaneously. He was standing up again and leaving the room. He found a chair in an empty, though grand, formal lounge area, and sat down with the letter. He would need to be able to read this properly, without anyone around…

Dear Brian

I want you to know that this has not been done to hurt you or your wife. I hope you will read this through to the end so you can hopefully understand why I'm doing this.

Many years ago, I was your daughter's friend. You might remember me, but I wouldn't blame you if you didn't. I was – still am – very non-descript.

Sally and I went to a party with some people from school one night in 1993. While there I was drugged and gang-raped, as the photos now in Sally and Dylan's possession will show. Dylan instigated and facilitated what happened to me.

I wanted you to know who your daughter has married. This was many years ago. Dylan has likely forgotten all about me – or maybe not. I don't know. Or care. But I haven't forgotten what happened that night. As though the rapes were not enough, a chain reaction was set in motion, resulting in the death of my best friend. Long ago I accepted indirect responsibility for her death, though the bulk of the blame must lie with Dylan and his friends. I was brutalised and humiliated over and over again. They took turns on me, while I drifted in and out of consciousness. They damaged me in ways most people will never understand, and that doesn't go away. No amount of time can wipe out the memories burned into my brain. And even if time could erase it, Dylan, Tony, John and Christian took photos, preserving that horrific time for eternity.

Sally — the beautiful bride — turned her back on me. Her rejection hurt as much as every painful thrust or punch delivered by the boys. I desperately needed a friend to turn to, and Sally abandoned me. She believed the rumours, believed I had enjoyed it — even instigated it — and threw me out of our group like rubbish. She didn't ask what happened, choosing to believe the worst of me.

Even worse, she had been there. A decent friend might have wondered where I was, or why all the boys were going upstairs. But she didn't. And while she wasn't involved directly, she hurt me too.

The photos came into my possession many years ago, though I'm sure you'll understand I had no idea what to do with them. I'm sure you will also be able to understand my need for retribution.

I could not go through the legal system, having barristers tear me apart on the witness stand. Having them expose me and violate me again. I had a couple of cans of cider, nothing more, but I would be ripped to shreds in a court room. I know that.

Despite the violent rage inside me, I refuse to break the law. I've served a sentence already. For years after that night, I felt imprisoned by fear. I've done my time, and I'm not doing any more. Today is my release date.

I've had to wait a long time, and this is my time.

I'm sorry to you and your wife. I have no doubt you will have saved up for this and been excited and proud to see your beautiful daughter on her big day. I know the humiliation of this happening right now will sting for a long time, and I know you'll feel anger towards me for spoiling the day. And I don't blame you for that.

But I need you to know why.

I had to humiliate. I had to publicly destroy. It feels only fair that I get to do this. It may seem petty to you. Vicious. Nasty, even. And it is. I know that. I've been filled with hate for a long time now and I'm done. I can't carry this with me forever. I need to move forwards and reclaim my life. But to do that I need closure, and that has to feel fair.

Dylan is getting away with his crime, as did the other boys – at least in a legal sense. They should be in prison for what they did. But I have spared them that. They will live their lives, but their secret – the one I kept as MY dirty secret – is out now.

Ask them for the photos that were in their envelopes. Go on, Brian. Have a look. Most of my high school year group did. I have nothing to hide – everyone's seen everything.

In case anyone ever wonders, yes there are negatives. And yes, they are in a safe place. A place known only to me and one other person. Destroying these photos won't erase what happened. I keep the negatives only because I want Dylan to know that I have them. I want him to know that his life, such that it will be after today, and his freedom are at my discretion. I want him to question if, and when, I might decide to use them again. I want Dylan to know that these photos will be the 'Sword of Damocles' for the rest of his life. I want him to know that any time he feels he has escaped my reach, or enough time has passed, those photos still exist. I want him to feel unable to settle, unable to enjoy anything, unable to forget, until the day he dies. I hope that won't be until he's an old man – I wish many years of torment and discomfort for him. Death would be an easy way out.

Why would I want anyone to see these photos? That's a question I've asked myself many times. After all, they show me exposed, vulnerable, at the lowest point of my life. I've held on to these photos for a long time now, pondering what to do. I couldn't destroy them, poisonous though they are. They're evidence. For years, people thought I invited these boys to play with me. Now, even if they go no further, someone else knows the truth. And there's another reason. I don't want my grandkids, decades from now, to find them as they clear out my belongings and wonder: why has Nana got these photos? What the hell happened? Who is the girl in them? I don't want them looking for answers.

For the record, it's taken a long time to decide what to do with the pictures. It's also taken a lot of time for me to separate myself from the young girl – no more than a child – being savaged in those images.

I moved away, though remain close enough that I hope to hear whispers of the fallout. Time has of course helped in changing the way I look – not that any young girl would be recognisable from the bloody, pulped face you will see in the pictures.

Sally, Dylan, maybe even you, might walk past a woman in the street and wonder . . . is that her? I expect this may happen often. I hope so.

You may be able to control the damage. And that's okay. Of course, I'd prefer if everyone in that room knew the contents of this letter, but I'm sure they won't. But questions will be asked. What was in the letter? Why did Brian leave the room? Why are the bride and groom not looking happy on their wedding day? Why won't they tell us what the big surprise is? Is that the clue to why they're having the marriage annulled?

And even if the secret is never leaked, YOU know. The responsibility is yours now. This letter is the grenade I threw into your daughter's wedding day, and now any damage is your problem.

Again, I'm sorry for the hurt this will cause to others, but the truth needs to be told. Now you and Sally both know. I've resented Sally ever since, but I mean her no real harm. I know she will get over this and move on. She'll find a decent man, get married again (maybe not after this), and will live a great life. Dylan is in karma's hands now.

Regards

Lydia

EPILOGUE

The Finale – Five Years Later

THE DIM LIGHT FROM the stage bathed the audience in a soft glow. In the darkness, I sat in the stalls, my fingers resting loosely on the armrests, eyes fixed on the stage.

Somehow, we had made it.

Annie was breathtaking – a vision of fragile elegance, her body bending and twisting with an ethereal grace. I was mesmerised. The light caught every single one of the 3200 hand-sewn crystals, as she moved through the final act of *Swan Lake*. Every leap, every pirouette, was a testament to the tough years of discipline, of sacrifice. The audience watched, entranced, unable to see the scars hidden beneath the delicate layers of fabric. But I could. I always could.

In the pit of my stomach, something stirred – not quite pride, but something colder, sharper. A satisfaction, perhaps. The faintest of smiles played on my lips as I leaned back in my chair, letting the music wash over me.

The theatre pulsed with an undercurrent of tension,

the kind that came in the brief moments before an eruption of sound. It was almost over now – the final act, the final movement. My daughter was on stage, luminous under the dim light, her body like something no longer human, something better than human. The swan's tragic descent was unfolding, the orchestra's strings trembling in perfect unison with each graceful, deliberate motion. But to me, this was more than a performance. It was the culmination of everything.

I thought of all the choices, the quiet manipulations. A ruined costume. A few tiny shards of glass in a nasty little brat's tap shoe. The odd laxative here and there. My personal favourite was the rubbing of a raw onion on costumes and clothing – that had been the most entertaining. Poor kid had no idea. They were minor things, really, in the grand scheme. Aside from the decision to messily eat a peanut butter sandwich just before panto – to be fair, that one could have ended up being pretty bad – these were all fairly low-key attempts at sabotage. Hardly worth remembering, except for how satisfying they had been.

I thought back to when I was younger. I'd been unable to fight off the boys at that party as they hurt me, and I'd been unable to stick up for myself for a long time afterwards, being walked all over by people who believed the worst of me. No child should have to go through what I went through back then. But we're all shaped by our experiences – good or bad. And what happened back then toughened me up from the inside out. I'd not been able to protect myself when I was drugged, but they picked the wrong girl if they thought they would get away with it forever, that I'd never speak out. I'd used their own evidence against them to tear their lives apart, and I'd relished every second of it.

So, if I'd do that for myself, there was no question that I would do whatever it took to protect Annie. We'd moved to another county. A fresh start. All ties cut with everyone from VCS. It had been easier than I thought, and the best thing for both of us.

I could feel the stillness inside me, the cold certainty that had long replaced the softer things. Here, in the dark, I watched my beautiful daughter glide across the stage as though she had been born for this moment alone.

And then there had been the darker times. Annie's illness – the weight that fell too far, too fast. I had spent months watching it happening – seen my daughter shrinking before my eyes – but I never intervened, not at first. And I lived with that guilt every day. When Annie had faltered, I had simply watched, paralysed, waiting and not knowing what to do. In the early years, I had hoped it would toughen her up, get her ready for the highly competitive world she was edging towards. It was only when the breaking point seemed near that I had stepped in, and it had been too late. I would still never forgive myself for taking so long to act. I would spend the rest of my life trying to make it up to Annie.

Annie had recovered. Maybe not fully… but perhaps in a similar way to an alcoholic who hasn't touched a drop for years but could easily spiral quickly towards rock bottom if the road to recovery was paved with difficulties, pressures, stresses and crises. But Annie had become stronger, more focused. More perfect. The kind of perfection that only came from being completely broken down, and rebuilt, one piece at a time.

During the long recovery, I reminded myself every day of the promise I made to her – that I would support her, that I would have her back, whatever she decided to do. This wasn't what I would have chosen for her – this cruel, ugly world of nastiness, competition and pressure. But it was her choice, and I would keep my promise.

And I helped my daughter to rebuild herself. Just as I had broken those who might be a threat to her.

As the final strains of the orchestra swelled, Annie took her last steps across the stage, poised in a perfect, tragic silhouette. As the final note hung in the air, she lowered herself gracefully to the floor, her body folding in on itself like a dying swan, the tragic heroine in her last, exquisite moment. The crowd would rise in a moment, their applause thunderous, their admiration blind. They would see only the beauty. They would never know the cost. And they would never see the scars.

But I did. And as I sat in the dark, my eyes fixed on the graceful figure before me, I felt no regret. I remained seated as the applause thundered around me, watching Annie rise to take her bow. This was everything she had worked for, everything we had fought for. And I felt nothing but pride and satisfaction. No remorse for the paths I had altered, the lives forever changed that one day when I did nothing more than walk away.

My daughter had become everything I had always known she would be – perfect, untouchable, a star. Dance was not the choice I would have made for her, given everything that had happened. But it was Annie's choice, and she was finally living her dream.

In the end, that was all I had ever wanted.